2/25/16
$26.95

3/16

D0633433

THE
SQUANDERED

Also by David Putnam

The Replacements

The Disposables

THE
SQUANDERED

A BRUNO JOHNSON NOVEL

DAVID PUTNAM

Oceanview Publishing
Longboat Key, Florida

ISBN: 978-1-60809-165-2

Published in the United States of America by Oceanview Publishing
Longboat Key, Florida

www.oceanviewpub.com

10 9 8 7 6 5 4 3 2 1

PRINTED IN THE UNITED STATES OF AMERICA

To my best friend, partner in crime, and true love,
Little Sweet Mary

ACKNOWLEDGMENTS

I'd like to thank everyone at Oceanview Publishing for working so hard to turn my dreams into reality. Also, huge thanks to my big crazy family for all the love, support, and inspiration— especially Sheri for her party-throwing prowess and ideas for the progression of Bruno and Marie's love story.

Thanks to Matt Coyle for all his help with the world of marketing, and to Maggie Latimer for her great insight as a first reader of the manuscripts.

I'd like to give a special thanks to all the Asilomar and De Luz Writers who help and support me in so many ways. And thanks again to Jerry Hannah, my writing mentor and guru.

CHAPTER ONE

WILLOWBROOK, SOUTH CENTRAL LOS ANGELES, 1988

"IF YOU HAVE to go hands on with a suspect, you take him fast, down and dirty. You don't mess around. Forget the policy. Forget using the escalation of force they taught you in the academy. You understand what I'm telling you here?"

Trainee Robert Crews didn't look like he understood at all. He'd only been in my car for two weeks, after doing four years in the Men's Central Jail waiting for his turn to go out on the streets. Four years working MCJ—Men's Central Jail—had rubbed some of the shine off of him.

But not enough.

What his time in the jail did do, worked against him. He now thought he possessed all the information needed to handle the criminal element out in the real world. He didn't. Inside the jail, concrete walls and steel bars created a controlled environment, nothing even close to the unpredictability of the streets.

We stood outside the Los Angeles County Sheriff's black-and-white patrol car in Lucy's parking lot on Long Beach Boulevard eating HO, half-off tacos over the hood. The unit's PA blared, and the calls echoed off the buildings, the night hot even for July. Cars zipped by in the street and pedestrians moved both ways on the sidewalk, none of them making eye contact. Mostly coked-out thieves and degenerates lost to the world, and prostitutes, women and girls who'd fallen in love with the glass gun. One puff and they too disappeared from the real world. Coke ruined lives; rock coke ruined a generation.

Crews possessed that new-guy energy, that drive to get into the action that as a trainee you either overcame or it ate you alive. He wanted to be a ghetto gunfighter and didn't understand the job wasn't about the badge and the swagger. I grew up a couple of miles from Lucy's. This was my home. He drove in from yuppie town, USA, and went back there every night to his safe neighborhood, and to his girlfriend who worked in a middle-class job.

I didn't want the street to eat him.

He nodded, acknowledging the question, chewing his taco.

"What, I didn't hear you?" I said.

He swallowed hard. "Yes, sir."

"You don't understand, I can see it in that sappy face of yours. You're just paying me lip service. Look, when you step away from this cop car, you no longer have the radio. The radio is your umbilical cord to your fellow deputies, the guys who are gonna bust their ass getting to you if you call for help. But if you're out of your car, and you can't get to your radio, you're on your own."

Trainee Crews didn't understand, and his ignorance would get him in deep shit a lot sooner than later. In his four years at the jail, he'd used his time to work the weight pile at the Bauchet Street Gym, Bauchet being the name of the street MCJ occupied, an entire city block, miles north of Willowbrook, in downtown LA. The jail had a gym exclusively for the deputies to use on their time off and lunch breaks. Crews wore his blond hair in a standard buzz cut, his blue eyes alive with the desire for action, his uniform shirt tailored and stretched tight around bulging biceps and shoulder muscles. He oozed with overconfidence.

I'd lost my appetite envisioning Crews stepping out of his car on a call and walking into a problem he couldn't handle. "Okay," I said, "Let's say you go hands on. After you've first tried verbally to have the guy turn around and put his hands behind his back. You go hands on and try and take him down and dirty like I've shown you, but it doesn't work, he's a bad ass. You're fighting him in the street at a traffic stop or inside a house, what do you do?"

He let the taco he'd put up to his mouth sag as he thought about an answer I wanted to hear, and not what he needed to know as the truth. He shrugged, "I guess I beat his ass."

"No. No. What did I tell you? You better pay attention to what I'm saying here or someone's going to hand you your ass. And it's not going to be some big muscle-bound criminal. It's going to be some highly motivated, skinny little punk.

"If you're fighting all out for sixty seconds, no matter who it is, and you're not getting the upper hand, you disengage and get away from him. You run if you have to. After sixty seconds the odds of overcoming your opponent start moving against you in a serious way. Don't be too proud to run. You understand?"

He nodded again and I thought I broke through to him this time, until he let the essence of a smile creep in. He just didn't believe me. He'd have to find out for himself; an ugly proposition.

I shook my head and took a bite of taco just to help mask my disapproval.

"What?" he asked.

I didn't have time to answer; another Lynwood unit on the street slowed and stopped. The Good Johnson piloted the black and white. He, too, had a trainee in the car. Too bad. Good Johnson would instill all his own biases and prejudices in the fresh-faced new guy. I wish I could say Good developed these horrible traits and cynicism over a long, storied career, but he'd only been on the street one year longer than my two. I feared his hatred came to him genetically, and if true, what chance did this world have?

He went by the nickname Good. He was the white Johnson. I was the black Johnson. When I first arrived at Lynwood, right from the gate he started calling me "boy." With the confusion in the names, the veteran deputies called me the bad Johnson. We became the good and the bad, and I was Bruno-the-Bad-Boy Johnson. He harbored an unwarranted dislike for me, and I wanted to believe it wasn't solely based on skin color. I'd never given him any other reason to treat me the way he did. I tried to get along even though the man didn't possess any redeeming qualities and worked as a detriment to the community.

Good smiled from his open car window and nodded to Crews as he pointed at me. "Hang in there, kid, you only have another two weeks with this weak sister, then you'll be in my car, and I'll teach you all that you need to know."

Crews didn't know how to react and just looked down at his taco and nodded. Crews nodded a lot, a generic response that kept him out of trouble with the deputies during his hazing period. Most trainees were not allowed to eat standing at the hood of the patrol car, not until they'd earned the right to, usually in phase three of their training. They normally ate sitting in the right front passenger seat, the "bookman" seat of the patrol car, alone, listening to the radio, completing the shift log, or hand writing the crime reports. I didn't believe in treating him like a grunt.

I didn't give Good the satisfaction of telling him to take off. It wouldn't have worked anyway. Good would do whatever he damn well pleased.

Over the loud patrol unit PA, Dispatch said, "251 to handle, 251 Adam to back a 211 silent at the Stop and Go, 16711 Platt Avenue cross of Century Boulevard."

A 211 silent. An armed robbery call where the clerk had tripped the alarm.

I wadded up the rest of my dinner and tossed it in the trash can. "Come on, let's go. That's not us, but we're close."

Good took off from the curb, his unit tires chirping and his engine roaring as he put his foot in it. I got in the unit and started up. "Stay off the radio. Let the assigned units coordinate the call." I pulled out of the parking lot and tried to catch up to Good.

Two fifty-one Adam, the deputy in the other patrol car, came up on the radio. "251 Adam, I'm going 97 and I have a vehicle leaving at a high rate of speed. I'm in pursuit."

I turned on the lights and siren and slammed my foot on the accelerator.

CHAPTER TWO

LUCK WINKED AT us. Frank Wilson, in 251A, a new guy who'd just finished his training three months earlier, changed direction and chased the robbery vehicle our way. Good Johnson, up ahead, kept going north on Long Beach Boulevard. I waited for traffic to clear and pulled a U-turn, went to the curb, and waited. I watched the rearview.

Behind us, at the next intersection, a Chevy Impala busted through the red signal, sending east- and westbound cars skidding into each other to avoid a broadside with the robber. Wilson, with nine months total on the street, hung on the guy's tail far too close. Traveling ninety miles an hour, he should've stayed back a couple more car lengths. He knew better. I'd had him in my car during his phase two. His excitement in the chase overrode his good sense and training.

I took a second to look at Crews twisting in the seat next to me to see behind us, his eyes wild with excitement, his body humming with it.

The Impala blasted by close enough to see two suspects, the driver in the front and the passenger in the right rear, an odd configuration for only two. They wore the folded and tied blue bandanas on their forehead just above their eyes, standard garb for the Crips, a violent street gang. These two paid our patrol car no mind. They looked straight ahead, intent on shaking Wilson loose before the airship could catch up to the pursuit and their chances of getting away dwindled to nonexistent.

I pulled out right behind Wilson and put my foot on the accelerator, the back tires screaming and sending up a cloud of white smoke. We now had the number two position in the pursuit. Policy dictated we take over the job of calling out location and speed so the lead car need only drive. Crews knew the job, picked up the mike and called out our speed and DOT—direction of travel.

Behind us, Good made a dangerous U-turn in front of other responding units instead of waiting for them to pass. He'd put the other deputies' safety at risk to make up for his poor positioning at the onset. He'd also slowed the other units' response to the pursuit.

Up ahead, the suspect continued to blow through north-south intersections, unheeded, all of them red signals.

Two streets later the Impala careened around a corner in a wide sweeping right turn and banged off an uninvolved civilian headed eastbound. Over the loud sirens of both our units, Crews spoke calmly but rapidly. "253, we just turned westbound on Rosecrans."

I corrected him. "We're on Compton."

Crews said into the mike, "We're on Compton, not Rosecrans."

He'd just earned himself some major verbal abuse from the veterans later on in the locker room.

The Impala let up on the speed just a little, not much, though. "Okay," I said, "they're looking for a place to foot bail. When they do, you stay with me, you understand? You stay right on my ass, you understand? And if it goes to guns, watch your backdrop."

He didn't answer, too caught up in the chase.

"Hey, pay attention, you hear me? You understand, stay right on my ass and do exactly what I tell you."

"Yes, sir."

The Impala took the next left down a narrow street with cars parked on both sides, leaving room for only one car to travel north or south—our cars. If anyone came north, the Impala would be trapped with no outlet. The driver must've realized his error, because he increased his speed.

Up ahead, headlights appeared just beyond the next intersection. If that car made it past the intersection, headed right at us, the Impala would only have two choices: stop, or ram the car head on.

The Impala almost made it to the intersection in time—almost. The Impala turned hard, cut it too short, and bounced over the curb. The driver lost control, his terminal speed for the turn too great, at least sixty miles per hour. The Impala bounced like a billiard ball across someone's front yard, mowing over the fence, kicking shrubs out the back, and smashing head on into the front wall to the house. The impact, an explosion that shook the entire structure, sent up a cloud of steam and dust and pulverized plaster.

The Impala was shoved deep into a dark living room that glowed with the subdued and flickering light from the television.

I locked our brakes up, skidding to a stop. Our stopping took only seconds. In that time the two suspects bailed out of the crashed car and instantly disappeared into the night.

Inside the house, a woman shrieked and shrieked, "My baby. My baby. Oh my God, where's my baby?"

The exterior gaped open, exposing the television on the left and the Impala impaled into a couch, which was now shoved deeper into the house, the interior a compressed wreck.

I jumped out and drew my service .357 and pointed it at the car. In my peripheral vision, Crews followed Wilson, who had taken off after the suspects. "Crews. Get your ass back here. Now."

Crews stopped and looked to where Wilson had disappeared, wanting to follow and knowing what was right: doing what the training officer told him.

I advanced on the Impala, my focus entirely on the car. "Cover the car. Clear the car first. Always clear the car first if you don't want to get shot in the back."

He returned and took up a position beside me, breathing hard. "They ran off. We're missing the foot pursuit."

"We clear the car first. Wilson shouldn't have moved on past before he cleared the car. That's the fastest way to get yourself shot."

"I told ya, I saw both of the suspects run off."

"Pay attention. Take that side. I'll cover this one, and we move up together."

We advanced across the torn-up front yard as more sheriff units skidded to a stop behind us.

From seven feet away, still moving up, I pointed the flashlight beam into the car, which appeared empty from where I stood. Crews moved up on his side faster, intent on getting it done too quickly. All of a sudden he stuck his gun out farther and yelled. His voice hit that squeaky high note that told everyone he'd crossed over into a fear he'd never yet experienced. "Freeze. Show me your hands. Show me your hands."

"Crews, go easy."

"I got one in the back seat," he said. "He's on the floor between the seats. I can't see his hands."

He'd gotten that part of the training right: the gun never killed you, the hands did each and every time.

I didn't have time for these asshole crooks. I had to get inside the house and help the woman find her child. What a nightmare we'd dumped into her life. Who wouldn't believe their world safe behind a closed and locked door, watching their favorite sitcom? And then out of the blue their house comes down around them?

I yelled, "Just hold and cover. Don't move up any farther."

I shuffle-stepped up and peered into the car. Dust from the torn-up yard and the demolished wall settled in a cloud, dimming the view and diffusing the flashlight beams. In the rear compartment, a fat black guy lay facedown, wedged in between the back of the front seat and the backseat. He wore khaki pants and a gray sweatshirt shoved up, exposing his back. The light black skin was tattooed with "Dust Town Hoggs" and the bust of a woman wearing a bandana, topless, her breasts huge, artistically well-defined. The right breast of the tattoo bled profusely from a large entry wound. This kid of seventeen or eighteen had been shot in the back in a bad place, the liver.

"Watch him," I said to Crews.

I moved up and shone my light into the front compartment and found a second suspect. He was on his back, his head shoved up under the dash, with his legs on the front seat. Nobody in the car wore seatbelts, and the impact had created havoc with their bodies, tossing them around like crash dummies. The guy in the front seat didn't move, his legs spread eagled. The right one canted off at an unnatural angle, the blue denim sopping wet with blood, the indentation of the seat filling with it. I looked closer. An exit wound out the front of his leg gaped through a tattered hole that exposed white bone reflecting in the flashlight beam. This damage also came from a large-caliber weapon. This kid had also been shot from behind, his leg all but blown off.

The woman inside the house continued to scream. A deputy

on the street directed his unit's spotlight on the scene, and then another and another until the whole place was lit up bright as a sun-filled day.

Backing deputies moved in to assist. I let them take control. I holstered and climbed across the hood, boots thumping on crumpled metal and on into the house.

A black woman stood pinned at the knees by the couch, her back up against the far wall in the small living room. Her hands up by her face as she keened over and over, "My baby, where's my baby?"

I grew sick to my stomach with the fear of what I'd find in that room.

CHAPTER THREE

THE DUST FROM the outside wafted in thick and obscured the room, but not enough to hide the terror in the mother's eyes.

"It's okay, take it easy. I'll help you find your baby. I'll find him, I promise."

"My baby," she shrieked. "My baby."

I climbed across chunks of the folded wall and over the couch to get to her. The dust now filled my lungs and I coughed as I hugged her trembling body. "It's okay, I'm here to help."

I let go of her to move the couch, but she glommed onto me. I couldn't budge the couch. Her legs had to be compromised at least to some degree, broken or crushed. "Where's the last place you saw your child?"

"I don't know. I'm not sure anymore. Over there, I think. What happened? Was it an airplane? Did an airplane crash into our house? My baby, please help me find my baby."

"How old is the child and what's his name?"

"Delbert Fawlkes, I named him after his daddy. Everyone calls him Del, jus' like his daddy. His daddy works for Papa Dee. You know Papa Dee?"

In her hysteria she'd gone to jabbering to help bury the reality of the moment. Of course I knew Papa Dee; everyone in South

Central LA knew him. He controlled all the rock cocaine in the projects—Jordan Downs, Nickerson Gardens, and Imperial Courts. Word went around that Papa Dee was on the move to expand. The poor bastards gunshot in the Impala—if they lived, it wouldn't be for long, not once Papa Dee found out what happened to his people, driving a car into their house like this.

A child cried.

"My baby, that's Del. Help my baby. Please, Lord God, help my baby, mister."

Not ten feet away, the length of a car, six or eight deputies dragged the wounded suspects from the Impala and not too kindly. Their racket covered the baby's cry.

I moved toward the direction of the sound and coughed some more.

Del cried again. I shone my light into the darkness. A toddler stood in the hall that led to the back of the house. He wore a Teenage Mutant Ninja Turtles pajama top and a diaper, his chubby little legs slightly bowlegged. Tears glistened on his smooth black skin. Blood trickled from his lip and his nose, not much, not enough to worry about unless it came from internal injuries. He must've been in just the right position to be shoved into the hallway when the car came through.

One lucky little guy.

I made it over to him, cooing, saying his name. The poor child shook with fear, half-scared out of his wits. Who could blame him? I picked him up and carefully carried him back to his mama. Her legs were still pinned to the wall by the crunched-up couch. I handed him to her just as firemen climbed through the opening with a large light, tools, and medical boxes. I left them to it and went to find my other obligation, trainee Crews.

* * *

Crews stood off to the side with three trainees, in a separate group
from the field-training officers and other patrol deps. I headed toward Crews, weaving in and out of the emergency vehicles now jam-
ming up the street and blocking in our patrol car, just as Sergeant
Foreman came out of the darkness. "Bruno, get your ass over here."

Foreman always made it a point to go out of his way to make my
life miserable. I deserved it. Not all that long ago, I'd gone to a call,
one that always popped up in my memory tagged as *The House
That Bled*. I found a gunshot child at the location and rushed him
to the hospital in the patrol car against Foreman's direct orders.
He had wanted me to wait for paramedics. I should've been repri-
manded, but instead, the station captain squashed the reprimand.
He said to Foreman, loud enough for witnesses to hear, "Now,
just how the hell do you think that would look if Bruno fought
this reprimand and the press got a hold of it. The kid lived, you
dumbass. Get the hell outta my office."

Further rubbing salt in the wound, the training lieutenant
made me a training officer.

Deputy Good stood among the other deputies gathered for
Sergeant Foreman's briefing.

Foreman looked at me when he spoke. "Okay, no guns were
found in the car."

Wilson, the new guy, who'd gone on scene of the robbery and
started the pursuit, said, "How'd they get shot, then? Without
any guns in the car, how'd they get shot?"

Good Johnson grunted, said, "Rookie."

Foreman nodded in agreement to the rookie comment and
said, "In all the excitement the guns discharged inside the car, and
then when you got onto them, started the chase, they tossed the

guns out the windows." He looked from Wilson to me, "That's why I want you, Bruno, to take all three trainees, divide up, and walk back the entire length of the pursuit. We gotta recover those guns. We can't afford to let any kids get a hold of them or it'll give the sheriff's department a black eye."

I wanted to say, "Right, and also endanger some kids as well," but I held my tongue.

"Yeah, have a good time with that, Bad Boy," Good said, "while us real deputies handle the tough calls." He laughed, along with some of the others who held the same prejudices.

I left that group without further comment and went over to the three trainees. "Okay, follow me." I kept walking right on by them and moved between the cars.

The pursuit hadn't lasted that long, but at eighty miles an hour, we'd covered a lot of ground—ground that in reverse and on foot, would take hours to search. I moved out of the street and up onto the sidewalk. "You two take that side, one in the street and one on the sidewalk. We're looking for guns tossed during the pursuit. Do a good job, because if you miss it, and it's found later, there'll be hell to pay. Me and Crews here will take this side. Keep your partner in sight and don't separate for any reason. We're still deep into Indian country, and you cherries don't know your heads from your asses and you will get eaten. You understand?"

All three answered in unison, "Yes, sir."

"Get to it."

They moved out.

Crews and I started our sweep. The more I thought about what happened, the more I knew Foreman and the others were wrong. I thought I knew what had happened, only I couldn't leave to check it out, not when left with the responsibility for the safety of three new guys.

We made it to the main artery we'd turned off of, Compton Avenue. I stopped. Crews looked up from scanning the ground with his flashlight. "What? You find something?"

"No, but this is ridiculous."

"Why?"

"Never mind."

He came over close. "How am I going to learn if you don't tell me?"

I waved the two trainees across the street to keep going, then looked at Crews. "Okay, back there at the scene, inside the car, before anybody was moved, what did you see?"

He thought about it. "Two suspects with GSWs, both dressed like gangbangers. Two shot, two got away on foot, total of four. What am I missing here?"

"Entry, exit?"

He took a second to think about it. "I didn't really look when—"

"Details, pay attention to the details, they'll save your life one day."

"Okay, I got that. What did I miss?"

"Both were shot from behind."

He shrugged. "I'm still not following you. Oh, wait. Sergeant Foreman said he thought they were ADs, accidental discharges. I gotta tell ya that sounded a little screwy to me when he said that."

"Why?"

"Well, I could see one AD, inside the car. The assholes get excited and the gun goes off. But not two." He snapped his fingers. "And then you add in that they were both shot from behind and no way could that happen like that, especially in the car."

I snapped my fingers like he did and pointed at him. "Give the rookie a cracker."

He beamed. "So what are we going to do?"

"Foreman already hates my ass, but what's right is right." I yelled at the other two deputy trainees across the street. "You two, keep going, stay together and stay on your side of the street. We're gonna be right back." They nodded and kept looking, intent on being the ones to find the sought-after evidence that I knew wasn't there and they believed would make them look good in the eyes of their FTOs, their Field Training Officers.

"Come on," I said to Crews, and stepped into the middle of Compton Avenue to flag down a passing car.

CHAPTER FOUR

A NEWSPAPER DELIVERY van drove us the short three miles to the Stop and Go where the robbery occurred. We got out. I shook the long-haired driver's hand. "Thanks, man, I owe you."

"No problem, dude. Glad to do it. Good luck." He backed up and drove off.

Deputy Wilson's patrol car sat in front of the Stop and Go. His car had been lead in the pursuit and not boxed in like ours. He'd been assigned the handle on the call and came back to get a formal statement from the clerk.

The bright light from inside lit up the parking lot. Wilson stood at the counter, notebook in hand talking with—

"Oh, shit."

Crews stopped when I did and said, "What? What's the matter?"

The clerk made eye contact with me and lost his smile. "Nothing," I said. "Tonight just went from bad to worse."

Crews nodded. He opened the door and we entered the store.

The clerk pointed at me. "I don't want that nigga in my store."

Wilson turned and looked at me, confused.

I moved right up to the counter, staring the clerk down, not believing who, of all people, it turned out to be. I didn't know that Noble had gotten a job, let alone worked in a store on my beat.

Wilson said, "Bruno, you know this guy?"

"Yeah, I do." I still looked at the clerk, "Noble, give me the gun."

Noble raised his hands, open, spread wide. He feigned surprise, "What're you talking about, Deputy?"

"Don't make this any worse than it already is. Gimme the gun."

Noble instantly shifted to violent anger, which he was prone to do. He pointed at me and yelled, "Get him out of my store, right motherfucking now." His body vibrated with pent-up rage. He fought to keep from coming over the counter at me. We'd done battle before, a number of times, and what he lacked in skill he made up for with an innate, brutal violence that usually left his adversaries lacking body parts: eyes, noses, and ears.

I didn't break eye contact and said, "Crews, read this suspect his rights. Do it right from the card, no mistakes."

"No," Noble yelled, "No, this ain't right. I'm tellin' you right now. I was defending myself. They came in here and stuck a gauge up in my face, Bruno. I only did what I had to do."

Wilson's mouth dropped open. "What? What are you saying? What's he talking about? What gun? Who'd he shoot?"

I pulled my gun in a quick, smooth draw and pointed it right at Noble's forehead. I didn't want to, Lord knows I didn't want to, but this crime would send Noble over the edge. A two-time loser at only twenty-one and on parole, this would send him back to the joint for a long stretch. If anyone back in that Impala died, he'd be eligible for that *forever* kind of time. This impending arrest made him as dangerous as a wounded lion. I'd pulled the gun not for me but to protect the two new guys standing with me who didn't have all the information.

He raged, "You're pointing a gun at me? At me? You son of a

bitch." He vaulted the counter, a human torpedo. I hit him with the pistol on the top of his head. He wilted to the floor.

Crews jumped on him.

"No. Get back. This is my cross to bear and mine alone." I pulled Crews off, holstered my gun, and handcuffed Noble, hands trembling.

His scalp bled from the laceration.

I rolled him over and patted him down. Under his Stop and Go smock I pulled from a shoulder holster a Ruger Redhawk .44 magnum with an eight-and-three-quarter-inch barrel. I broke open the cylinder; five of the six rounds had been fired. I handed the small cannon to Wilson as Noble's eyes rolled from the top and came down into focus. "Bruno, man, you can't do this. It was self-defense. You do this, I'll never get out. Never. They'll kill me in the joint. You know that. They'll shank my ass."

I helped him to his feet, my stomach churning with emotion. "You shot them in the back after the threat had passed. It's not up to me. The DA will make the determination."

"Come on. Come on, man. Can't you for once in your life step across that perfect line and not do what's right? I was tryin' here. I was tryin' real hard to do right. I got this fucked-up straight man's job doin' the eight ta five thing. I wasn't slingin' no more for Papa Dee. I was only packin' heavy tonight 'cause Del, Dee's main man, was gunnin' for me, said I still owed him. I don't owe him shit. Can't you see that? I was tryin' hard, Bruno."

I swallowed down the lump in my throat. "You made a poor choice bringing a gun to work. You're on parole, Noble. Jesus, you're on parole."

Tears filled his eyes. "You and your 'what's right is right' bull-shit. What's our daddy gonna say? Huh, Bruno? What's our daddy gonna say about you arresting your own brother?"

CHAPTER FIVE

FROM THE HALLWAY of our house, I peeked inside. The tall door was open only a crack. All ten kids quietly played with each other on the floor, in the chairs, and at the low table. Their sitter, a tired old man—my father—slept in the recliner.

I still wore my work clothes, an issued floral shirt and white pants from the La Margarite, where I tended the outdoor cabana bar. The nameplate read "Bob Johnson," a not-so-clever alias.

Marie, my dad, and I had scooped up these endangered kids in South Central Los Angeles and fled with them down to Costa Rica, where they at least had a chance to be safe and to survive. My grandson, Alonzo, had been placed by the court with my in-laws, the same parents who'd raised Derek Sams, the man who'd abused Alonzo's brother, Albert, until he died. Rick and Toby Bixler, brothers burned in a failed PCP lab. Those two would've gone back to the same hazardous and toxic environment had we not intervened. Sonny Taylor, the cute, hungry little kid who ate his mother's meth and then, after the judge gave him back to her, got locked in a closet. What chance did he have? Marvin Kelso, his mom's child-molesting boyfriend—I couldn't even think about that horrible scenario. Randy Lugo, with five broken bones—how long before it would have been his neck?

Tommy Bascombe, his mother a speed freak who took Tommy to the most dangerous parts of LA to score dope. She had even traded him off for a while, but always got him back in time for social services to do their home inspection. She wasn't going to miss out on her welfare check. Eddie Crane, Elena Cortez, and Sandy Williams, the most recent arrivals, made ten total. They ranged in age from ten to five. All present, I breathed easier each and every time I came home and found them safe and sound.

The Feds back in the States were still looking for me hot and heavy, but wouldn't bother to come this far south to scoop me up, not on suspicion only. Not for children who would be no better off if returned. At least, that's what I wanted to believe.

We were a family now. The latest three kids, Eddie Crane, Elena Cortez, and Sandy Williams, had only been with us a short time. Marie and I had gone back to the states three months ago to rescue them from a violent kidnapper. In the process, I'd managed to anger every member of the Sons of Satan outlaw motorcycle gang, yet another good reason to be in hiding down in Costa Rica. Eddie, Elena, and Sandy had assimilated well and now acted as if they'd always been there with the other seven.

Ten kids, what a handful, what a responsibility. One so large it sometimes scared me when I thought about how much these kids depended upon me. Depended on us.

I eased the door open. The hinges creaked. All the children still possessed survival instincts honed sharp from the constant threat of abuse in their old environments. They turned to look at the door and froze, waiting to see who came through, friend or foe. I could only hope that one day they'd grow to feel safe like children should.

I raised my hands, fingers splayed like a monster. I put on a monster's grimace and pushed in the rest of the way. When the kids saw me, their frozen expressions shifted to smiles. I stepped into the room like Frankenstein's monster with long stiff-legged steps. "I just got off work," I said, in a louder than normal voice, "And!" I stopped. The younger children shrieked with joy and crawled around to hide. I took another step. "Suddenly, I'm feeling kinda hungry." The rest of the children scrambled about; two of the older ones from the original seven charged right at me. I roared like a monster, grabbed them both up, and wrestled them to the floor, tickling and rolling around with them. The other kids piled on, all laughing and having a wonderful time.

We rolled around and around. I pretended to eat arms and legs and they pretended to be a town mob fighting off the monster. I roared, they shrieked and laughed. We played until I couldn't breathe. A man on the backside of forty, pushing fifty hard, I couldn't keep up with ten healthy and vigorous children. I gave up and lay flat on my back. Everyone piled on. Tommy said, "Come on, play some more, play some more." Some of the others took up the mantra. "Come on, play some more."

"No, no, I can't." I struggled up to all fours and tried to stand as they hung on like koala bears to a tree.

I froze. They did, too. I waited a long second and then said, "Suddenly, I'm feeling kinda hungry." They all yelled and shrieked and piled on harder to fight the monster. We rolled around some more until my old body said it was enough. The kids sweated and breathed hard. I peeled them off one at a time. The older ones knew the game had ended and moved back to the low table and their board games.

I caught a glimpse of my girl Marie standing at the door, smiling. "How long have you been there?" I asked.

"Long enough to see that you're not working hard enough at the hotel if you have that much energy left when you get home."

She smiled and, in a lower tone, said, "You'd better have saved some of that for me."

Back in the States, the love of my life, Marie, had been a physician's assistant at Martin Luther King Hospital before she threw in with me and became a federal fugitive dodging the law for taking children out of their toxic homes. Now she volunteered at the local clinic just to stay fresh in the career she dearly loved, helping people who were sick or injured.

I, casually so she wouldn't notice, reached down and felt my outside pants pocket to make sure the small lump was still there after all the rough and tumble, and relaxed some. Relaxed as much as I could, given what it represented. To be honest, it scared the hell outta me, and I thought I'd rather go back to the States and do battle with the Sons, rather than have it in my pocket.

Dad touched my back and said, "Hey?"

I turned around expecting to see his glowing smile. He liked to watch me wrestle around with the kids. This time, though, his expression remained neutral.

"Bruno," he said, "I need to talk to you for a minute."

"Sure, Dad." He rarely called me by name. Most times he called me "Son." This did not bode well. Maybe one of the kids needed something extra, additional tutoring for math or history that would put an added drain on our already limited budget. He'd become their de facto advocate. I never denied him anything, but we'd periodically dance this dance.

I turned back to look at Marie and, at the same time, said to him, "First though, would you mind watching the kids tonight. I'd like to take my lovely girl out to dinner at the El Toro, in San José."

Marie smiled. "The El Toro, Bruno, really? I'll call Rosie, she'll help watch the children, give your dad a little break. A night out, and at the El Toro, I can't wait."

Dad took hold of my hand. "This is important, Son, can I talk to you, please?"

I turned back; his expression remained grim. "Sure, sure, Dad. Come on, let's go outside." I gently turned him and guided him out the double French doors to the patio.

The weather varied little, with sporadic showers throughout the day. Water sat in puddles and dripped from the tropical plants and trees, a far cry from the desert-like conditions in South Central Los Angeles. Even so, I missed LA.

I grew more scared with each step as my mind started to spin out the possibilities. Dad had been battling stomach cancer. He'd had the surgery, the chemo, and now they were finishing up with radiation. Like a scared child, I'd put aside the reality of it. He used to be strong, well built with muscle he came by naturally. I remembered him most often the way he was in the 1970s when I was growing up, with his glistening close-cropped hair and a narrow waist and broad shoulders. He'd worked forty years for the postal service as a mail carrier and never called in sick, not even one day. The USPS thought this an amazing feat and honored him when he retired with a special plaque. He told me later, "Pshaw, thanking me for doing something that was the right thing to do, anyway. That's ridiculous. They should save their honors for those who deserve it, those who keep their families together and safe from this crazy, out-of-control world."

Of course, the crazy world to which he referred had been all about Albert, my grandson, Dad's great-grandson, who died at the hand of Derek Sams. I'd tracked Sams and gunned him down like the mad dog that he was. I went to prison for two years for that little indiscretion and lost my job as a detective on the Los Angeles County Sheriff's Violent Crimes team. A job—and a position in the community—Dad had been so damn proud of.

Moving out to the patio, Dad looked emaciated, a mere shell of what he used to be. In my heart I knew what he was about to tell me, that he didn't have long to live.

What the hell would I ever do without him?

Outside, he turned and looked up at me. I swallowed hard and fought the huge lump growing in my throat. He took my hand and held up a white paper folded in thirds. "I want you to read this. I know you don't want to, but I want you to do it for me. Please?"

I swallowed hard. "What is it? Is it from the hospital? Is it from the doctor?"

"No, of course not. What's the matter with you? It's a letter from your brother Noble."

CHAPTER SIX

"No, I'm sorry, I don't want anything to do with him." I shoved it away.

Dad's eyes flared. "Don't be a horse's ass, don't you dare. You made yourself a party to this twenty-odd years ago, so you're going to read it." He stopped short of saying I'd been the cause for all of Noble's problems.

That wasn't fair. Dad had never blamed me for Noble's troubles, or his crimes.

Dad rarely used words like horse's ass, and his body trembled with a fury I didn't know he still possessed. "Sure, Dad, sure, take it easy. I'll read it." I took the letter from him. "Come on, let's sit down over here."

I gave in easily. He had another card to throw: my hypocrisy, something I knew he'd never do, so I owed him that.

We sat down on a raised flagstone planter. I held the letter still folded and rested my other hand on his. "Dad, first I need to know. It's important that I know how this letter made it here?"

"Don't you worry about me. I mailed everything to Tommy Tomkins. Noble does too. We both go through Tommy Tomkins. Nobody knows we're corresponding. Tomkins works as a middleman. No one knows where we are down here. We're still safe, I promise you. Okay? You know me better than that, little man. I'd never risk the safety of our kids."

I like that he referred to the kids as *ours*. But I didn't like so much the reference to me as *little man*. He hadn't used it since I attended elementary school.

I knew Tom Tomkins, an old buddy of Dad's who'd worked with him for several decades at the post office. They went albacore fishing every year during the season. Tom Tomkins wasn't much better off health wise. Last I'd heard he'd been laid up with twenty-four-hour care. No way did he receive or mail his own correspondence. That made at least one more person in this already dangerous loop.

"Okay," I said.

I had been concerned about our security, no doubt about it, but in reality I only wanted to stall. I didn't want to see what the letter contained. The words could only hurt and dredge up old emotional wounds of regret and again make me rue that Christmas day the neighbors' house burned down, killing a little boy and girl.

Dad didn't push me and waited patiently. I couldn't wait forever and needed to get this done for Dad's sake, and so I could move on with my life. I looked forward to the dinner with Marie and tried to think about that instead.

I took a deep breath and unfolded the paper. One page typed and dated ten months earlier. Dad had held on to the letter for a while.

> *Dad,*
> *Thank you so much for the money. I can't tell you how much it helps with Ricardo and Rebecca's school tuition.*

I stopped reading. "He has children? How can he have children? He's in prison, been there for twenty-five years."

"Read, read, would you just read it, Bruno?"

I understand your situation and why you can no longer visit. I get it and I'm glad you're no longer living in South Central, in Willowbrook. The place where you are, the way you describe it, sounds absolutely wonderful and if anyone deserves it, you do.

I knew Noble better than anyone; we'd been brothers for too long. Before reading on I sensed a very large "but" coming, I could feel it. He wanted something, and it would be something big just by the way he had worked to build up to it.

Dad, let me get right to the point. I did something to Bruno long ago, and it rips my heart out that I can't make it right. I think I know what it is, but time has clouded it, sanded off all the sharp edges. So much so, the reason now seems petty and infantile. Time has slipped through our fingers for him and me and now we don't have much left. I don't want something to happen to either one of us before we have a chance to make this right.

Could you please ask Bruno again to come and see me? Please? I really need to see him.

Always Yours, (and desperate)
Your favorite loving son
Noble Johnson

He'd put that *favorite loving son* part in there as a jab. He'd always joked that he was the favorite. I truly didn't care, but it seemed to matter a great deal to him.

I handed the letter back to Dad. "I can't go see him. I'm sorry. You know the reasons why. The cops are looking for me. It's not worth the risk." Being wanted by the cops worked only as a façade I hid behind.

I wanted to tell Dad that Noble had made his own choices, but couldn't, not anymore. I no longer had the high ground to defend. Years later, I, too, had made the choice to cross over into lawlessness. First with the killing of Derek Sams, and then by taking those physically and emotionally wounded children from their toxic homes and rescuing them. By anyone's moral compass, a correct and just motivation, but, at best, legally ambiguous. The social welfare system protecting the children was broken, but it was the only system we had.

Reading the letter forced me to reevaluate my stand on my brother Noble. He'd sold rock cocaine for Papa Dee. He ruined hundreds, if not thousands, of young lives with that poison. So no, he and I were still not in the same category. I tasted a hint of my own snobbery—*the moral high ground*—what the hell had I been thinking? He was my brother just like the twins in the house, the Bixlers. I'd watched the Bixlers; they would argue and fight with each other like normal kids do and then band together against a common interloper, another kid trying to take undue advantage. Noble and I had acted the same way through school, until Noble had dropped out his junior year to sling the rock. He made lots of money and flaunted it in Dad's face. Told Dad that he was a fool for working for the government making peanuts when all the money in the world lay just outside our front door in the ghetto.

Noble didn't understand that the coke crushed the breath out of lives and families.

I came home from school one day and found Dad with skinned knuckles and one eye swollen shut. I knew what had happened even though Dad wouldn't say. Noble had come over and goaded Dad one time too many. Dad had put Noble in his place. Still, I'd turned furious that Noble would raise his hand to our father. I went looking for Noble that day and didn't find him. Good thing.

Noble had to have been laid up somewhere licking his wounds from the thrashing Dad had given him. I never saw Noble again until the night he shot and killed two gang members who were trying to rob the Stop and Go.

Dad gently took the letter from me and handed me another. He patted my hand as he struggled to his feet and left me to it. I watched him hobble back through the doors into the dining room and disappear into the gloom.

This one was really the letter he wanted me to see. He'd given me the first one to force me to think things over, to gently ease me into what the next one held. And his strategy worked. I had relived our past, reexamined my own life with its errors and omissions, some that had turned deadly. Dad had done this without saying a word. If I lived to be a hundred, I'd never possess the natural insight Dad had into the human psyche.

And now, this bombshell, the folded paper that lay in my hand.

CHAPTER SEVEN

I SAT A long time with the folded letter, the paper turning unnaturally warm in my hand, the sensation generated entirely through imagination. I wanted to tear it up, walk away. I couldn't. I don't think I'd ever been so conflicted.

Noble had come over that day long ago and fought with Dad, and yet Dad still loved him unconditionally. I thought about little Alonzo, my grandson, inside playing with the other kids. I'd do the same for him. I'd defend him to the death, no question. All the kids for that matter, I'd do the same for them.

I didn't want to unfold the paper, to read the words written by Noble. Words I knew would suck me back into his vortex of emotion, his violent world that would glom onto me, pull me down and never let go. The first letter had been bad enough—this one—well—

I closed my eyes and unfolded it. After a long moment, I looked down at the words. The letter was dated from the previous week, the time it took to make its way through the cutout Dad had set up with Tom Tomkins and for Tomkins or Tomkins' agent to re-mail it.

* * *

Bruno,

My big brother, I'm in terrible trouble and need your help. I admit, when I was younger, to being a fool, a hateful, immature fool. And I am sorry. Sorry more than you know. You have to believe me when I say I've changed. I'm not like that anymore, not at all. I went to school while behind these walls and earned my degree. I'm educated, big brother, can you believe it? Me, of all people, with a degree in theology, a certified ordained minister.

No more excuses, though. As I said, I am in deep trouble here and only the Lord can help me. I've asked Him for His guidance. He came to me, told me I could only help myself. That help can only come from one place. The only option left to me. My big brother.

My past life has come back to teach me the same lesson all over again. I am desperate. Please come. I have no one else to turn to.

Bruno, it's my family, evil stalks my family and I can do nothing about it, not from behind these walls. It's so damn frustrating and scary. More scary than I can describe. Think about it. How would you feel in a similar situation, if the tables were turned?

Your favorite little bro
Noble Johnson

I wadded up the paper and threw it as hard as I could. How could he ask me something like this? Not after twenty-five years. Not after never hearing from him at all and then asking for something I couldn't give even if I wanted to, not without jeopardizing the welfare of my own family. I spun and kicked the unforgiving flagstone planter. I hopped around, fighting the pain. This kind of pain came as a welcome relief to the alternative, the emotional bombshell Noble just dropped in my lap to smother and ruin everything I'd worked for.

I stomped over to the door, hesitated, turned the knob, stopped, went back, picked up the balled paper, and shoved it down deep into my pocket with the other item. I stopped, thought about it, and took out the wadded paper. I shoved it in my other pocket. I didn't want Noble's words to taint the planned evening with Marie.

I took several deep breaths and went looking for Dad to tell him. No way. No way in hell.

Dad had retreated behind his locked bedroom door and wouldn't answer my knock. He knew me better than I did. Without Dad present for me to rail at, Noble's words would eat a big hole in my gut. I stood at his door, my forehead pressed to the wood, eyes closed, angry, not with Dad, but with myself. I respected Dad more than ever for his ability to read and understand the way I thought and acted.

That wadded-up paper in my pocket again started to glow warm. I put aside the thought that I might be losing my mind.

* * *

Rosie Beltran, a rotund, happy woman with long black hair down past her waist, appeared in the living room area where Marie and I sat with the kids, talking and just enjoying the early evening with our family. Rosie never knocked; she acted as an extended part of our household. She loved the kids, and when we added Eddie, Elena, and Sandy, I offered to hire a second housekeeper/sitter. She said with sixteen brothers and sisters, this well-mannered group had yet to give her problems.

Dad still had not come out of his room. He wouldn't until we left for dinner.

I kissed the top of Alonzo's head and lifted him off my lap. Marie got up before I could, came over, and offered a hand to help me out of the deep easy chair. "I love you dearly," I said, "but when you do that you make me feel . . . ah, inadequate."

She smiled, "Don't be silly, you'll never be inadequate."

I stood and kissed her lightly on the lips. "Thank you, babe."

"Never inadequate, just old." She jumped away laughing. I grabbed at her. The smaller kids saw the game and chased her, laughing.

Marie wore her dark-brown hair back in a ponytail the way I liked it. Her peasant blouse, covered in local colors, revealed just enough décolletage to entice and yet remain classy. From her neck hung a plain gold crucifix on a thin gold chain that dangled in the cleft of her breasts. Sexy beyond belief. Her smile, the best I'd ever seen, acted like a switch that lit up my world.

I watched her with the kids and, for the millionth time, couldn't understand what she saw in me. I gently brushed the kids aside, took her by the waist, and pulled her into me. Her head nestled nicely just below my chin. I took in her scent, tropical, hibiscus and orchid from the flowers she wore behind her ear. I kissed the top of her head and hugged her tight. Too tight, I knew, and for a different reason.

The wadded-up missive from Noble in my pocket would bring her a grief she didn't deserve and make our evening bittersweet.

Maybe I'd wait and tell her tomorrow. Yes, tomorrow would be soon enough.

She pulled back a little. "Hey, what gives? I'm not a tube of toothpaste, you know."

Before I could answer with a smart quip, the doorbell rang.

I took her by the hand and led her out of the room and into the hall. Rosie herded the children, kept them from following. I held tight to Marie's hand as we walked to the door.

"Who could that be?" Marie asked. "It's dinner time. How inconsiderate."

I didn't reply and opened the door.

The man, a Costa Rican native dressed in a tux, said, "Good evening, sir, ma'am." He'd doffed his hat. Behind him, parked at the curb, sat a gleaming black stretch limo.

I watched Marie and ate up her smile. I loved the way she beamed. It made the night worthwhile, and we hadn't even started out yet. She turned to me and gently socked me in the chest. "Really, Bruno? How can we afford this?"

"You're right, what was I thinking?" To the driver I said, "I'm sorry we won't be needing you after all. Thank you for coming."

"Very good, sir." He turned to leave.

"Wait," Marie said to me, "As long as he's here. You'll have to pay for it anyway, right?"

"Sure, of course."

"Bruno, honey, don't do something like this again, please?" She smiled, went up on her toes, and kissed me, then pulled my head down, whispered in my ear. "Thank you, you big jerk."

I took her hand and followed the driver, who opened the back door for us. Inside, a champagne bottle dripping with condensation waited in a silver ice bucket.

"Oh, my God. Bruno?"

She grabbed my hand and pulled us in. "What's the special occasion?"

The driver closed the door. The little subdued light inside stayed on.

"I don't tell you enough how much I love you," I said. "You deserve a lot more than this."

Tears filled her eyes, the emotion contagious. I swiped at my own.

I already wanted this evening to never end and tried hard to imprint it on my memory.

At the same time, I forced Noble's words into that part of my mind where I didn't often venture. Try as I might to believe differently, I knew he'd end up ruining this absolutely perfect occasion.

CHAPTER EIGHT

THIRTY MINUTES LATER, the limo pulled up to the front of El Toro, where the valet for the restaurant opened the limo door. We'd managed to drink two glasses of champagne each on the drive. I didn't drink much, and the wine really hit me and smoothed off the hard edges to the evening. I'd started to relax, not realizing how pent-up I'd been.

Marie stepped out and, at the same time, leaned her head back and kissed me. "I wish you would've told me ahead of time. I would've worn a nicer dress and my good shoes."

"You'll still be the most beautiful woman in the joint." And I meant it. I followed her out and feigned a little limp.

She gripped my hand tight, "What's the matter? Why are you limping?"

"Oh, it's nothing, I think I picked up a little rock in my shoe."

The hostess escorted us to the prearranged table—best in the house—on the patio overlooking the ocean, out under the stars. A billion stars. On the horizon, a fat and happy full moon rested for a moment on its journey across the heavens. The waiter set a bottle of champagne on the table, also prearranged, as I pulled Marie's chair out for her.

"Bruno, more wine?" She lowered her tone. "If you're looking to be rewarded later tonight for being a good boy, you had me with the limo."

I leaned down and kissed her on her exposed shoulder. When confronted with a situation she wasn't accustomed to, my lovely girl, a fiery Puerto Rican, tended toward the vulgar. Okay by me.

I moved my chair around closer to hers so I could hold her hand. Sometimes I couldn't get enough of her and needed to be touching her in order to feel whole. She rested her head on my shoulder. I had to scrunch down to get it done.

She nodded to the flower arrangement on the table. "Nice touch with the red roses."

"Can you believe that moon?" I said.

The warm and moist ocean breeze blew in, caressing our skin, and making the candles on the table gutter.

The waiter popped the cork and poured the champagne just as the music came on, the song I'd requested ahead of time: "Every Little Thing She Does Is Magic," by The Police. The song we loved to listen to together.

She gripped my hand tighter. "Bruno, what's going on?"

My voice caught. "You want to dance?"

She froze.

"Oh, my God, Bruno." Her hand flew to her mouth as she figured me out.

I stood, took her hand, and walked her to the hardwood dance floor. We danced slowly, our bodies together. Her tears wet my shoulder.

The song ended where it was supposed to, far too soon.

I went down on one knee. Her shoulders shook with happiness as tears streamed down her cheeks. I took the ring box from my sock.

All the diners in the restaurant turned silent, no longer talking or clinking glassware or silverware. They melted away until only Marie remained in my world.

I had to swallow hard. "I don't ever want to wake in the morning, not a single morning, and not be with you. Will you marry me and spend the rest of your life with me?"

She couldn't speak and nodded vigorously. I put the ring on her finger, a large marquise-cut diamond with a gold setting, one we really couldn't afford.

Patrons, who'd paused their meal, clapped. The world started up again.

She held up her hand to look at the ring as I stood. She threw her arms around my neck. I swung her off her feet. We stayed that way a long time, slowly turning around and around. I didn't want the moment to end. I had never seen her happier.

I set her down and we walked hand in hand to the table. I held her chair for her and scooted her in. She held the ring up again, moving it from side to side in the light. The facets twinkled right along with her eyes. "Oh, Bruno, I had no clue, really I didn't." She looked at me, "This was the supposed rock in your shoe? You were having fun with me?"

"All part of the service, ma'am."

The waiter brought the menus. We ordered sautéed mushrooms, steak and lobster. The mushrooms came as we both finished our third glass of wine.

Marie's words held just a hint of slur, but it might've been caused from the smile that had never left her lovely countenance.

"There's this young girl," she said. "One I treated at the clinic today. She came from the orphanage. She's so damn cute, Bruno, you just wouldn't believe it unless you saw her."

I stopped the fork halfway to my mouth as I looked at her.

"What?" she asked.

"You have a heart the size of Texas, my love, but we just don't have the room. Ten is our limit. That's the number we agreed upon. And if that's not enough, we don't have a fake ID and passport for her. You know what we have going on. If the Sons of Satan come looking for me, we're going to have to drop everything. We'll have to leave at a moment's notice. The escape plan is already set. We might be running to Panama at any minute."

She play-slapped my shoulder. "Oh, don't be ridiculous. That's not at all what I meant. Of course we couldn't afford another, silly."

"Oh, really?" I put the mushroom in my mouth and chewed.

"And about that other thing, it's been three months; no one's coming after us. I like it here, Bruno. I think we should stay right here. Panama's not as modern."

I ate another mushroom. We had a plan and an emergency code in place: *Rosebud*. Dad thought of it, he took it from the movie *Citizen Kane*. If I spotted something suspicious at work or on the way home, I had only to call and say the word *Rosebud* to get things rolling, to start the family evacuation. I'd evade and distract and, when safe, meet up with them in Panama.

"This poor little girl, Jenny, her name's Jenny, she lost her arm in some sort of agricultural accident. It must've been absolutely horrible for her." She put her fork down. "And, Bruno, you ought to see her, she acts like nothing ever happened. Goes about life as if everyone else in the world only has one arm. She's only ten. With her personality and drive she's . . . she's going to grab the world by the tail."

"I'm sorry, no."

"The biggest brown eyes, you ever did see."

"No."

The music shifted to Joe Sample, "Hippies on the Corner." I

scooted my chair out, got up, and held out my hand. She stood and swayed just a bit from the wine. On the dance floor, we moved with the music as I continued to ride the wave of perfect elation, euphoria I'd not experienced my entire life.

I held on to her too tightly as she snuggled in closer. We'd have to eat something more substantial before we drank any more wine.

In the evenings at home, after work and when the children were all in bed asleep, we'd sometimes dance in the dark. Not a dance really, more just clinging to each other, not wanting to let go, lost in a melody and love song lyrics. She liked to shove her balled-up fists in my front pants pockets and pull me in tighter, a move not appropriate in public. The wine dissolved the minor social improprieties and this night she stuck her balled-up fists in my pockets. Another minute passed. She melted into me even more. We became one as we moved in a trance, unaware of the world around us.

When I looked up next, the music had stopped. I had no idea for how long. Over at our table, the waiter set down our meals.

"Come on," I whispered. "Time to eat."

"No, I want to stay right here."

"Me too, but I'm hungry and we both need to get some food into us."

She nodded. We parted. Her hand came out of my pocket with a wadded-up piece of paper.

"Here," I said, "gimme that, it's just trash." I tried to suppress my panic.

She pulled the wad away from me, took a step back. I had not masked my panic well enough, and she'd detected it.

"Marie, babe, please let me have it."

"Bruno, what is it?"

No way could I lie to her. "I'll show it to you in the morning."

I held my hand out, waiting for her to give it to me, kicking myself for putting it back in my pocket when I changed into my suit. Somehow Dad's strategy had burrowed deep under my skin, and I could not let Noble get away from me again, not after twenty-five years, my younger brother in the form of a wadded-up piece of paper I kept in my pocket.

She looked into my eyes for a long moment and then unwrapped the letter.

CHAPTER NINE

HER LIPS MOVED as she read the words. Her mouth dropped open. The worst of it was her eyes, the betrayal she saw in me. She looked up shaking her head. "No. Not this time, no. Never again. You promised me. You said never again, remember? You promised. You're not going back."

We stood there. I didn't want to hurt her, especially on her special night. I held my hands open. "I'm not going."

She hesitated, as if she didn't believe me. "Good. Bruno, you can't continue to tempt fate like you're doing. The odds are . . . no, *they will* fall against you, and then what?" Her voice caught.

"I'm not gonna go."

She turned, walked back to the table, sat, shook out the napkin on her lap, picked up her fork, and took a bite of the braised asparagus.

I sat down and cut a piece from the perfectly grilled steak. I put it up to my mouth just as she said, "I'm going with you."

I brought my fork down. "I'm not going, okay?"

She nodded and took another bite, this time of baked potato. She pointed the fork at me. No words came out, at a total loss as to what to say.

"Babe, we're not going. Neither one of us. No, we're not. We're not going."

She dropped her fork, her eyes went big, her mouth dropped open.

"What?" I asked. "What do I have to do?"

"No," she half-yelled. "This," she held up her ring, not minutes old now, and waved her arm around, "All this. You asked me to marry you because you wanted me to be all right with *this*?" She held up Noble's crumpled letter.

Now my mouth dropped open. "No, no, no, listen to me, please. Dad gave me the letter this afternoon. I've been planning this, all this, for a month now."

She shook the paper in her fist. "Doesn't matter. You had this information before we started out tonight and you chose to go ahead with it? To go ahead with it before you told me about this?" Tears filled her eyes. "You ruined it, Bruno. You ruined all of it. The memory we were making." She got up and rushed out.

I tossed some money on the table and ran after her.

Out in front of the hotel, the wind had come up and clouds blew in, slowly obscuring the stars. Marie stomped one way, turned, and stomped the other. "Where's the limo? I wanna go home. Now, Bruno, I want to go home."

The lump in my throat had grown so large I could hardly breathe. The last thing in the world I wanted to do was to hurt her. And that's exactly what I had done.

I reached down and slipped my loafer off, took the room key out, a large metal one. "I got us the honeymoon suite." My voice low, barely audible.

She crossed her arms, held herself tight, and shook her head, her face crumpled into tears. I stepped over to her and took her in my arms. I hugged her a long time. I guided us toward the room, a bungalow right on the sand.

The clouds caught up to the other side of the hotel and started to eat the moon alive, the night growing dark. I stopped, scooped her legs, and carried her the rest of the way. She put her arm around my neck and nuzzled her nose in close, her tears wetting my neck.

The warm breeze turned cool.

I stuck the key in the lock without setting her down, opened the door, and went in. I carried her over to the bed, pulled down the spread, and set her gently on the blanket. She wouldn't let go of my neck and pulled me down on top of her. She kissed me, hot and passionate. Her breathing got faster and faster. She pulled at my tie, at my shirt, turning more and more frantic. I tried to stand to take my clothes off. She pulled me back down. We rolled, switched position with her on top. She shucked her blouse, unhooked her bra, and tossed it. She took my face in both hands and kissed me. A ravenous kiss.

*　*　*

She got up naked and shivering, went to the double French doors, and closed them, her curvy outline erotic in the shadowed relief. She hurried back to bed and snuggled in close under the covers.

Two hours had passed since we'd fallen into bed and made love, two hours without a word.

"Bruno?"

I struggled to get a look at her. I needed to see her eyes. If I could see her eyes, I would be able to tell if she forgave me. I needed her to forgive me.

"No," she said, "Stay right like that." She gently pushed me down and kept her head resting on my chest, my arm around her.

"I'm scared, Bruno. Really scared."

"I know, so am I. I'm sorry I hurt you, really I am. I didn't mean to."

"I know, and I acted foolish."

"No, you didn't. You—"

"I did, and you know it. Thank you, though."

I pulled her in tighter next to me.

She didn't say anything for a long time. We had all night.

"When I opened that letter," her voice cracked with emotion, "do you know what I saw?"

I didn't want to talk about it anymore and could only shake my head.

Her fingernails dug into the flesh on my chest. "I know this sounds creepy and juvenile, but what I saw was . . . a death warrant. Yours, Bruno. I saw your death warrant."

I peeled her away from my body, put one hand on her forehead, and moved my nose close to hers. "I'm not going."

"You sure?" She hiccupped, trying to stifle her tears.

"Yes."

"Thank you, Bruno." She kissed me.

I made love to my fiancée for the second time that night.

CHAPTER TEN

WHEN I WOKE, Marie sat on the edge of the bed with two cups of coffee, her hair down about her shoulders, her expression a vibrant glow. I sat up and took one cup from her. She took hers in both hands and sipped, all the time watching me.

I sipped the hot coffee, black, like I'd always drank it when I worked the streets of LA.

She stared deep into my eyes with a connection we never had before but should have. "I'm going with you," she said.

In the light of the new day, the idea of not going was no longer an option. The night before, fatigue had fueled the denial and masked the reality. If I didn't go, I couldn't go on living a normal life. I'd be forever enslaved, forced to drag around a giant emotional anchor that would continue to grow and overshadow all else. I nodded and sipped, not letting go of her stare.

She sipped again and said, "We're going to be married first, no argument."

I nodded. And tried to hide a smile.

"What? This isn't funny, Bruno Johnson."

"Is this the way it's going to be from now on?"

"What are you talking about?"

"You keeping my balls on top of the refrigerator, and, if I have to go out, I have to ask permission to take them along?"

She turned away to keep from smiling. "Yes, that's right, you're not responsible enough. Your balls are grounded until further notice."

"There's no one I'd rather have as custodian over those little fellas, Marie Johnson."

She beamed, this time smiling with her eyes as well.

*　*　*

The limo dropped us off in front of our rented house. We went through the side gate and entered the house through the dining room doors. The whole family sat at the table eating breakfast, chicken and eggs cooked by Rosie. Some of the younger kids started to get up to welcome us. Rosie spoke firmly and they stayed their advance.

Dad, at the head of the table, looking surprised to see us so early, got up as fast as his rickety bones allowed, and made for a quick exit.

"It's okay, old man," I said, "Marie knows, and we're both going to make the trip."

He stopped and turned, flashing a huge smile. "Good to hear, thank you, Son. Thank you, Marie, for being so understanding."

"You better have yourself a seat again, though," I said. "There's other news."

He lost his smile. We'd had a lot of news lately, the last couple of years, most of it not good. I still held Marie's hand and now raised it high in the air. "It's official; we're going to be married."

The older kids cheered, with the younger ones following suit, unsure what had just happened. Dad smiled and hobbled over to hug us both. Rosie got up, eyes welling, and hugged us each in turn.

Dad said, "We'll have a huge wedding when you get back."

"No, Dad, it's tomorrow morning at ten. We have to catch the twelve o'clock to Los Angeles."

He lost his smile. I put my hand on his shoulder and eased him away from the small crowd all talking at once to Marie.

"Listen," I said, "I don't want you to think you had anything to do with this. It's just the way things worked out. I sowed these seeds twenty-five years ago, and it's now come time to harvest, that's all. This is all on me."

He patted my back. I pulled him into a hug. I didn't have a lot of time left with him, and now I was about to embark on an escapade that might suck me in and keep me for the rest of my life. That was, if I slipped up and got caught and thrown in prison.

"While you're there," he said, "could you check in on Tommy Tomkins?"

"Sure." I hugged him, his bones' hard ridges poking through too-thin muscle.

"I know it's asking a lot," he said, "but could you take him a hot link sandwich from Stops? He loved those hot link sandwiches."

It was real nice to be a friend of my dad's.

"Will you take good care of our kids for us?"

He nodded and wiped tears from his eyes. "You know I will."

* * *

The preacher was late. The plane would leave in one hour and fifty minutes, with a half hour drive to the airport, a half hour without traffic.

All the children, in their Sunday best, their hair coifed or slicked down, stood out in the patio, the sun shining bright and the tropical birds in the trees singing. Rain had passed through earlier, making everything fresh and more vibrant. Dripping.

Marie and I had both been married before, each to other spouses, long ago. Disasters, mostly due to immaturity displayed by everyone involved. This one meant so much to me. The meaning of "man and wife" carried with it a sacred trust, an obligation I now understood more clearly than ever before.

The doorbell rang.

"Everyone stay put," I said. "I'll get it."

I hurried to answer it, to usher the preacher in. I swung the door open to find a Costa Rican woman in sandals and a loose dress, her gray hair hanging below her shoulders. She carried a Bible and nothing else. She offered her hand. "Sorry, I'm late," she said with a thick Spanish accent.

I took her firm and weathered hand. "No problem at all. But we are kind of on a tight schedule. Everyone's ready and out on the patio." I held my arm up to let her lead the way. She nodded and we headed to the ceremony, my heart swelling.

CHAPTER ELEVEN

THE FLIGHT TOOK six hours and touched down at LAX at six thirty in the evening. Marie, emotionally exhausted, slept from the moment she sat down and clicked in her seatbelt. My body hummed with stress the entire flight. I didn't know if American intelligence—CIA, NSA, FBI, INS—would somehow be sharp enough to pick up the fake ID and passport I used to travel under. Would they be waiting at the other end when I stepped off the plane, back on American soil?

We moved down the skyway with our carry-ons. We hadn't checked any bags, as we didn't intend on staying more than a couple of days. The skyway spilled the passengers out into the main terminal. No one made eye contact, no uniformed police waited. We'd made it.

Now fatigue hung on my shoulders like twenty-pound weights. Marie's eyes continued to scan, her head moving from side to side, alert, ready for any threat. That's the way I needed to be. Our roles had reversed. Marie made a great partner, and I trusted her implicitly. I let her guide us, first through customs and then to the shuttle that took us to the rental-car kiosk. The bus bounced and jostled us, and still I had difficulty keeping my eyes open. Marie leaned over, whispered, "You look like ten miles of bad road."

"You always know just the right words to cheer me up."

She held up her new ring. "Yep, that's why wives were put here on this earth."

"Really, you've started already? We've been married less than eight hours. You know there's a twenty-four hour lemon law in Costa Rica so let's not jump the gun here, okay? Lemon-law status means I can return you if you turn out to be a lemon. You're on probation, if you wanna pass your prob—"

She socked me in the arm. The husband and wife sitting across from us, a rosy-faced couple from the Midwest, based solely on their ultra-white skin, whispered when they witnessed the spousal abuse.

I'd only catnapped in the bungalow on the beach the night this all started, with the storm, the wonderful lovemaking, and the argument. Then, of course, the next night, with all the plans to be made for the wedding and the impending trip, I hadn't slept much, and now I was feeling every bit my age.

Marie rented the car, a silver Ford Focus, and drove us to our hotel, the New Otani. We'd decided not to stay at a cost-effective fleabag motel, which tended to draw life's more undesirables and, in so doing, the cops. We went the other way, a midrange hotel where we could more easily blend in and fly under the radar.

In the room, I let the roller bag handles fall to the floor and dropped onto the hotel bed.

I woke to darkness. And no Marie.

I didn't recognize my surroundings, and it took a moment to remember we'd flown to LA.

The door opened. Marie came in carrying a bag. "Come on, get all that up, we have to eat and get over to the jail."

I swung my legs over the edge of the bed. "What? What's going on?"

She reached in the bag and tossed me a package containing a disposable cell phone, the kind you use by purchasing blocks of minutes.

"The jail? No, no we need to go to Chino, the state prison, not the jail."

She sat next to me on the bed, reached in the bag again, and came out with a pack of Sno Balls, half-round chocolate confection cakes covered in pink coconut, my favorite, and a carton of chocolate milk. "Enjoy it," she said. "When we get back, you're back on the low-carb, low-cholesterol diet."

My stomach growled. I tore open the pack, took a big bite, and savored the taste. They didn't have them in Costa Rica. "Are you going to answer any of my questions?"

"Not really, because you're just going to get mad."

I stopped chewing. "What'd you do?"

"Hell of a honeymoon, you taking me to Los Angeles to visit your brother in jail."

"Marie?"

"All right, Noble Johnson is housed at MCJ, Men's Central Jail. He's here from prison on a subpoena to testify in a Black Guerilla Family murder trial. He's testifying as a character witness for the accused, a member of the BGF who offed an Aryan Brother in the yard up at Soledad."

I leaned back to get a better look at her. "And just where did you get all of this information?" She didn't normally use so much police jargon. She'd talked to someone and given it back to me verbatim. I started to wake up; the sugar gave me a jolt and kick started my brain. I mentally searched through all the possibilities and landed on the only possible answer.

"Ah, Marie, I told you not to call him."

"Stop it right now, Mr. Bruno Johnson. He's your friend, and it's ridiculous that you're afraid to see him, let alone talk to the poor man. You owe him a lot, more than you can ever repay him. Not after what he's done for us."

"I know, don't you think I know? I'm ashamed of what happened and—"

"Ashamed? There's no reason at all for being ashamed. He's an adult and he knew the risks."

"I know it doesn't make sense. Maybe it isn't shame and it's guilt. I really screwed up his life and . . . and look at us, how happy we are. All that mess happened and I fled back to Costa Rica like some sort of Butch Cassidy running for the Hole in the Wall. I feel like I abandoned him when he needed me most."

"If you stayed, you would have been in prison. He knows that. He knew the rules of the game before he asked to play."

I nodded.

John Mack had been a deputy with the Los Angeles County Violent Crimes Team, the same team I belonged to before I crossed the line and took out Derek Sams, my son-in-law. Three months ago, Mack was with me when we hit the clubhouse of the Sons of Satan. They caught us inside and beat us, kicked the livin' hell out of us. Mack took more of it than I did and almost died from internal injuries. The Sheriff's Department fired him for committing the failed robbery that the District Attorney declined to prosecute on. He lost the job that he lived and breathed for. I knew how he felt, I'd been there; I'd had the same job and loved it dearly. He did it all for me. I needed to see him and tell him in person how sorry I was.

"How did he get the information?" I asked.

"He fought his termination order and won. They put him back working the jail."

"What? You're kiddin' me."

"Nope."

"Well, hell, let's get going then. What time are we set up in visiting to see Noble?"

She checked her watch. "Forty-five minutes."

I stood and went over to her. "Ten minutes' drive time, five-minute shower, I guess we have time." I pulled her into me and kissed her.

She half-pushed me away. "Bruno."

"Babe, you're the one who called this our honeymoon."

She checked her watch one more time and quickly started to unbutton her blouse. "Okay, but we have to hurry."

CHAPTER TWELVE

Since I knew the way, I drove. I wanted to see Noble alone, at least for the first time. Marie didn't even ask and only nodded when I suggested I drop her somewhere. I let her off at a diner three blocks from the jail. The place used to be a Denny's. Now it looked a little more rundown and shabby, and went by the name the Double Yolk.

I'd worked the old MCJ as a deputy before the Twin Towers, the new jail annex, had been built, and stuck my face into the windshield to look up at the towers as I drove by. I parked the rental in the large parking area and made my way toward the main entrance to the old jail across from the towers and mingled among the stream of other visitors.

Law enforcement only deals with six percent of the population—a whole lot of tax dollars and effort for only six percent. The visitors walking in made up part of that six percent, at the moment anyway; right then, it just wasn't their turn on the merry-go-round.

Women of every ethnic background herded their children along, most of whom were unwashed and in raggedy clothes, their mothers speed freaks or wedded to the rock pipe. Mothers should not bring their children to a jail to visit the fathers. It presents the image that jail might just be a part of a normal life, something to adjust to and live with. The sight of the kids made me glad I'd dropped off Marie. She wouldn't have been able to hold her tongue. She would've confronted the mothers, given them the what-for in how not to raise their children. As it stood I, too, had difficulty not saying something. What chance did those children have? None, not one chance in hell.

The lines just to get to the desk inside to check in snaked out the door and down the side of the building. This would take a while. I dialed Marie and she picked up on the first ring. "You done already?" she asked. "That was fast."

"No, I've been in line for twenty minutes and it's barely moved. This is gonna take hours."

"Do you want me to come over there? I can walk. I need the exercise." Eagerness in her voice said she really wanted to be present when this dysfunctional reunion occurred.

I already missed her. I just didn't know what would happen once Noble and I met for the first time after being apart so long. No, not just being apart, but what would happen when all those festering emotions collided, guilt on my part and the anger on his for me having been the one to put him there.

"Sure, come on. I miss you."

"Be right there."

MCJ sat in a large commercial area that didn't have a lot of sidewalks and did have lots of high chain-link fences topped with concertina wire. I watched for Marie and, after only a few minutes, regretted having her walk. The jail acted as an epicenter for criminals, a vortex they all swirled around and around in a revolving door, coming in or getting released. With their sentences served, the crooks were let out the front door and left on their own to find their way home. Most get rides, but many, having alienated family and friends, have no one and nowhere else to go and have to hoof it.

Marie appeared, walking up the long driveway that was really a dedicated street. I breathed easier. The line moved into the inside. I moved in before Marie caught up. Three deputies in Class B uniforms stood among the crowd, monitoring and keeping the peace. I didn't look at them directly. I didn't need the heartache. Predators recognized other predators, and I tried to make myself small, unassuming, and watched my feet. The beige linoleum floor wore through to the smooth concrete underneath in the path to the visitor check-in, a testament to the hundreds of thousands of people who'd come to visit, a sad commentary on humanity.

Marie came up and gave me a hug.

I whispered into her neck, "Sorry, I shouldn't have dropped you off. I don't know what I was thinking." Before I let her go, someone tapped me on the shoulder. I froze. The visiting deputy wanted to see my ID. Just be cool, turn around, and smile.

I did and found Deputy John Mack standing there in the Sheriff's Class B uniform, smiling, his eyes alive with adventure. He still wore his hair buzzed close. He'd changed a lot in three months. Weight had melted off him. He used to be a bull of a man with huge shoulders and biceps. Getting the hell kicked out of you by five biker assholes and then three surgeries could do that to a person. I stuck out my hand to shake his and swallowed the lump that rose in my throat. He knocked my hand away and hugged me. I hugged him back as hard as I could. When I let go, Marie swiped at the tears in her eyes.

"Bruno, damn good to see you, man."

"Yeah, good to see you too." The line moved, we moved with it.

I forced myself to hold his gaze. "Hey, you know that I—"

He smiled and gave me a little shove in the chest. "Stop it. Really, I mean it."

"No, let me say it. I have to say it. I owe you more than I can ever repay you, and I'm sorry I haven't called or come to see you before now."

"Yeah, right, a federal fugitive, how could you do that? I understand. I'm just damn glad to see you."

I cringed. I could only hope the other deputies hadn't heard the fugitive part.

He gave Marie a big hug, lifting her off her feet. He set her down. "Come on," he said, "I fixed it up. I got you put in a segregated interview room and not out here in the zoo."

We followed him, weaving in and out of the crowd to the front desk. The deputy behind the desk handed over two mauve visitor badges that Marie and I clipped to our shirt pockets. Marie looked at me. "You sure you want me there the first time?"

"Absolutely."

Mack guided us into one door, down a long hall, and through another door. The odor changed as we passed through that second door. It shifted to a reek that spoke of body odor, urine, and a sour hint of vomit. I'd been in many county jails when chasing and booking violent criminals—the ones we weren't forced to shoot, or run over—and the odor remained the same no matter what county. I always related the stink to despair.

Mack stopped at a barred sally port and waved to the invisible person in the booth, who opened the first gate to let us pass and closed it behind us. I watched the gate roll closed, and, with each inch it moved, I found it more difficult to breathe.

Once it was closed, the booth bitch, the name of the invisible operator that had nothing to do with gender, opened the next gate in front of us. Mack took us down a hallway rife with inmates dressed in blue. The common misconception of the other 94 percent of society was that everyone in jail was locked in a cell. Not true. On the other side of the sally port, the jail turned into a self-contained city, with chow halls, a hospital, clinics, a church, law library, visiting areas, and lots of crime. The inmates were locked down during the night, but otherwise they could move about with hall passes. Passes that allowed them to go to personal visits: doctor visits, church, chow, things of that sort. Being criminals, naturally some didn't go where they were directed and snuck off to other modules to caper: sell dope, rape, rob, blackmail, and even murder. Deputies in the jail learned how to take first reports and to do follow-up.

I couldn't help feeling vulnerable. The inmates gawked at Marie.

Mack took us to a room with a white resin table and four chairs. He stuck out his hand again. I shook it. "I have to go," he said. "I'm working High Power, 1700-1750, and it's feeding time. You know the way out; just go back the way you came. Good seeing you again. Call me tonight. Marie has my number. You better call me, Bruno, or I'll come looking for you." He smiled.

He went out and closed the door. Now the waiting began. The memories flooded back. Who knew how long it would take? Visiting carried a lower priority, and if something else occurred, visiting got pushed back. I hoped while we waited that an event didn't occur that caused the jail to go to red bells and lockdown. We'd be stuck. When the guards came off of red bells, they might look closer at who we were. We should never have walked into the lion's den.

Marie, aware of my anxiety, said, "Why don't you tell me about your brother?"

I'd not talked about him before. She knew nothing about him. "He's not really my brother."

"What? What are you talking about?"

"It's a long story."

"Well, you better start talking, mister. I didn't come all this way to help some criminal not related to the family."

I nodded and began at the beginning.

CHAPTER THIRTEEN

ON THE CHRISTMAS of my eighth year, Mrs. Gloria Bingham, the grocer's wife, became the first white woman I'd ever seen bare-assed naked.

My best friend and neighbor, Johnny Noble, had come over on Christmas Eve to escape his always-menacing younger brother and sister, little Jakey and Kari. That's what Johnny said, anyway; that's what he used as an excuse.

The dusk settled cold and crisp over our little two-bedroom home on Nord Avenue in South Central Los Angeles, an area nicknamed "The Corner Pocket." A dark, moonless night came in close on its heels. Outside smelled of burnt wood from all the homes in the area using fireplaces. We could afford the gas heat and a small canned ham for dinner. Dad rated the cold nights one through four. Tonight we had four burners on the stovetop going full blast. Our living room shared a space with the kitchen, and the walls let in some of the cold from outside.

Dad still wore his blue-gray postal pants and a t-shirt with the sleeves rolled up above his thick muscles as he lay on the floor and struggled to get our tree to stay up in its too-rickety stand.

Me and Johnny stood by holding the green-and-red string lights, ready to put them on as soon as Dad said go. My stomach growled loud enough for everyone to hear. Not my fault. The heavenly aroma from the canned ham heating in the oven, with circle-cut pineapple and brown sugar on top, overpowered the room, overpowered even the fresh pine-tree scent. I wanted to get the lights on, decorate the tree, eat, and get to bed. The sooner I got to bed, the sooner I could get up and find whatever surprises the Christmas tree held. "The Christmas stockings are next," I said. "Tomorrow morning they'll be filled with little prizes and candy canes."

Johnny shook his head, "There's no Santa Claus. I'm not fallin' for that bunch of hooey, not anymore."

Me and Johnny, we'd had this same discussion at least fifty times in the last three days. Johnny only said it to show off for Dad. He liked my dad, but wouldn't come right out and say so. He wanted to sound grown up.

Dad said from under the tree, "If you don't believe in Santa Claus, then you aren't going to get anything for Christmas."

"Huh?" Johnny said, "Oh, yeah, right. I'm not buyin' that. Like I said, it's nothin' but a load of hooey."

When Johnny had said it to me, those umpteen times all those days before Christmas, he used "crap" instead of "hooey."

Dad came from under the tree. His expression of concern scared me. I didn't believe in Santa Claus either, but this new development, Dad defending the charade, shook me up a little. What if I was wrong not to believe and there really *was* a Santa? I wouldn't get the complete set of the *Hardy Boys Mysteries* like I asked for, or the real pipe dream, the two-wheeler bike. Dad saw my look and tried to hide a smile. I saw it and relaxed. Life turned good again.

Someone knocked on the door. I jumped, only because I hadn't been ready for it. Dad got up, slapping his hands together to knock off the errant pine needles stuck there with sap. Like he always did, he stepped to the side window to check before open-ing up and "letting in the world."

When he opened the door, a gust of ice-cold wind blew in. The blue flames on the stovetop fluttered.

Eli Noble, Johnny's dad, stood on the stoop. He wore a stylish Afro, full and thick, compared to Dad's hair cropped close to his scalp. Dad always said, why pay someone to do your hair when you could do it yourself for free.

Eli Noble wore black Dickie pants, a white shirt, and a black tie. He worked at Big Ed's Grocery way up Central Avenue at 20th, a stocker and box boy. Seven years ago, after the Watts riots burned down our part of the city along with all the stores close to us, the rich storeowners never rebuilt. We had to drive a long way to find a good grocery if we wanted something the little corner market couldn't supply.

Eli Noble said, "Evening, Johnson." He said it in a haughty tone spiced with a hint of anger. I always thought Mr. Noble jealous of Dad's great job with the postal service.

Dad said, "Merry Christmas, Eli."

Eli Noble moved to the side to see around Dad. "Come on now, Johnny, time to git your ass on home."

"Can't I spend the night?"

We had not discussed spending the night, and Johnny looked at me with pleading eyes. "Can he, Dad," I said, "please?"

Eli Noble said, "Hell no, not on Christmas Eve. Now come on." He held out his hand to usher his son from the warm house out into the bitter cold night.

Dad said, "I'll thank you not to talk that way in front of my son."

Eli Noble opened his mouth and then shut it as if he'd been slapped.

Dad hesitated. "It's fine by me, Eli, if Johnny wants to stay over."

"Hell no, not on Christmas Eve." He tried to reach around Dad to take hold of Johnny's arm.

Dad shoved him as he stepped out on the porch and eased the door closed all but a crack. Me and Johnny moved up to peek through the crack and listen. Outside in the cold, Dad spoke. His words mixed with white fog from his mouth. "It's not right what you have goin' on over there, Eli. It jeopardizes the safety of your family."

Eli Noble raised his hand and pointed at Dad. "That's none of yore damn bidness, you hear me. You'd better mind your own bidness before I make you eat those words."

Dad stiffened. He eased the door closed the rest of the way until it latched. Low murmurs came through the door that we couldn't understand.

Two minutes later, Dad opened the door. The cold blew in. He shut it behind him, his face flushed with anger. He took a long moment, then pasted on his best fake smile. "Johnny, you can stay over, but you have to go back first thing tomorrow, in the mornin', you understand? Now you boys get washed up for dinner. Do a good job, you hear. I'll be checking under those nails."

Me and Johnny hurried into the bathroom and shoved back and forth over the hot water and fought over the one bar of soap. I shouldered him to get a better position. "What'd my dad mean 'bout it's not right what your dad's got goin' on over there?"

"That's none of your damn bidness, Bruno Johnson. Keep that big nose of yours outta my bidness or I'll show you why." He'd taken on the words and demeanor of his dad.

His eyes came at me fierce like a lion. I didn't like it. If I took him to the deck like Dad taught me and gave him what for, Johnny'd be spending the night at his own house with a shiner, and I'd have a tanned butt. Then I'd have no one to talk to on Christmas Eve. I had plenty of time to work on him, to soften him up tonight after lights out. He'd eventually tell me. Nothing softened up a stubborn fathead like a canned ham with circle-cut pineapple, crusted over with glazed brown sugar.

Me and Johnny stood by the oven when Dad took out the ham. My stomach growled loud enough to be a pet dog.

My mouth dropped open.

The ham had shriveled something terrible.

"What happened to that big ol' ham, Daddy?" I didn't want to cry, but man, that was one sorry lookin' ham.

Dad, in his big oven mitts, chuckled as he set the pan on the counter. "There's plenty here for three hungry men."

"That's good to hear," Johnny said with a straight face, "'cause there's only a man and two boys."

Dad turned away to snicker, then said, "Bruno, you pour the milk. Johnny, get the butter on the table for the bread."

Dad put the ham on a dinner plate and sliced it. He took some butter squash off the stove and put that on the table as well. Steam rose into the air, filling the room with an aroma I forever after related to Christmas.

We ate all the ham and half the loaf of Wonder bread.

* * *

I woke and didn't move. Johnny lay on the bunk right below. He'd snored as soon as his head hit the pillow, so we didn't get to talk. He had told me many times that his brother and sister usually kept him awake all night. They slept on their bunks. He got the one bed at his house, in the same room. His brother and sister would get out of bed at night and wander, get into trouble, and make a lot of noise. His dad didn't wake up or didn't care. At our house, without anything to disturb him, Johnny slept like the dead.

I smelled something.

Smoke?

Through the wall of our house came a distant squeak, not a regular kinda squeak, and I identified it before it came again. Far off, a woman screamed. I jumped up and ran barefoot to the front door. Dad's loud feet thumped on the wood floor behind me. "Wait, Bruno. You wait."

I didn't, and instead, threw open the door to let the world in. Dawn, in light grays and blues, peeked over the horizon that I only saw for a quick moment. A black cloud of smoke drifted across our front porch, obscuring all else.

I went out onto the porch, the morning bitter cold and absolutely still. The smoke caught in my lungs. I coughed. My eyes teared.

I whispered, "Fire."

Dad caught me by the shoulder, pinching hard, hurting me. He wouldn't let me move another inch. To the right, bright yellow and orange and red flames with black smoke roiled and roared behind the downstairs windows of my best friend Johnny's house, batting the curtains around and eating them in big gulps.

CHAPTER FOURTEEN

I STARED AT the wall while telling the story, transported back to another time, another world.

Marie snapped me out of it when she said, "What happened to Johnny's brother and sister, little Jakey and Kari?"

I looked at her, not seeing her at first, my lovely wife. "What? Oh, I ah . . . you sure you wanna hear this?"

"Yes, of course I do."

I nodded, wishing she'd said no. "Johnny's dad and Mrs. Bingham, a nice white lady, the wife of the owner of the grocery where Mr. Noble worked, climbed out of the second-story window, both stark naked. I still remember exactly what she looked like, her skin whiter than white next to Johnny's dad. Her skin instantly turned pink in the cold. Naked. I couldn't believe she was naked. I was eight years old and I'd never seen a naked white woman. For that matter, I'd never seen any naked woman.

"Up on the roof, flames jumped out at them from the bedroom window, where they'd just escaped. They moved to the edge of the overhang. They were still ten feet off the ground. Mr. Noble yelled at my dad, 'Xander, for God's sakes, get the children. Get my son and daughter.'"

Marie gripped my arm, her nails digging in.

"Dad stood next to me and said, 'Oh, my God.' He ran toward the house as a black-and-white sheriff's prowl car zoomed up to the curb and stopped. Two deputies got out and ran to the burning house. Dad stopped running and yelled, 'There's two children still inside.'

"The black deputy didn't hesitate or even slow down. You should've seen him. He bounded up on the porch and kicked the door in. Fire burst out and blew him back, laid him out flat. Mr. Noble kept on keening, again and again, 'Get my babies. Please, get my babies.'

"The black deputy got up and went at the open door again, which now had billowing flames four feet long that ate the desiccated wood. Instantly charring it black, turning it to that alligator kinda skin. His partner grabbed him and wrestled him to the ground. I couldn't believe that guy, his unflinching bravery."

I paused, took a breath.

"The fire department arrived in time to rescue Mrs. Bingham and Mr. Noble."

I swallowed hard. "Johnny's sister and brother perished, smoke inhalation. That's what they said, but I don't think so, not as hot as that fire burned.

"The horrible part, the absolutely horrible part about this whole tragic Christmas morning, was that Johnny's dad had gotten tired of the two younger children getting up in the night and tearing up the house. He used soft restraints and tied the two kids into the bunk beds. They couldn't have gotten out of that house if they wanted to."

Marie's mouth dropped open. "And you saw all that when you were only eight? Oh, I'm so sorry, Bruno."

She sat and watched me for a long moment.

Now, decades later, I could look back at what happened with a more mature perspective. Or maybe telling Marie about the event, talking about it for the first time in more than thirty-five years, I realized that Mr. Noble might've tied those two children in their beds because he didn't want them to get up and see Mrs. Bingham, see what their father was up to. That had been what Dad referred to that Christmas Eve when he spoke with Mr. Noble out on our stoop, when he'd said, *With what you got goin' on over there.*

"Mr. Eli Noble," I said to Marie, "went a little crazy. No, that's not true. Eli, he went over the edge deep into batshit-crazy. I felt so sorry for Johnny. He hurt something fierce over the loss of his siblings. He cried at night when he thought I was asleep.

"Mr. Noble, he just up and disappeared three days later, never saw nor heard from him again. Six months after that, long about June—I know because it was summer vacation—Johnny was still living with us. When social services came looking for him, Dad told them he didn't know what happened to the child called Johnny Noble. Two years after that, Dad filed the papers and officially adopted him. He gave Johnny the choice of his name. Johnny no longer liked the name *Johnny*. I think because his dad ran off and left him without so much as a good-bye. But Johnny also wanted to keep his last name so Johnny Noble became Noble Johnson, my brother." The door to the visiting room rattled.

* * *

The door opened. Noble stood there and stared at me. His face looked so much older, the wrinkles, the droopy skin over his eyes, I hardly recognized him. Gray laced his eyebrows and his hair. A long jagged scar started on his forehead and came down across his left eye, the eye milky and dead, an injury I was sure had been earned in gladiator school, the state prison system.

We looked at each other, our expressions grim, neither one of us wanting to blink first. His presence sparked a thousand images and events that flashed by in one beat of the heart and made me ache for days past.

Marie jumped up and without hesitation hugged him. Noble broke his concentration and looked down at Marie. A smile leapt to his face and instantly reminded me of the Johnny Noble from our childhood: ice cream socials, marble games, trick or treating, basketball, foot races, and just staying up late at night talking about the future.

I smiled, too, and stood. That's when I noticed what I should've seen right off. Noble wore the green jail uniform of a K-nine, a keep-away, an "escort only." Green was one level down from the highest, a red suit, an escape risk. The green meant segregation, it meant he wasn't housed in genpop, general population. Green meant protective custody for one of two things: he'd ratted, or he was what the inmates called "a baby raper," booked in on a child molestation charge.

Noble couldn't return the hug; waist chains restricted his movement, as did the leg irons on his ankles. He held onto Marie's waist. I fought the desire to pull her away from him. I didn't want him touching her. Old emotions died hard.

The escort deputy put his hand on Noble's back and eased him farther into the small confines of the room. Noble's chains rattled. The deputy reached for the door. "I'll be right outside if you need me." He closed us in with Noble Johnson the brother, Noble Johnson the killer, and now, apparently, Noble Johnson, the rat.

CHAPTER FIFTEEN

MARIE TOOK HOLD of Noble's arm. "Please, sit down."

Noble waited, watching my eyes. I nodded, barely moving my head. He let a hint of a smile creep out as he wiggled into the chair, his chains restricting him.

"Why are you a K-nine?" I asked.

Noble closed his eyes and shook his head. "After all the years we missed together, that's the first thing outta your mouth?"

"I wouldn't be here at all if it wasn't for Dad."

"Well, believe you me, I wouldn't have asked you if you weren't the very last choice in this entire screwed-up world."

"That right?"

"That's right."

"Boys," Marie said, "play nice."

He smiled at Marie, gave her the big smile that he kept exclusively for wooing the girls. You can bet there hadn't been a lot of girls or women in the last two-and-a-half-decades. "You got yourself a real looker here, Bruno, you lucky son of a bitch."

"Watch your language, this is my wife." The word wife sounded alien and reminded me of a much larger responsibility.

"Your wife? Well, congratulations. My big brother definitely got the better end of that deal."

"Why, thank you," Marie said. "I won't stand on modesty here and I'll agree with you." She leaned over and gave me a light kiss on the cheek. "My name is Marie."

"Nice to meet you, Marie."

"What can we help you with, Johnny?" I asked.

"Don't be that way, Bruno, you don't need to call me that. You know my name's Noble."

Marie jumped in, "So, your letter said you're having problems with your family. I'm kinda tryin' to catch up here, and without being too insensitive, what family are you talking about? I thought you only had Bruno and Bruno's dad, Xander."

Marie had only seen the second letter and not the one that mentioned Dad giving Noble supposed tuition money for his son Ricardo and daughter Rebecca.

Noble looked surprised. "Dad didn't tell you about my grandson and granddaughter?"

"What?" I asked. "What are you taking about? Grandchildren? I thought these were *your* kids we were talking about?"

"Wait, wait." Marie waved her hand. "Excuse me, but I thought that . . . I mean, I was told that you've been in prison for twenty-five years."

"I have been, and he's the one who put me here." He pointed a finger with a hand restricted to his waist.

I jumped forward in my chair. "How dare you blame this on me. You killed two kids, gunned 'em down as they ran away from the store."

Noble struggled up out of his seat "That right? That's the way it's gonna be? I say bullshit on you, big brother. I wouldn't be here if it wasn't for you." His voice went higher with each word. "Those dumb-assed cops wouldn't have tumbled to who shot those armed robbers, tryin' to take my life, if it hadn't been for you. *The Great Bruno, The Bad Boy Johnson.* That's right, I heard the stories about you. I've had to live in here with the people you threw in the slam. Every one of 'em came in here shot or beat ta shit. What was that all about, brother, huh?"

"Violent people live a violent life," I yelled back at him.

The deputy outside opened the door, shoved his way in. The door banged into the chair, which pushed into the back of Noble's legs. "All right," the deputy said, "that's it, this visit's over." He took hold of Noble's arm and yanked on him as Noble's words echoed around in my head.

Had classification in the prison PC'ed Noble because of me? Had they put him in protective custody because of the murderers and violent offenders I had chased, caught, and convicted? Had he lost that eye because of me?

I stood. "Wait, Deputy," I said, "Can't we please have another minute?"

He didn't have time to answer. Noble struggled with the deputy, trying to stay in the room. The deputy put Noble in a headlock and pulled him out the door. Noble grunted, his feet slid on the slick concrete floor. On the top of Noble's shiny pate, a jagged scar stood out like a fat earthworm, a memento from the night I arrested him, pistol-whipped him when he came over the counter at me. He disappeared out into the hall as the door eased closed.

The room fell silent. My heart pounded in my chest. "I didn't want that to happen." My voice came out more of a croak.

"Yeah, well, it did, and right now, I'm not too happy with my new husband." She came around and hugged me. I hugged her back and waited a few minutes to allow time for Noble to get clear of the hallway. If he saw me again, he might go off on the deputies worse than he already had.

Marie, her head on my shoulder, her arms wrapped around me, said, "Is there a lemon law for husbands as well?"

"Nope," I said. "Double standard. You're stuck with me, no money-back guarantee."

"Not fair, I'm going to write my senator."

"You do that, pretty girl."

After a while, I said, "Come on, let's get outta this hellhole."

Inside that room I could fool myself that we were not trapped like animals in a cage and needed to escape. Back out in the hallway, with all the inmates moving to and from locations, all of them loose, some of whom, I'm sure, I'd put there and might recognize me, the reality was inescapable; likewise with the old salt deps who worked the jail. My skin itched to be back outside in the fresh air. I put my arm around Marie, lowered my head, and quietly talked with her as we moved to the sally port.

I looked up periodically when an inmate would move in and out of our personal zone. I needed to be ready if one suddenly turned aggressive.

Two deputies escorted a long line of fish, new inmates fresh from IRC, the Inmate Reception Center, or the transfers from other jails or prisons. The fish walked in a line with their shoulders against the wall. The deputies watched them closely, didn't allow them to talk or come off the wall, a part of the indoctrination to make them understand who ran the zoo.

One of them looked up and we made eye contact. I recognized him, a Son of Satan, one of the many who'd been arrested three months ago when we tried to rob their clubhouse. I glared back at him the way animal predators did to each other. I didn't want him to think me weak, especially not with Marie at my side. I needed to protect her.

One of the escorting deputies saw the violation and quick-stepped over to him and got right up in the guy's face. "What's your problem, asshole? Can't you follow simple directions? Look straight ahead, or I'll put you on the brick for three days. You understand me?"

The biker looked out of place without his denim cut, flying his colors, and his heavy black motorcycle boots. Back when I worked this same jail, we didn't threaten with the brick, a burnt piece of compressed protein meted out as discipline for minor violations. We face-planted the inmates into the wall, a violent move that busted their lips, or noses, and sometimes broke teeth. Not done out of hate or vehemence but to control the six percent of our population who choose to walk on the wrong side. Twenty-two thousand inmates in custody at any one time, most of those in MCJ, supervised each shift by less than a hundred deputies. You couldn't supervise with those percentages; you could only rule.

Times change, and the inmates had taken one giant step closer to running the zoo.

We made it to the sally port. The first gate opened and let us pass inside. The gate behind us closed and the one in front of us opened. We'd made it out.

CHAPTER SIXTEEN

WE STOPPED OUTSIDE and reveled for a minute in the unbridled freedom. The outgoing and incoming visitors with their children passed without taking notice, taking their own freedom for granted.

We walked slowly to the car and didn't look back at the windowless concrete monolith, not wanting to imagine what it would be like to be trapped in there, or to relive the memories of when I had been. Once in the car and underway, Marie spoke for the first time. "We have to go back, you know."

I nodded and took the curve of Bauchet Street that ended at the Double Yolk and made a right, headed to the heart of downtown LA. I played back the entire scene in my head, the way Noble's anger had turned so suddenly.

Noble wrote in his letter that he'd earned a degree in theology. His behavior didn't match that of an ordained minister. Had all of that, the degree, being a minister, been a sham to trick the parole board?

If he truly wanted help with his family, why didn't he keep his temper and his festering hate for me under control? Only one reason: that deep-seated hatred was far worse than I imagined. Grandkids, though, what a mess.

Marie put her hand on my arm as we turned onto Los Angeles Street, a block away from 2nd in Little Tokyo, and a block from our hotel, The New Otani. "Didn't your father say he wanted us to visit Mr. Tomkins?"

"Yes, he did. Thank you for reminding me." I made a quick turn and headed toward Alameda, not the quickest way down to South Central Los Angeles, but I needed time to think. Marie sensed that need, slid over, cuddled in close, and didn't say a word for several miles, until her curiosity got the better of her. "Kids, Bruno? He's really got grandkids and he's been in prison the whole time?"

"Looks that way."

"How?"

"You really don't know how this works?"

"Would I be asking?"

"Okay, okay, here it is. In the glorious State of California, you can get conjugal visits with your wife if you're going to be in for an extended period of time."

"You're kidding, right?"

"Nope."

She thought about that for a minute. "And if you don't have a wife? Noble didn't have a wife when he went in twenty-five years ago, did he?"

"That's right. You can marry while in prison, have conjugal visits, and your wife can have the kids."

"Wait, wait, wait, I can't believe this. That is wrong on so many levels, not to mention the worst one, how it affects the kids having a father in prison for life, never getting out. Who pays for the kids?"

"We do, well, I mean the taxpayers do. The state pays the mother for each child all the way up until the child turns eighteen, then the child is eligible to get welfare. That is, if the child, who is now an adult, is not a contributing member of society. And the statistics show that most of them are not. Once hooked onto the entitlement system, that's where they stay."

"Didn't you tell me once that one crook costs about a hundred and twenty thousand dollars per year?"

"That's an old number, I'm sure it's higher now."

"And then on top of that we're paying for a wife and kids?"

"That's right."

"What's that, about two hundred to two hundred and fifty thousand a year for every jerk who can't live in society and goes to prison?"

"That's probably a good number for those with only one child, sure. You add in medical and more kids, it goes a lot higher."

"How many people are in prison in California?"

"About two hundred thousand, but not all of those are in for life. And about another seventy thousand are out on parole, rotating back in and out of the system."

Marie shook her head in wonder.

I turned from Alameda onto Imperial Highway, westbound. In five more minutes we came to Nickerson Gardens, the low-income housing on the right. I pulled into Stops parking lot, now infested with weeds coming up in the cracked asphalt. The roadside restaurant that had been open for five or six decades, a historical landmark, now sat abandoned and all boarded up. The last time I'd been there was with Robby Wicks when he was chasing me, trying to find the children Marie and I had stashed away in a house with Dad. Not much more than a year ago.

On special occasions, Dad used to take Noble and me to Stops for chili fries and hot links. I didn't dwell on the loss. I pulled around, drove out onto the street, and headed to the Corner Pocket.

No hot link sandwich for Tommy Tomkins.

* * *

Tom Tomkins lived just south of the Corner Pocket in the area called Fruit Town, all the streets named after fruit trees. He lived on Cherry. I parked in front of the house, which was no longer immaculately maintained. Every day after work, Tom had gone out into his yard and trimmed and pruned and mowed. His yard had stood out from all the rest on the street. Now the paint peeled on the house. The weeds had long ago won the battle and then the war. Branches from the fruitless mulberry hung down, obscuring the front windows.

I got out and opened the door for Marie. She looked at the house, and I read her mind; no way did she want to go in. The disrepair of the house stood as a clue to what we'd find inside.

"You want to wait outside?" I asked. "It's okay with me."

"Don't pull none of your crap with me, Mr. Bruno Johnson. I'm official now, and you can't shield me from the world anymore. Not like I let you do when I was just your girlfriend, so don't even try."

"Not like you let me do?"

"That's right."

"Can I get a copy of this new rule book?" I asked, "'Cause I'm tellin' you I'm starting to get a little confused."

She patted my arm. "You're a husband now. You're supposed to be confused."

I took her hand and we walked past the broken-down fence. "Is that what I've been doing, shielding you, before I said those two horrible little words?"

She stopped and yanked on my arm. "What two horrible little words? You better not start with that already." She tried not to smile. "Tell me what two words?"

I'd been about to say *I do* but decided not to. Not if I didn't want one of her socks to the arm. "Why, *I love you*, of course, the two most important words in the world, and they're not horrible. I misspoke. They're wonderful words."

"You're a rotten liar, Bruno Johnson."

I put my hand to my chest. "I'm hurt. You hurt me to the bone."

She laughed. "You're a liar who can't do math; you can't even count to three. Which, after I think about it, maybe you're not a liar, 'cause you don't know any better."

I laughed with her.

We stepped up onto the porch and knocked.

After a couple of minutes, the door opened. A short Filipino woman dressed in a floral nurse's outfit looked at us.

"We're here to visit Tom Tomkins," I said.

She didn't answer and probably couldn't speak a lot of English.

She turned and escorted us through the small house, which was tidy but in need of dusting and a good scrub. The air hung thick with antiseptic mixed with a sour odor. From deeper in the house, the wheeze of a respirator grew louder as we moved toward it.

The nurse stopped at the small bedroom. I stuck my head in, knowing what I'd see.

Tommy Tomkins had not been of this world for a long time. Not really, not conscious as a functioning human. The medical profession had only kept his body alive, his mind spoiled long ago. He'd shriveled to nothing more than a raisin with tubes and wires running out of him. The poor man. For a brief moment I thought about having Marie distract the nurse while I did the moral thing and unplugged him. He'd been Dad's best friend for many years and didn't deserve this. Then the terrible image of Dad going out in this manner hit me. No, I wouldn't let that happen, not to Dad, not if I had a say in it. I shook off those thoughts and forced my mind back to the purpose of our visit. Poor old Tom had been incapacitated for a while now.

The big question was, who had Dad been corresponding with? Who had been taking the letters from the mailbox from Dad or Noble, repackaging them with the next address, and passing them on?

CHAPTER SEVENTEEN

MARIE AND I rode the elevator down from our room on the tenth floor, relaxed and semisated. I'd called John Mack, and he agreed to meet us downstairs in the hotel bar. Marie held my arm, and I loved the feeling of being married, the feeling of finally being whole. She had dolled up, took her almost two hours, but she looked absolutely stunning. She'd taken a dress out of her carry-on, a wadded-up little thing that looked more like a red silk handbag. She shook it out and disappeared into the bathroom. I changed into the best clothes I had brought, black slacks and a wrinkled white-on-white long-sleeve dress shirt. After a long time, she reappeared looking like the Puerto Rican version of Julia Roberts in *Pretty Woman*. Stunning. The silky red dress, smooth now, hugged all those glorious curves. I looked down at myself and then back at her. "Babe," I said, "I really don't know what you see in me."

She smiled. "I'm not sure I do either."

I shook my head. "I guess the honeymoon's over."

She came over and kissed me, "Don't kid yourself, cowboy. It hasn't even started." She pushed me backward until I fell on the bed.

On the way down in the elevator twenty minutes later, we both looked a little more rumpled. The doors opened and we hurried to the bar, Marie's high heels clacking on the marble floor.

The bar opened off the lobby. Barbara Wicks and John Mack sat at a high-top table deep in the mostly empty bar. He smiled hugely when he saw us walking up.

John had said he was bringing his girlfriend, Barbara Wicks, the chief of police for Montclair, a little city in San Bernardino County at the far eastern edge of Los Angeles County. Barbara used to be the wife of Robby Wicks, the lieutenant and leader of the Violent Crimes Team. I'd been a member of that team before I switched teams and became what I had chased.

John Mack had also been a member of the Violent Crimes Team. The relationship between Barbara and John shouldn't have worked out at all. A year and a half prior, John Mack had shot and killed Robby, Barbara's husband, when Robby had shot me and was about to shoot my dad.

Then, three months ago, I'd convinced John Mack to go into the Sons of Satan clubhouse on a wild-goose chase to recover money from a twenty-five-year-old armored-car heist, money we needed to trade for three kidnapped children, Eddie Crane, Sandy Williams, and Elena Cortez—children now safe in Costa Rica due largely to the actions of these two people.

We'd gotten in the clubhouse just fine; getting out had been the problem. We were caught, and the Sons literally beat John to within an inch of his life. Barbara still blamed me for Mack almost losing his life, as she should.

We entered the bar. They stood. We took turns and hugged and then sat down with them. Two near-empty martini glasses and an empty basket of bread crowded the little table. "Sorry," Mack said, "I was hungry."

Barbara looked at me. "And you're a little late."

Marie smiled. "That wasn't his fault." On purpose, she casually brought her left hand up to brush her hair back. The facets in her diamond caught the light, giving her the desired effect.

Barbara's mouth dropped open, her eyes going wide. "Oh, my God, you two got married, didn't you?"

Marie nodded, overwhelmed with emotion, her expression crumpling as she fought tears. I loved her for it, but wasn't sure why it hit her right at that moment. I mean, we'd already been married going on thirty or forty hours.

Barbara got up and came over to Marie. "You know you're crazy for marrying the likes of him."

Marie dabbed at her eyes with a cocktail napkin and nodded. "I know."

"Hey," I said, "I'm sittin' right here."

Barbara said, "He's right. Come on, girl, let's go powder our noses."

We watched them disappear into the ladies' room.

Mack turned to me and held up his cocktail glass. "Thanks, buddy, now I'm really gonna get the pressure laid on nice and thick."

"Hey, not my fault, not really, not the way it happened. I was having a glass of wine after dinner with Marie, minding my own business, the next thing I remember I wake up—" I held up the ring on my finger "—and I find this." He held onto my hand to see the gold band on my finger. I said, "Then she tells me I'm married. She must've slipped me a mickey."

Mack laughed. "Yeah, and I'm going to believe that one."

It was good to see him laugh.

"Hey," I said, "I'm sorry about you getting bounced from the Violent Crimes Team."

"I was getting tired of all those extra hours anyway. And I told you, I made my own choices."

The moment hung long and heavy between us. "When are you and Barbara going to get engaged?"

He looked over at the closed ladies' room and reached into his pocket. He pulled out a ring, a gold setting with a round-cut diamond surrounded by little sapphires. "I've been carrying this around since I got out of the hospital and haven't had the balls to ask. I'm scared to death she's going to panic. That she doesn't feel the same way, and thinks I'm some sort of lovesick puppy and breaks it off." He quickly stashed the ring.

I remembered how Barbara acted with Mack in surgery. I put my hand on his shoulder. "Do you trust me?" I asked.

He nodded. "You know I do."

"Then listen to what I'm tellin' you. She feels the same about you and, the longer you wait, the madder she's going to be at your dumb ass for waiting so long."

The door to the ladies' room opened, and our women came out arm in arm.

We ordered drinks, wine for us, and two more martinis for them.

CHAPTER EIGHTEEN

THE NEXT MORNING right when the jail opened for visitors, I sat in the same windowless, concrete-walled room with Marie at my side. We again waited for my brother to show. Marie sat close, her head resting on my shoulder, her hand locked in mine.

She squeezed my hand. "Do you want to talk more about your brother?"

"No."

She nodded with her head still on my shoulder.

We waited some more.

"I don't know what happened to him, really I don't." I said, "He had the same of everything. Dad treated him the same as me. Dad even gave him a little preferential treatment. At least that's what I thought at the time. Maybe not, I could've just been jealous."

She didn't nod this time, only listened.

"You know," I said, "In high school, they called him Knight as in the Noble Knight. He played JV basketball, first string. He . . . "

A lump rose in my throat at the thought of the way things could've turned out. How we could've been a family, the contented kind with holiday get-togethers and birthdays, grandkids, and growing old with each other. What the hell happened?

"Then somehow chance interceded." I said, "Something just

clicked in his head, and he went to the other side. Dropped out of school, and fell in with the likes of Papa Dee and Del Fawlkes. On the street they started calling him Not-so. He back stabbed everyone, cheated, and played dirty with anyone he dealt with. For the life of me, I don't know why. Why would he do it? You think he was genetically predisposed?"

"Or maybe," Marie said, "the death and loss of his family took that long to manifest the emotional symptoms. It happens. It does, Bruno."

"Maybe."

The door opened and Not-so came shuffling in with his chains rattling. He looked haggard, as if he'd not slept at all. He wrangled the white resin chair around and sat, his eyes locked on mine.

The deputy, dressed in a Class B uniform with a green-and-black cloth name patch that said "B. Stanford" over his right breast, closed the door. Not the same deputy as the day before.

Noble started first. "I'm sorry about yesterday. I don't know what happened. I really don't. Something inside me, something I don't have any control over, just took me by the throat and . . . I'm sorry." He broke eye contact with me and looked at Marie. "And to you, beautiful lady, I hope you can forgive me for my behavior. You must think I'm some kind of an animal by the way I acted. Especially the first time we meet. I'm so sorry, I was a fool."

"It's okay," Marie said. "I understand. You don't have anything to be forgiven for."

"Noble?" He looked back at me when I said, "Dad told me about the cut-out you used, Tommy Tomkins."

Noble squirmed a little in his chair. "Yes, that's the way Dad wanted it. He said it would be okay if we communicated that way. I didn't mean to put you or your family at risk."

"I know, I know, it's okay, I understand, but we went by there yesterday and he's laid up in bed on a respirator, has been for the last year or so."

Noble's eyes focused into the distance as his mind tried to process this new information. "That doesn't make sense. The letters went through without any problem. Maybe his nurse passed them on for him?"

I shrugged. "Maybe."

I didn't think the nurse did; the service rotated the nurses on a regular basis. I let it go. "So we're here now, tell us what's going on."

"I didn't think you'd come back. I didn't sleep all night because I thought I screwed up royal. You had no reason to come back, Bruno. I know that. I owe you for this. I'll repay you somehow, I promise. You hear, I promise, you have my word."

"I know, my brother. How can we help?"

He nodded, and looked down at his hands, shame plain in his expression. "I'm not proud of how I ended up here. I'm not. You were right yesterday when you said I was the one who shot those two boys. I did. I'm guilty of that and I'm paying for it. I have no problem with that. Though, I disagree with you, I had to shoot those boys. It was them or me and I'm not proud of it. I did other things though, things I'm not proud of, and like I said, I deserve to be in here. No doubt about it."

His words cut me deep, his admission, the words I'd thrown at him in anger, repeated back in this humble way. What Marie said only seconds ago, about what had motivated my brother—the loss of his family—I'd never thought about that event and how it must've impacted him. Of course, that's what had happened, delayed post-traumatic stress. I'd read about it. Why had that obvious solution eluded me all this time? I'd been too close to it, or maybe I, too, had been impacted by the experience that Christmas morning. I went around and sat on the edge of the table, put my hand on his, and helped him up. I hugged my brother for the first time in twenty-five years. He couldn't hug back. The waist chains restricted him. He put his head on my shoulder and pushed down. We stayed that way a long time. He finally said, "I love you, bro."

"I love you too." I let go and leaned back against the table. "We don't have much time. Tell us what's happening."

He sat down and nodded, then took a deep breath and looked up at me. "I did it again. I somehow got myself in deep trouble without even trying. Got in trouble out there, when I'm in here. It's amazin', isn't it?"

I said nothing and waited for him to tell it.

"I worked for Papa Dee. You know that part already."

"Dee's dead," I said. "He got gunned, payback for the hate he inflicted upon all those thousands of lives, ruined them with bullets and rock coke and his hateful ways."

"I know," Noble said. "We heard about Papa Dee and Del getting gunned in here, that someone took them both off the board. They never solved it."

He paused for a long moment.

"Okay, so here it is," he said. "I was movin' up in Dee's organization. I'd made it to second under Del. It was Del, then Fat Chuck, then me. Del didn't like the way Papa Dee had been askin' my opinion. I could see it in Del's eyes. Fat Chuck, he could care less, he ran those two gamblin' houses off Central and never got close to the dope. That was where all the big money was anyway, in the dope. Del, he was just overprotective of his precious Papa Dee."

Noble again paused.

We waited.

"Okay," he said. "What happened was that Papa Dee slapped around his girl, banged her up pretty good. She was no bigger than a minute." Noble gritted his teeth in between the words; telling this angered him even today. He said, "She needed a hospital, but Dee wouldn't allow it. It was too dangerous. If we took her to the hospital, Johnny Law might tumble to Papa's brutal ways and toss his happy ass in the can. Papa Dee called in Grover Porter. You remember old Grover, don't ya, Bruno?"

"Yeah," I said. "He lived in that boarded-up library and gambled his life away, right? Wait, Wait. Okay, now I remember, Grover came to me when I was still working patrol, said this girl needed help. He said the girl belonged to Papa. Yeah, that's right. As I remember it, I talked to her, tried to get her to go into a battered women's shelter. She'd have none of that no matter how hard I tried to convince her. Her name was . . ." I turned my head to the ceiling and closed my eyes. "Her name was Sasha, she was eighteen or nineteen, and she—"

"Yeah, yeah, that's her," Noble said, "I didn't know about that, that she talked with you. That's really crazy, ain't it, that we're talkin' about the same girl all these years later?"

"Not really, I worked patrol in the same area and—" I stopped. The complete memory of her bubbled to the surface: her soft, gentle voice, her porcelain-smooth skin, her deep-brown eyes, large and vulnerable. She'd been one of the most beautiful women I'd ever seen. I opened my eyes and looked at Noble. Now I thought I knew what had attracted my older brother to the wrong side of the street.

CHAPTER NINETEEN

Deputy B. Stanford stuck his head in. "Time's up."

Marie stood and shot him a smile. "Please, could we just have a few more minutes?"

The deputy shook his head, "No. Hell no. This mope isn't even supposed to be on this side of the jail. My ass is hung out a country mile on this."

"I know," she said, "and we really appreciate it, we really do, but we just need a few more minutes, please?"

"I'm only doin' this as a favor for Johnny Mack. Tell him he owes me big." He closed the door and left us alone.

"Hurry," I said.

"Okay, I . . . I fell hard for her. I know it's sappy and I never admitted it before, but . . . I mean, I fell in love the first time I saw her at Roscoe's Chicken and Waffles. She came into Roscoe's with Papa Dee and Del and bam! Jus' like that I knew I couldn't live without her. Call me a fool, I don't care. That's how it was, crazy jus' like that, bam!

"Bruno, I couldn't eat my chicken, I just stared at her. Even after she got up and left, I couldn't eat. I followed them out to their Lincoln. I couldn't for the life of me understand how a woman would go with—"

"Noble."

"Right, right sorry. Anyway, I left school and I started slingin' rock for Pigman, a guy way down the food chain from Del and Papa Dee. It took two years, but I worked my way up just on the hope of getting another look at her. And I did get a look at her every now and then. I did. I even had a few words with her here and there.

"Ah, all right, all right, no, that's a lie. I'm older now, smarter, I can tell you the truth. I wanted her from the start. All of her. She's all I thought about every waking minute. I never gave up thinkin', tryin' to put somethin' together, some sorta plan. I knew it was all a fantasy that she and I could run off together. Pure Alice in Wonderland kinda shit.

"She didn't even know I existed, even though I'd said 'hi' to her twice, and had asked her how her day was once in two years."

So this whole mess had started over a woman. I looked at Marie and realized that, without reservation, I'd do the same for her. So what Noble described wasn't that far of a stretch, not really.

Noble's expression shifted to a huge smile. "At least I didn't think she knew I existed. Papa watched her close, like some kinda national treasure. But I was patient and bided my time. Papa Dee slipped up and let his guard down, and I was right there when he did. Me and Sasha, we got together one night . . . ah, yeah, I'll skip that part ta save ya all the embarrassing details. Anyway, we hit it off. I mean we really hit it off. Fell in love, the both of us."

"That wasn't too smart," I said. "Not with Papa Dee's girl."

"You don't have to tell me that, big brother. We were damn careful about it. And we knew, we sure did, that it was just a matter of time, Papa Dee would figure us out. Especially with Del all up in my ass all the time, afraid I was movin' in on him, tryin' ta get his job. I wasn't though, I was jus' trying to get close to my girl. That's all."

"Go ahead," I said.

"Papa liked me. He had this big deal goin' down, this huge deal, and he asked me to run security on it."

The night I'd arrested Noble, when he came over the counter at me and I pistol-whipped him all those years ago, he'd said that Del had accused him of a rip-off.

"You took off the load, didn't you?" I said.

He stared at me for a long, fat moment. He shook his head. "I wanted to. I did. I planned it all out. I'll admit to that. But I didn't. I felt bad, Bruno. I didn't want to sell all that rock to those kids, to those street whores ruinin' their lives, to Joe College comin' into the ghetto to cop some dope. I felt bad, I'm tellin' ya. So I thought I could kinda make up for it by takin' off this load."

I shook my head. "Bullshit, brother. Call it like it was. You wanted out and you needed a stake to get it done. How could you save the people if you had to sell the load to get your stake? You'd be putting it right back out on the street."

"Don't you judge me, asshole. You shot Derek Sams." He instantly shifted emotions and started to run up that uncontrolled rage again, his face bloated, the veins in his forehead pulsing. He caught himself this time.

I *had* shot and killed my son-in-law, Derek Sams, but only after he'd killed Albert, my grandson, and only after Sams got spit out the other end of the justice system, walked away clean. I couldn't let that happen and I didn't. As much as Noble wanted it to be the same, it wasn't. "How much did you walk away with?" I fought down my anger. This whole fiasco hadn't ignited over a woman. Maybe it started with that, but in reality, it came down to a twenty-five-year-old dope rip-off. Marie and I had come all this way over dope?

He glared at me.

"Well," I said, "how much?"

"Four hundred and fifty kilos. But it didn't go down. I'm tellin' yeah, Bruno, it didn't go down."

"A half ton? You're kiddin' me, right?"

"Exactly, that's a lot, right? I didn't do it."

I pointed my finger at his face. "Noble, don't you dare lie to me. You lie to me, we're outta here."

Then it hit me. I said, "Wait. Wait. Papa Dee found out about you, didn't he? That's how Sasha got beat. Papa Dee found out about you two and took it out on her."

His expression drooped, shifted from anger to sorrow. He looked away. His voice cracked. "She got hurt because of me. I'll never forgive myself for it. Papa did find out. So naturally he took me off the deal. Hell, he tried to take me off the board. He sicced Del on my ass. He put up a contract, a fifty-thousand-dollar bounty on my head, to get every swingin' dick, poo-butt crackhead on the street to stick a shiv in me or bust a cap in my ass."

"So why did you get a job at that Stop and Go?"

"Exactly, if I took off a half ton of coke, why would I be workin' as a clerk in a damn corner grocery, huh? Tell me that, huh? I worked there 'cause I'd hit rock bottom. I got a straight job to earn some money, to do it the right way, to show Sasha I could do it. It was the only damn job I could get. And I needed that job. I needed to prove to her I could make it work."

"No, you're right," I said. "It doesn't make sense. Why would you get the job if you had nine million dollars in coke?"

Marie cut in. "Nine million dollars? Nine million?"

"Yeah," I said, "that's a lot of motivation."

"So let me get this straight," Marie said. "The reason we're here is because someone is menacing your family over some cocaine they *think* you stole twenty-five years ago?"

"That's right. My son and his two kids, Ricardo and Rebecca."

"Someone thinks you have all of that coke," I said. "A half ton of it stashed away somewhere for twenty-five years and no one's ever found it. That doesn't make any sense. Why now? What's changed?"

He shrugged. "Who knows? The story's been goin' around the prison system for years. They're callin' it *Noble's white gold*. Talkin' about it like it's some kind of pirate's treasure."

I smiled. "And I bet you haven't done anything to discourage it either, have you? Why would you? If people thought you had that kind of secret, killin' you off wouldn't do them any good."

That explained why he'd survived so long in the prison system that should've eaten him.

"Now they've gone after my family," he said. "Last night I called home. My son said they grabbed Becca and Ricky yesterday. Went right into the school to show they don't give one shit about the authorities and took 'em right out of their classes."

Marie jumped up. "They kidnapped the kids? Who did this? Who?"

"I don't know who, but my son said they snatched them right outta their preschool."

My stomach turned sick. These children were family. Using children as pawns, a negotiating tool, made my blood boil. Didn't they know what it did to the children? "Why didn't you say something when we first walked in?"

"I didn't wanna scare you off. I was at my wits' end last night. I didn't know if you'd come back. Not until I got the call on the PA from the booth bitch that there was a visit. That's when I knew you'd come back. That was the longest night of my sorry-assed life, Bruno. You're my last hope, and I didn't wanna scare you off, so I didn't tell you right out the gate. I wanted to explain the whole thing first. Believe me, I'm all tore up inside. You gotta help me, please. I'm beggin' ya, man."

"What do they want?" Marie asked. "Is it really all about this mysterious load of coke you have stashed?"

"I don't have any coke stashed. You gotta believe me. That's ridiculous. Where could you hide a half ton all these years and not have someone find it, huh? These guys are crazy, completely off their nut, ta even think it."

"You're sure it's about this coke, then?" I asked.

"Yeah, I'm sure, what else could it be? But they haven't contacted my son yet. So I don't know for absolute sure."

"Your son has to call the police." Marie said it more like a demand.

He finally broke eye contact with me and looked at my wife. "He called the police. My son called the police for sure. The police are in it now."

"Shit."

"Bruno, watch your mouth, please."

I didn't have time for her language scolding. "Noble, with the cops involved, you have to know it's difficult for us to get mixed up in this."

His face flushed and the veins in his temples pulsated. "Brother, I knew if it got a little rough, you'd turn tail and run. I was so careful, being so nice, and it didn't matter a damn, did it? You're still jus' gonna turn tail and run, pissin' in your pants at the first mention of the pol-eese. What happened to Bruno The Bad Boy Johnson, huh? What happened to that guy?"

Marie said, "Shut up. No one's going to run."

I said, "Just what do you expect us to do with cops crawlin' all over this thing?"

"If you don't have the balls for this, then jus' help get me out, help spring me, and I'll take care of my own."

"Like that's gonna happen."

"It's easy. I've got a foolproof plan."

"Foolproof plans are for fools. The jails are full of 'em."

"Get out then. Go on back to South America or wherever it is you go where it's nice and safe." His voice rose higher into a yell.

The door burst open. "Okay," Deputy B. Stanford said, "that's it, game over, time to go back to your cage."

"And it's Central America, not South," I said.

"Where can we find your son to talk to him?" Marie asked with the voice of reason.

Deputy B. Stanford took hold of Noble's elbow and tugged him out the door. "He's living in Dad's old house on Nord."

We followed him out into the hall. We stopped and they kept moving, the deputy tugging, trying to get Noble to move, no more than a few feet away.

"What's your son's name?" I asked.

Noble struggled to look back. "Bruno. I named him Bruno."

CHAPTER TWENTY

I STOPPED DEAD. *Bruno?* He named his son after me?

Marie stood next to me, her hip touching my leg, her hands grasping my arm. She gripped tighter when Noble said the name. "Oh my God, Bruno."

I couldn't say anything. The words clogged and wouldn't come. Noble continued to move a little at a time, not yet ten feet away. I raised my hand to him, a silly, insignificant gesture, but I had to do something in response. How come I hadn't known? How come Dad had not told me? Had I been that much of a tyrant about right and wrong—that much of a vindictive fool who wouldn't listen to reason and made them afraid to tell me?

All at once Noble's expression shifted from a smile to one of abject fear, his eyes no longer on me. "Look out!" he yelled.

I spun, shoving Marie out of the way and toward the closest wall.

Three men descended upon me, all of them Sons of Satan. Large men with shaved heads and tattoos, black and ugly on their scalps, faces, and necks. The first two came in as blockers, the ones meant to restrain the victim while the one with the shiv came in and finished the job—the lamb offered up and ready. I instantly recognized their play. I sidestepped out of the grasp of the first one on the left and swung wide and hard at the jaw of the one who came in low on the right. My fist connected hard with bone and shot pain through my wrist, up my arm, and into my shoulder. I'd not hit him hard enough. He pivoted, his arm going around my waist and spinning me back around into the path of the guy with the shiv.

Marie screamed like a banshee and jumped on the guy that I had hit, who now had a good hold of my arm. Marie swung her arm around his neck to hold on, and with her other hand took hold of his ear and pulled with everything she had. The guy screamed like a pig but wouldn't let go of me.

This all happened in nothing more than a blink.

I tried to shake both men off and couldn't. They had me locked up tight. The shiv came in low and fast, headed right for my belly.

Noble had moved from the onset to intercede. His chains rattled as he came up from behind, passed by, and jumped in between.

He couldn't swing his arms or kick his legs. All he had was his body. He yelled. I could only see his back. His body convulsed as it accepted the shiv. Skin and muscle and intestine parted to let it in. His body jerked and shuddered from the violent intrusion.

I yelled like a bull moose and head butted the man Marie had. His nose mashed flat, his eyes rolled. He let go of me. Marie rode him to the floor, kicking and scratching.

Deputy B. Stanford, late on the upswing, jumped in it now and punched the guy with the shiv. The shiv came back and went into Noble again. The deputy bore in with both fists, battering the assassin with unchecked brutality.

Red bells went off. The entire jail banged again and again as the place went into lockdown, the steel doors clanging closed. I spun on the last guy, who had me around the waist, and brought my knee up into his face. I did it again and again. His grip loosened.

I peeled him off and raised his shoulders to get at his face. I punched him as hard as I could. Battered his face over and over, driving him back to the opposite wall.

The hallway thundered with boots. Two deputies tackled me. More took down the attacker I had pinned against the wall. The floor turned into a writhing pit of arms and legs and blood.

Blood.

The smooth, polished concrete floor went slick with blood.

Noble.

My God, Noble.

One of the deputies wrenched my arm behind my back, and then the other, and put the handcuffs on.

"Marie? Marie, are you okay?"

"Let go of me, you pervert."

I struggled up to see. She stood by the far wall, shrugging off the deputy trying to restrain her. "Let me go. I'm a doctor," she said. "I need to tend to that man."

The throng of deputies still kicked and punched the Sons on the floor, trying to get them handcuffed, trying to knock the bejesus outta them for daring to disrupt their jail. Marie pulled away and went to Noble, who was lying on the concrete with a puddle of blood expanding around him, his hands chained to his waist, unable to put his own hands to the wound to stem the flow. Marie got right down next to him, put pressure on his stomach with both her hands. Her hands instantly turned red. She yelled to the deputy who'd had his hands on her a moment before. "*You,* gimme your shirt. Do it now."

"Who the fuck do you think you are?"

She didn't answer and gave him a glare that should've burnt a hole right through him. She pulled her top off over her head, leaving only her red lace bra, exposing smooth tan skin and cleavage.

She bundled up her shirt and firmly pressed it against Noble's wounds.

From far off down the hall, the watch sergeant, an old salt with gray hair and a belly, walked, unhurried. An old salt who knew it didn't matter that much when he arrived; his young deputies knew how to handle the situation.

Deputy B. Stanford grinned and said in a voice altered to mimic a PA, "Cleanup on aisle seven. We have a spill on aisle seven." Jailhouse humor. Another deputy chimed in, "More like a hazardous-waste spill."

The deputies pulled me to my feet, my hands cuffed behind. "It's okay," I said, "I was just here visiting my brother. My brother's right there, the one that's hurt real bad. Can you take off these cuffs, please? I'm a visitor." I checked around on the floor for my plastic visitor's badge, which had been yanked off in the melee. I tried to speak as an affronted victim. Suddenly, I realized I'd made a fatal mistake. In all the excitement, I'd forgotten where I was and let down my guard.

The sergeant got up to us, looked around. "Are we secure? Can we secure from red bells?"

The deputies had the Sons cuffed and pressed hard into the concrete floor, their knees shoved in the bikers' backs. The Sons' faces were battered and torn. Two deputies answered at the same time, "Yes, sir, Sergeant, code four."

The sergeant took a radio off his belt. "Three Sam, code four, secure from red bells."

"Sergeant," I said, "I was just here visiting my friend. He's over there on the floor, hurt. Can you get him medical aid please?"

Another deputy said to the sergeant, "We have the nurse coming and paramedics are en route."

The sergeant pointed at the tall deputy who had just spoken

and then at Marie. "Son, take your shirt off and give it to that woman."

The deputy didn't hesitate. He yanked his shirttails from his pants, unbuttoned it, and handed it to Marie. She put it on. The uniform shirt went down to just above her knees.

"Sergeant," I said again, "I'm a visitor, can you take these cuffs off, please?"

He turned to give me his attention. "What happened here?"

"I don't know. We came to visit my friend and then this fight somehow broke out. I don't know why. My wife and I were minding our own business when these three guys over here—"

The sergeant cut me off and turned to Deputy B. Stanford, who now looked a little sheepish as the sergeant pointed his radio at Noble on the floor. "What in the hell is that K-nine doing visiting in a room next door to 1700 and 1750?"

Nobody answered.

The sergeant shook his head and took his cell phone out. Only supervisors were allowed to carry them. A couple of the deputies figured out what was about to happen and started to edge away. The sergeant held up his phone and said, "Nobody move." He snapped some pics to memorialize who had participated in the incident and to preserve the crime scene.

"I want a memo from everyone here, on my desk in one hour." He looked at the deputy closest to him and pointed his radio at me, then at Marie. "I want both of them locked down until we figure out what the hell happened here."

CHAPTER TWENTY-ONE

MARIE SAT ON my lap, still clad in the deputy's uniform shirt, which smelled of cologne mixed with body odor, a strong manly stink incongruent with her soft vulnerability. They'd put us back in the same room we'd sat in minutes before with Noble. She nuzzled my neck, her tears cool and wet.

Outside the door, in the hall, paramedics continued to work on Noble, my brother. "How bad is he?" I whispered in her ear.

"He could be okay, really. I've seen them like that before where the wounds only need to be sutured, where the knife missed everything vital. There is a chance the knife missed everything."

"And you've also seen them where the knife didn't."

She nodded. "What are we going to do? What if they fingerprint you?" She wanted to change the subject.

She already knew the answer to that one. If fingerprinted, I'd be arrested for kidnapping, a crime I had technically committed, legally wrong, but morally correct, a private morality and a costly luxury.

"Their case is circumstantial at best. I can beat it, no problem."

"Don't you blow smoke up my dress, Mr. Bruno Johnson," she whispered. "You don't even know what kind of case they have against you."

"Well, let's just hope they don't fingerprint me, then. How's that? And you're not wearing a dress, you're wearing slacks."

She pushed on me with the flat of her hand. "You know what I meant."

We waited.

"You know," she said, "on our tenth anniversary we'll be sitting together on our veranda in our swing chair and laugh about all of this."

"Hey, what happened to the other nine years in between? What, we won't think it's funny until it ages for ten years? Or that's when you think I'll get out?"

The door opened, a female deputy outside. "Ma'am," the deputy said, "please come with me."

Marie kissed my forehead and gave me a hug. "See you in a little while, babe."

"I love you," I said. I couldn't bring myself to lie, to say I'd see her in a *little while*, because I didn't know for sure if I would.

But I did know. I'd worked the jail, and investigations, long enough to know. They would find me out, no question. I'd slipped up and made a mistake, a fatal one. Nobody's fault but my own. I only hoped the mistake didn't pull my beautiful wife into it.

I'd walked into the lion's den, fat, dumb, and happy, the way Robby used to say, and now had to sit still while the lions ate me.

Thirty minutes later, time enough to do a background check on the phony name I'd given them, time enough to let me fester and wind up my paranoia—the door opened again and in walked a lone detective in denim pants, a blue chambray shirt, and a blue blazer. When he sat in the chair Noble had occupied, his blazer opened. He wore an empty pancake holster on his right hip. No guns of any kind came into the jail.

He offered his hand. "How you doin'? I'm Deputy John Harris."

I shook his hand and said, "Jason Minor," the name on my forged driver's license, the name I'd used to enter the country, the one the detective now had clipped to his Posse Box in the form of my driver's license.

"How's my friend? Is he going to be okay? How bad is he hurt?"

He leaned back in the chair and looked at me for a long couple of minutes, trying to make me squirm. I knew the routine, had used it myself in the past. I didn't want it to work on my paranoia, but it did. His gaze burrowed right down into the bottom of my spine and made me want to shudder.

"We know—" he pointed to me, then to himself "—you and me, we know that this façade you're trying to feed us is a bunch of bullshit, right?"

I gave him my best confused expression. "No, I don't know what you're talking about. How come you're holding us? I don't think this is right. You don't have the right to hold us, do you? I mean, we didn't do anything wrong. I want to see my wife." I tried to say all the things a victim would say, an act more difficult than I thought after living a predator's life for the last twenty-seven years.

"You're going to play dumb, is that it? I don't think that game would be in your best interest, not when we have your wife on ice, ready to book for any number of offenses."

"What're you talking about? We haven't done anything wrong."

"Come on, man, cut the crap. I'm not some rookie detective you can run a game on. You slipped up out there. I interviewed everyone involved before I got to you."

Smart. Always have as much intel as possible before you interrogate. This guy knew his way around the games criminals played. He was right; I wouldn't be able to bluff this guy.

I said nothing.

He leaned in close. "You referred to our illustrious, rat-bastard inmate, who calls himself Noble Johnson, as your brother. Noble Johnson only has one brother, and you and I both know his name, don't we?"

Now he'd gone and played it too smug. I needed to shake him up a little if I wanted to have any chance at all. "What . . ." I stammered. "What're you talking about? Oh . . . oh you mean out there in the hall. You're right, I did. I did call him my brother. But we're all brothers in the eyes of our Lord."

He sat back. His mouth dropped open for just a second before he caught himself and regained his composure. I had him. I needed to press the advantage. "Sure, sure, I'm sure you've heard us black folk, heard us call each other bro, or brother, or brother-man. That's all I meant. Is that what all this confusion's about? I'm sorry, really I am. It's all a mistake."

His eyes narrowed and a smile slowly spread across his arrogant mug. "All right, *Mr. Jason Minor*, then I guess I'll just have to let you go."

I didn't fall for it. His smugness served only to make me shrink deeper in my chair. He had me before he said another word, and knew I couldn't do anything about it.

"I give you my word," he said, "as a deputy sheriff, that I'll let you go if you do one thing for me? Just one. And if you do, I promise you that you can walk right out that door."

I said nothing and didn't move.

"Show me your right bicep."

Ah, shit.

He had me cold.

Way back when, I'd been a young and dumb fool. While on the Violent Crimes Team, I fell for the camaraderie, the competitive spirit, and once I'd made my bones on the team, I, too, like all the other members, tattooed BMF—Brutal Mother Fucker—on my body. Just like the ignorant, misguided gangsters that I chased down, bludgeoned, ran over, or shot if they didn't want to give up.

He stood and, making a show of it, came around the table, his eyes boring into mine. His hands, in my peripheral vision, moved to my shirt.

He pulled the sleeve up.

CHAPTER TWENTY-TWO

Detective Harris laughed.

I can't say that I wouldn't have done the same thing in his place had I caught a heavyweight fugitive as simply as he had caught me. In fact, my capture was one for the books. I'd come into the jail, of all places, and all but begged to be found out. Back in the day, when I'd been younger and less enlightened in the ways of the criminal mind, and I'd caught one running a game on me, I'd say, "Peek-a-boo, asshole." Detective Harris at least spared me that indignity and embarrassment.

Harris left.

A short time later, two deputies, B. Stanford and W. Smithson, came in. While they chained me, they talked between themselves about the next transfer list due out at the end of the month and wondered if they'd be on it. B. Stanford had in for The Devil's Triangle: Lynwood, Firestone, and Carson, now known as Century Station. W. Smithson had in for Norwalk, Alta Dena, and Industry Stations. They talked as if I didn't matter as they put on the waist chains and leg irons. Cool metal on my wrists and ankles, metal that snatched at the air I breathed and made the walls close in around me.

I wouldn't be a K-nine like Noble. Once processed through

classification, they'd make me a red suit, an escape risk. Then I'd be housed in High Power, 1700 and 1750, a jail within a jail with no chance at all to escape.

I didn't see any way out, none. "Hey, can you guys at least answer me one question, please?"

"You're an asshole, comin' in here like this," B. Stanford said "You put your buddy's ass in a sling. They just suspended him. And I liked the dude too. So no, you get nothin' from us."

"They suspended John Mack?"

W. Smithson shoved me in the back. "What'd ya think was gonna happen, comin' in our house and starting that kinda bullshit? We gotta write paper out the ass on that little dust-up. And now I heard there's gonna be an internal affairs investigation on it. No. No, you definitely got nothin' comin'. Get movin'."

They walked me in short half steps, steps restricted by the leg irons. Walked me through the old jail all the way over to IRC, where they took off the cuffs. They left the waist chain hooked around my waist and the leg irons on my ankles. In the walk from the jail, the leg irons had enough time to chafe the skin, and it burned whenever I moved.

They left me in a long line of fish waiting to have their fingerprints put into the LiveScan system, thirty to thirty-five people in front of me, the line moving slow, but still too fast for me. Once my prints entered the system, the *Alert* would pop and confirm what Detective Harris already thought he knew. They should not have left me unescorted, not as a high-power inmate. But I had not officially been classified, so they could get away with the error in judgment if anything happened.

IRC had one large room in the center, like a hub with four slightly smaller adjoining rooms; the whole place opened like some kind of church. The room off to the right contained a hundred or so naked men who stood with their hands covering their eyes while a uniformed deputy hosed them down with a delousing chemical. The chemical reeked bad enough to overpower every other odor in the IRC. The reek overpowered body odor, the acidic and sour scent of barf, and the worst odor of all, that always present smell of despair.

The line behind filled up with fifteen or twenty more men waiting to be fingerprinted. No one spoke; the order of silence had been given by the deputy who patrolled the line.

Everyone wore different types of mostly raggedy street clothes. Some wore no shirt, their chests burnt brown from the sun, dirty, and up close, too close, they smelled of body odor. Hispanic and black gangsters all eyed each other. Bikers, with their heavy street boots, and a few guys new to this world, Joe-citizen types who'd made a big mistake like not paying a drunk-driver penalty and now would have to wait to get processed before afforded the opportunity to bail, their eyes wide in fear and wonderment at this horrible little glimpse of someone else's reality.

IRC, with the new fish, had always been the most volatile place in the jail; the crooks fresh off the street, wild and anxious, sometimes went off if not properly supervised. Proper supervision meant keeping a thumb on them, constantly getting in their face, keeping their minds busy, keeping them worried that they were, at any moment, about to get their ass beat. That's how so few deputies controlled the vast number of loose and unclassified inmates, all that fresh meat off the street.

The line edged up some more.

Over by the main entrance, a line of inmates came in escorted by trans deputies, called *bus drivers* by fellow jail deputies. The line comprised a mixture of gang members coming back from court, or in from other booking stations, all chained together. The trans deputies, one at each end of the long line, unhooked the inmates, eager to hand them off to the IRC deputies.

A large black gangster, a Crip by his tattoos, caught my eye. He stared at a short white dude with Aryan Brotherhood tattoos who stood at the back of our line, waiting for the LiveScan. I looked around to see if the deputies saw the same thing I saw. They didn't.

"Deputy," I said to the passing IRC deputy walking line security, "You're about to have a problem."

He didn't know me, and rushed right up into my face. "What's your problem, asshole? What were you told about talking in line?"

I lowered my voice and took a big chance admitting my past affiliation to his brotherhood. "I used to be a cop, and you're about to have a problem over there. Look."

The trans deputy had already taken off the black gangster's leg irons and one wrist cuff on the waist chain. He'd started on the second one when the deputy I'd warned tumbled to my admonishment. "Hey!" he yelled, and moved quick, but not quick enough. The second cuff came off.

The black gangster shoved the bus driver out of the way and went after the Aryan in my line.

The deputy I'd warned yelled again and moved to block the black gangster's path. The man, who was far larger than the deputy, bowled him over. The deputy caught the gangster's leg and held on.

With the sudden call to action, everyone in our line moved away, scattered everywhere. Some went for a wall, trapped, unable to go any further. They tried to get next to it, tried to get small. Other deputies reacted but were too far away. The black gangster pulled back with his free leg and kicked the hell out of the deputy holding his leg. When he pulled back to kick the deputy again, I slugged him in the head. Gave him a long, sweeping roundhouse that connected solid to his jaw.

Unfazed, the gangster pivoted and came at me, dragging the deputy, who was still hanging on. The man dwarfed me. I couldn't run, not with leg irons.

I didn't want to. I needed someplace to vent my frustration. I went at him with both fists, hit him twice, quick, with a right-left combination. He moved slowly, his big size a hindrance. He only hit me once, with a fist that came in right out of the sky and landed on my cheek. The blow shook my world, made the walls and the lights quake and waver.

I stumbled backward, legs tangled in the leg irons, and fell on my ass. The deputies swarmed the big man, took him to the ground. More deputies came into the huge room, some jumping on. Others yelled at the inmates, "Get on a wall. Get on the wall, and stay there!"

Two deputies had seen my involvement and came at me to "council and advise," regarding fighting in the jail. That's how their reports would read tomorrow, a veiled attempt to cover what really happened, a beatdown. Mine.

A second before they reached me, a second before they started to put the boots to me, the deputy who'd been on the ground holding the gangster's leg saw what was about to happen to me and yelled over the din, "No, no, he's cool. Leave him be."

The two stopped and redirected their attention to controlling the other fish who had just entered IRC. A dozen deputies, the total number in all of IRC, against three hundred unclassified crooks and court returns. Not good odds. Not even close.

The near riot started and ended in eighty or ninety seconds, averted by quick-to-action deputies.

I shook off the punch, my face swelling, my vision still a little wobbly. Someone said, "Hey." I turned around.

My friend John Mack stood close, wearing his Class B uniform, minus his usual smile.

CHAPTER TWENTY-THREE

MY FACE THROBBED and continued to swell. John Mack worked at taking off the rest of my leg irons and waist chains. Deputies still yelled orders. Inmates moved in waves, groups small and large obeyed and started to calm as the IRC returned to normal.

John didn't look at me as he worked at the chains. "You can't ever stay outta trouble, can you?"

"I'm sorry about what happened," I said. "I heard they suspended you."

John stopped what he was doing and looked around to see if anyone stood close enough to hear. "Hey, can it, would ya? Wait until we get outside."

"What? Are you kiddin' me? John, you can't help me escape. It won't just be your job, it'll be a criminal act. You'll go to prison. I can't hold with that. I won't be a party to that." The words came out of my mouth without the devotion they needed. I wanted, with all my soul, to be reunited with my girl, my wife Marie, and to be on our way back to Costa Rica and the kids.

"Bruno, do me a favor and shut the hell up for five minutes, would you? Can you do that much for me, huh?"

"I'm not going, John, I'm not doin' it."

He moved up close to my face. "What kind of ignoramus are

you? I got to you before you were fingerprinted. You're not officially here yet. You get it? If you're not here, not booked in, you can't escape, so just do me a favor and shut your trap until we get out of here, okay?"

I didn't understand. "What about Detective Harris? He knows what time it is. He's the kind of cop who'll yell foul, blow the whistle on you."

John took hold of my elbow and, at a fast pace, headed us back toward the old part of the jail, the way we had come.

Once away from everyone and moving down a long hall with long murals painted by inmates, he said, "I don't know how you do it, but you always manage to find some kind of guardian angel. This guy I'm talkin' about, this guardian angel, whispered in Harris' ear, made it right with Harris."

"What're you talking about?"

He stopped and faced me. "The captain of the facility heard about what went down in the hall with the Sons and with your brother. I'm sorry about your brother. It never should've happened, and if Stanford had been doing his job, it wouldn't have."

"How's Noble doing? Is he okay?"

"He's in surgery, Bruno. I don't have any information other than that."

"Where'd they take him?"

"LCMC. Come on, we gotta keep movin'."

Los Angeles County Medical Center was the best hospital in the county for emergency surgery. It had to be, given the amount of experience their docs got with all the car crashes and shootings that entered that hospital.

I'd heard docs working LCMC compared to those docs who'd worked a MASH unit in Vietnam.

After the surgery, now that was a whole other matter. I felt better that Noble lived long enough to make it to LCMC and then into surgery. In my book, his odds had just increased exponentially.

We continued to walk, but I slowed our pace. "What captain?" I asked. "What're you talking about?"

"The captain showed up on the facility after he'd already gone home for the day. He pulled me into his office. The L.T. had suspended me, took my badge and gun. A deputy found me in the locker room. I was cleaning out my locker. To tell you the truth, I was glad, relieved really. I hate working this hellhole. I thought if I could keep my head down, I could eventually work my way back onto the Violent Crimes Team. But after tonight, I realized I couldn't wait it out, not here, not in this job. So those assholes, the Sons, did me a favor tonight. The captain calls me in, sits me down, and asks me what happened. I was mad, fed up like I said, so I told him. Really let him have it."

"Not about me, not my real name, not the truth."

He smiled, happy with himself. "Yeah, I did."

"Ah, Jesus, Johnny."

Mack socked me in the arm, hard. "No, listen to this, your guardian angel hears everything I had to say, sits still for every word. He didn't ask any questions, not one. Well, maybe it was because I told him every detail and I didn't give him a chance to. I told ya, I was pissed. The captain, he's got his one leg up on the desk listening as he chews on this cigar. When I finish, he takes his leg down, reaches into his inbox, takes out a paper with a list on it. He hands it to me."

"Who is this guy, this captain? What's his name?"

"Aren't you going to ask me what's on the list?"

"All right, I'll play along. What kind of list was it?"

"It's a transfer list. And I'm on it. I'm going out to Century Station to work a two-man crime car. Bruno, it's not the Violent

Crimes Team, but it's the hottest place in the county. It's the old Devil's Triangle. It'll be a real kick in the ass to work there."

"I don't want to rain on your parade," I said, "but I thought you said the L.T. suspended you."

"He did. After the captain gave me a minute to figure out that my name appeared on the list he handed me, he reached in his drawer and handed me my gun and badge. Told me to personally go to IRC and escort you off the facility. Said I was then to forget I ever did it. Said that I had to hurry, that if I didn't get to you before you were fingerprinted, it would be too late, all bets would be off, and to leave you there."

I stopped walking. "What about Marie?"

"I'm not crazy, I got her out first. That's what took so long. Sorry I cut it so close getting to you, but I thought you'd want her safe first."

I let out a long breath. A huge pressure just eased up off my chest. I hugged him. "Thank you, man, I owe you big."

We started walking again, faster this time. I wanted to get to my Marie, hold her in my arms. Not many minutes ago I had resigned myself to never being able to hold her again. My smile grew so large it hurt my face. "Hey," I said, "you didn't tell me the name of this guardian angel, the name of this captain?"

"I never heard of him before." Mack said. "His name's Robert Crews."

I stopped dead.

"What's the matter? You know this guy?"

"Yeah, I do."

"Who is he?"

"My first trainee."

CHAPTER TWENTY-FOUR

THE VETERAN DEPUTIES joked and grab assed in the locker room, waiting until the time got closer to when briefing started, not wanting to be associated with the trainees. The diligent and always punctual trainee Crews sat at the long briefing table, working on the previous evening's reports, which were due at the end of watch. I always arrived early, left a time bumper of thirty minutes just in case something out of the ordinary happened to delay me, like a crash on the Long Beach Freeway. I didn't mind breaking unwritten protocol about being with the trainees and sat diagonally across from Crews. I didn't want to embarrass him too much by sitting close and looking over his shoulder. I'd get my chance to correct his reports later.

Veteran deputies always referred to the TOs, Training Officers, as the trainee's *daddy*. "Trainee, you better ask your daddy if you wanna get out of the patrol car." That sort of thing.

The second swing shift started at three in the afternoon. Right at three, the locker room started to empty out and the briefing room filled. The shift sergeant who gave briefing had yet to arrive. Crews kept his head down working on his "paper." I worked him hard on his paper, told him his reports went out far ahead of him and stood as an example of his work product, not only to supervisors, district attorneys, and judges, but sometimes even the sheriff's executive staff as well. I told him that to be a good street cop you had to have good paper.

Directly across from Crews, a new deputy, Atkinson, who'd only been off training six or seven months, sat with his chair tipped back slightly from the briefing table. Atkinson drew his gun and reholstered, drew and reholstered, practicing his fast draw. He'd bought into the ghetto-gunfighter image too heavily, and it would eventually get him in trouble. He violated policy drawing his gun without cause, especially indoors. Worse, he did it directly in the line of fire to my trainee. Atkinson, though new, now qualified as a regular deputy, and I couldn't tell him what to do, tell him to stop. Not without stepping outside the unwritten code. "Crews," I said.

Crews looked up from his report.

"Pick your shit up and move to the end of the table, over there."

He looked around at the other deputies, not knowing what he'd done wrong. He gathered up his reports and did as instructed while Atkinson continued to draw and reholster, the movement turned into an action without conscious effort, and compounded the hazard in the already dangerous situation.

Deputy Ortega came in from the locker room and sat in Crews' vacated spot just as Atkinson's trigger guard on his gun caught on his holster. His gun discharged with a huge explosion in the enclosed confines. Everyone jumped, including Atkinson. Two veteran deputies drew their guns, ducked, and moved.

A cloud of blue smoke rose. Ortega hopped around, holding his leg. "Son of a bitch. Son of a bitch, you shot me."

Crews looked over at me and let a hint of a smile slip out.

The shift sergeant came in at a run. "What the hell happened?"

All the deputies laughed except Atkinson and Ortega. Ortega

put his leg up on the table and pulled up his pant leg. The round had hit the floor between his feet and shattered the floor tile, which turned into shrapnel. The shrapnel peppered Ortega's legs. Small specks of blood beaded on his brown skin.

The shift sergeant said to Atkinson, "My office before you hit the streets. None of you other children better ever play cowboys and Indians again, not in my station." He turned to me. "Johnson, have your trainee dress down in street clothes, he's TDY tonight to work 647b's."

TDY meant temporary duty assignment, 647b's, working hookers. I didn't want to have him out with someone else watching over him, not when he'd had so little time on the street. "Sarge, if you can spare me tonight, I'd like to tag along."

The sergeant checked his shift roster, drew a line through my name, and adjusted the lineup. "Okay, Daddy, you can go along and babysit your rookie."

* * *

Thirty minutes later, we were dressed down in our street clothes. The station detective sergeant running the operation gave the briefing to three teams of three working Long Beach Boulevard on hooker suppression, called a "John" program.

All the crooks on the Boulevard knew my ugly mug, and I couldn't operate undercover in the area I'd patrolled for the last two years. That's why the detective sergeant had asked for some fresh meat, the three trainees, who were not yet known to the "B" girls.

I would work as Crews' cover team along with Detective Al Parks. Crews would cruise the Boulevard until he spotted a "B" girl or was flagged down by one. He'd pull over, get the solicitation, and then give his cover team the bust signal, flashing his brake lights by pumping the brake pedal.

I walked with Crews up to his small truck, a beat-up loaner, a trade-in from a local car dealer. His body hummed with excitement. "Play it back to me again," I said.

"I got this, Deputy Johnson, no problem."

"Listen to me. Are you paying attention?"

When I started a lecture this way, he knew to stop and pull his head out of his ass.

"Don't think of this as a cakewalk," I said. "You can't look at these suspects as women, you understand?" He nodded.

"No, you don't understand. I want you to think about them at all times as if they are armed and dangerous. As if each one is a street-smart gangster, armed with a handgun, and at any moment she's gonna throw down on you and cap your sorry little rookie ass. That's your level of alertness that I want. The trick is not showing it, while you act casual, like you're some kinda ignorant college kid. Okay? You got it?"

"Yes, sir."

"You're not carrying a gun because they *will* pat you down looking for a badge or a gun. You're not wearing body armor either, so when you get the solicitation, and you give the signal, you're out of it. You understand? Listen to what I'm saying here, you don't get involved. You let me and Al do the takedown. This is important. Stay out of it, stay away from the takedown."

"I got it. I got it."

"I hope you do." I gripped his shoulder. "Be careful."

Night set in early, making the street twice as dangerous. Al and I followed at a discreet distance. Crews worked the Boulevard like a pro and took down three "B" girls in as many hours. He could've done more if the booking process hadn't slowed us down. We broke for code seven, picked up our food from Lucy's, and ate in the back parking lot of the defunct library along with the other two teams. Crews ate with the other "Johns," the trainees, while I ate at the hood of the car with Al and the other detectives.

I ate my tacos, my stomach a little upset from the stress. With the last arrest, Crews acted a little overconfident. I'd told him about it, but he didn't let it sink. I could tell by his involvement in our conversation.

I listened to the detectives talk about a surveillance. In a couple of days, the detective bureau was going to set up on a heavyweight target, Papa Dee, the main man in cocaine for the entire area. I wanted to be in on that operation in a bad way, but didn't have the seniority yet or the experience to even ask.

Off in the darkness, over by the shrubs, I caught movement and hoped the others didn't see it. Grover Porter, an informant I used off and on, lived in the boarded-up library. I needed him on the street and not in custody on some kind of chickenshit trespassing beef.

Fifteen minutes later, we hit the Boulevard. Crews hooked up his fourth of the evening right away. He spotted a thick-bodied black woman in a stretch skirt that left nothing to the imagination and you wished it had. Crews pulled over to the curb with his passenger window down. The hooker stuck her head in the window, said a couple of words, reached inside, opened the door, and got in.

It was Al's turn to drive. He pulled up and stopped, but not close enough for my liking as I waited for the bust signal.

The brake lights flashed. I bailed out of the car, my attention glued to my trainee. Through the back window of the truck, I could see that an argument had started with Crews and the hooker. Something had happened. The hooker had somehow caught on. I tried to get there and couldn't make it happen fast enough. Al had parked too far away, not wanting to burn the deal. Up ahead in the truck cab, the verbal argument between Crews and the hooker escalated and turned physical. I yelled, "Crews, disengage! Disengage! Get out of the truck."

He couldn't hear. Or didn't want to.

The hooker opened her door and tried to get out, pulling Crews along with her. Crews, half in the truck and half out, was trying to get her in a control hold, a wristlock. I willed my legs to move faster.

Her free hand disappeared into her shoulder bag and came out with an ice pick. She raised the weapon, ready to plunge it into Crews' back.

CHAPTER TWENTY-FIVE

MCJ, Men's Central Jail, Downtown Los Angeles
Current day

Mack stopped us at the door to Visiting, the door Marie and I had passed through to come into the jail. "What happened?" Mack asked.

"That woman pulled back to plunge that ice pick into my rookie just as I got there. I cracked her across the head with my flashlight, knocked her out. I didn't have any choice. She flopped, out cold across the sidewalk." I chuckled at the memory. "You should've seen Crews' face when he saw that ice pick about to descend on his skinny little rookie ass."

"Scared shitless, I bet."

"That's a good description."

Mack shook my hand. "Well, this makes more sense now." He handed me a business card. On one side it read, *Captain Robert Crews, Commander, Men's Central Jail.* I turned it over. In perfect printing, Crews had written, *We're even.*

* * *

Out in the parking lot by the car, Marie waited for me. She wore a t-shirt with Bauchet Street Gym written on it. Mack must've given it to her. When I got close, she saw me and ran. Her joy and love for me struck me like a blow and made a lump rise in my throat. What did I do to deserve this lovely woman? I must've done something right in another life. I caught her up and swung her around and around. She buried her face in my neck.

"Oh, Bruno, I thought we'd never get out of that wretched place. I mean it, I thought we were through. Let's get out of here right now, please?"

I scooped up her legs and carried her toward the car. She lifted her head from my shoulder and kissed my cheek. "What are you doing? Put me down."

"Not a chance, lady."

"Bruno, people are watching." She said it without emphasis and let the last words trail off. With her arms around my neck, she rested her head back on my shoulder. I moved us through the line of cars, headed for our rental. She let her hand wander and caress my cheek. Her hand moved to the other side of my face. I flinched. She jerked back and looked. She saw the swelling from where the gangster socked me.

"Ah, Bruno, what happened?" She gently probed the facial bones, her fingers those of a doctor and not a lover. I flinched again, tried to hold my face still, and continued to walk to the car.

"Stupid, really," I said. "You're gonna laugh. I wasn't watching where I was goin' and I ran into a door." I made it to the car and set her down.

"I don't think anything's broken," she said, "but it should be x-rayed. What does the other guy look like?" She took up my hands to look. "Ah, Bruno."

She probed my skinned and swollen knuckles. "I think this one might be fractured."

"Ouch! Take it easy, Dr. Frankenstein."

"Don't be such a big baby. I think it is broken, really."

"I'm not surprised. The doors in that joint are made of solid steel." I hit the fob, unlocked the doors to the rental, opened hers, and ushered her in. I went around and got in. I drove back to the hotel while she used the cell and called LCMC to check on Noble. She knew her way around hospital personnel and quickly made it through to the nurse with the information. "Yes, thank you very much," Marie said, and hung up as I pulled into the hotel parking lot and shut the car down.

"Nothing yet," she said. "But the nurse I spoke to saw his vitals and doesn't think it's going to be that bad."

I got out, came around, and opened her door. The memory of the jail, the prospect of living in a concrete cell for the next ten or fifteen years without Marie, caught me up short. What a horrible proposition. I suddenly realized I couldn't get enough of my lovely wife, and I scooped her up again and headed for the hotel. With her close in my arms, the anxiety eased up a little.

She giggled. "What're you doing?"

"Ma'am, I've been remiss in my contractual obligations. Paragraph four, subsection two, line seven: 'The Lessor shall, as soon as time permits, carry the Lessee across the threshold of said abode described in paragraph two, line three.'"

She took hold of my ear, ready to yank. "I was liking it until you got to the part about me being leased property."

The bellman opened the door for me as I continued on in, headed toward the elevator. He smiled.

"Well, madam, I guess you should've read the fine print."

She yanked. I yelped and hopped around a little, juggling her, just as the elevator door opened to disgorge a load of passengers, aghast at our display. I moved into the car and turned to face them as they continued to watch us. I kissed my wife and she kissed me back while the doors closed.

* * *

We lay naked on the bed, still damp from a shower where we attempted, unsuccessfully, to use all the hot water in the hotel. My legs trembled from the exertion, trying to hold her up for so long.

She rested her chin on my chest, her thigh languidly across mine.

"I don't want to ruin this wonderful mood," she said, "but I think we really need to go see your nephew."

For the last hour, with the hot water sluicing off our bodies, I tried real hard to forget about what lay ahead. I might've succeeded if not for the two little people involved, Rebecca and Ricardo.

"What do you think?" she asked. "Tell me what you make of all this."

I let all that had happened in the last two days sink in. I tried to put out of my mind the wonderful time playing with the children, the engagement dinner, and the wedding, and focused on the ugliness we'd encountered since our plane touched down in California.

"The way I feel about Noble, the way I remember him, I can't keep from thinking he's working us in some way, that it's some kind of con and that it's going to jump up and bite us in the ass."

"How?"

"I was a cop a lot of years."

"I know that. I know you have some kind of sixth sense when it comes to reading people. I also know that what gets you in trouble most often is that part of you that believes in humanity and keeps you from *listening* to that sixth sense of yours."

Jesus, this woman could read me like nothing I'd ever seen. In our time together we'd somehow linked up as one. She now resonated from deep inside me. "So, you're saying that everyone's bad."

"No," she said, "and you know better than that. What I'm saying is, if you're getting a twinge in regard to your brother, we better tread easy. That's all I'm saying."

"I don't want to think ill of my brother, really I don't, but—"

"I know what's bugging you."

"You do?"

"Sure, you're a guy."

"Thanks for that verification."

"No, listen, guys don't believe in love at first sight. They say they do, but they just don't. You think Noble has some hidden ulterior motive, that motive being greed. You think he wanted to, or did, rip off all those kilos of cocaine. You think that job as a clerk was just a cover, an attempt to make everyone believe a story already far too difficult to believe."

I thought about it for a moment.

"You're right," I said. "We should tread lightly." I kissed her and continued to feel guilty about not trusting Noble.

CHAPTER TWENTY-SIX

AN HOUR LATER, we headed south on Central Avenue, driving toward the heart of South Central Los Angeles and to the old house on Nord. The sense of foreboding continued to shove its way into my thoughts when it shouldn't have. I had fond memories in that house, too many to count.

Marie sat close, holding my hand as I steered with the other.

I guess I didn't want to see Bruno, my nephew. How weird was that going to be? Then, on top of that, to see him living in the house where I grew up.

Too weird.

I turned down Nord, the house up ahead now, only a short distance away. Speed just twenty-five miles per hour. I kept going right on past.

"Hey." Marie pointed out the window. "Wasn't that it?"

"Yeah, I guess it was. I'll go around again."

"Honey, if you don't want to do this . . . "

"Don't be ridiculous."

I made the turns, pulled down Nord a second time, and stopped at the curb.

My childhood house looked the same, except now the exterior sported lime-green paint instead of beige, and the roof needed new shingles. Plywood covered the window on the right side of the front door. Dad never let the place look that seedy. He stayed up on it, tinkering all the time. I hadn't seen the place in over three years, and now it no longer fit comfortably in any past memory.

We sat and looked for a minute.

Marie pointed to the east, next to our house. "You drove me by this place once to show me where you used to live, where you grew up. I didn't notice the empty lot before. It just sorta blended in. Now it's like . . . it's like a missing abscessed tooth where Noble's house used to be."

I nodded. "Back then, for almost a year I mean, Noble's house sat gutted and caved in on itself. Transients and heroin addicts infested it. The city came out and condemned it. Another year went by before city workers bulldozed it down. All that's left is that concrete foundation right there."

"The city doesn't usually get involved in things like that, do they? Not this far south, do they?"

"I always thought Dad had something to do with it, that he must've called and complained enough times the city got tired of the problem and solved it. But, you see, he never made those calls in front of me and Noble."

"Did your dad do that because he didn't want Noble to have a burnt-out hulk as a reminder to his nightmare?"

I looked at her and nodded. "That's my guess. A little while after they razed the house, on warm evenings, Dad would sometimes set up a table and chairs and we ate dinner right out there on that foundation."

"Your father's one smart old man. He wanted Noble to make new memories on that spot to help cover the old."

"I never thought of it like that, but you're probably right. I always just thought it was nice to do something different. I never got used to it, though, not with the memory of what happened there. And we sat in our chairs right over the top of it. I'm not superstitious or believe in ghosts, you know that. It just didn't sit right with me, though. I don't think Noble got used to it either."

Without warning, that horrible Christmas morning flooded back on me, replete with all the colors and smells and emotions; too vivid, too much reality all at once, it caused a twinge of vertigo.

Two firemen had carried down Noble's little brother and sister, wrapped in bed sheets, and laid the little bundles at the base of the tree—a tree no longer there, not all of it anyway. The stump out front now looked like someone had buried an elephant and her one foot stuck up out of her grave, flat and round and gray.

My voice came out hollow. "I don't think it worked, even though Dad tried so hard. I just don't think it worked, not on Noble."

I got out, went around, and opened Marie's door. We walked hand in hand up across the short yard and mounted the porch. I raised my hand to knock. The door opened before I could.

The young man stood with his body bladed, his hand out of view behind the door. Not an abnormal positioning, not really, but still I sensed he held a weapon. More specifically, a handgun. I slowly tried to ease Marie behind and took a half step in front of her.

She gave me a little shove. "What's the matter with you?"

The young man said, "Can I help you?" He wore a black t-shirt with the Raiders football emblem, black denim pants, and big sneakers with blue laces. I took a closer look at his features. He did present a striking resemblance to Noble, but with lighter skin and a spray of freckles across his nose. Not as tall either, five-eight or nine and a hundred and sixty pounds, compared to Noble's six-foot, stocky build. I couldn't help the regret that came on strong enough to taste, hard and metallic. I'd somehow missed this young man's entire life. How had that been possible?

"We're here to see Bruno Johnson." The words came out alien and strange. I'd never said my own name before, not in that context, requesting to see someone named Bruno Johnson.

The young man kept his frown, "Who's askin'? State your business or get off my damn porch."

"First off, you can put that gun away. We're not here to hurt anyone, and it's making me nervous."

"Gun?" Marie said. She quit fighting me and moved behind to where I wanted her in the first place. "Bruno Johnson," she said, "meet your uncle Bruno Johnson."

The young man's frown slowly shifted to a smile, an expression that changed his entire personality, turned it youthful, washing away the seriousness of adulthood prematurely thrust upon him. Just as fast as the smile came, it fled. He stuck his head out the door and looked one way then the next. "Come on in, hurry."

Some of his paranoia immediately transferred to me. The cops working the kidnap would have the house staked out. They'd be photographing anyone and everyone who so much as walked by the front of the house.

We hurried inside. He closed the door.

I don't know what I expected. I guess I expected the inside to be the same as I remembered it.

Not even close.

CHAPTER TWENTY-SEVEN

THE AREA RUGS on the highly polished hardwood floors had been replaced with tired, wall-to-wall carpet. The high-traffic area through the living room cut a worn path, in some places right down to the weave. The interior white paint, which used to be beige, now sported fingerprint smudges and Crayola pictures from small tots—dinosaurs and stick figures, houses, and trees with green leaves. And Dad with his cotton-top hair plain as day.

Rebecca and Ricardo's artwork.

I more easily pictured the children now, and anxiety rose and started to hum inside my body. I wanted them back as soon as possible, back in the cradle of family.

Bruno did have a gun, a chrome 9mm, the cheap kind that tended to jam at the most inopportune moments, like when you tried to use them. He set the automatic on the stand right next to the door. A habit, I hoped, he didn't employ with the children present.

Marie and I took seats on an old-style divan stained with mac and cheese and purple squeezebox fruit juice.

Bruno picked up a book he'd been reading, walked the few paces into the kitchen, and placed the novel on top of the refrigerator. I liked it that the kid read. I just wondered what sparked his interest: mystery, crime novels, or thrillers?

He came and sat in the wooden rocker and rocked. He looked eighteen or nineteen, but could've been twenty or twenty-one, still too young to have children and to raise them without any help.

He looked at us and rocked and said nothing.

"Tell us what happened," I said. "Start at the beginning."

I wanted to get to know him, hug him, and welcome him into the family. All of that didn't work, not with the children in harm's way. There would be time enough later for tears and anger and apologies.

He looked away from us, his gaze far away as he remembered events he'd rather forget. I recognized the look, understood the feeling. I, too, had been in the same place too many times.

He bent over and picked up a wooden train with wooden wheels and tinkered with it, spun the wheels with the edge of his hand.

Marie leaned forward. "How old are they?"

He looked up. "Ricardo's four and Rebecca's three. I dropped them off at the preschool and daycare and went to work. The teacher called me and . . ."

He went back to tinkering with the train.

With those ages, that meant he had to have had the children when he was sixteen or seventeen. A terrible idea, kids having kids, but not that unusual, not in Willowbrook. It happened far too often.

"Hey," I said, "look at me."

He did.

"I'm your uncle. I used to be a cop. I'm good at this kind of thing, but we can't help you if you don't tell us what happened. We need to know everything, right down to the last detail."

He jumped up and threw the train against the wall. The vibration knocked off a framed award of some sort and the picture next to it. "*Now* you come around. Where've you been all of these years, huh?"

I stood.

Marie grabbed my hand and tried to tug me back down. I resisted.

"I'm here now. Shut up and sit your butt down. Your anger isn't gonna help anything. It's only gonna delay us. There's time enough for that later."

We stared at each other. He needed a moment to cool down. I went over and picked up the two framed pictures from the floor. The glass to the one with the photo cracked on impact. The picture depicted Bruno, my nephew, receiving the award. The award was the other framed picture he'd knocked down. In the photo, Bruno shook hands with County Supervisor Willy Jessup. Jessup had been on the board for years and held the most senior seat. With his experience, knowledge, and supporters, he garnered sway over the rest of the board. A year ago, maybe eighteen months now, I'd read in the *LA Times* that Jessup's long-time girlfriend drowned in his backyard pool. Controversy surrounded the incident, rumors of murder that couldn't be proven. Whether true or not, in politics it doesn't matter: some pundits thought he'd served his last term and would be ousted the next election.

Jessup's Afro had turned all white, and that made him what they called on the street a cotton-top. His politics had always been a little too liberal for me. In his mind, he wanted to continue entitlements forever, not leaving any motivation for a family to work to improve, to earn back their self-esteem. Sure, people needed a helping hand, but not for a lifetime. I'd never vote for him.

I hung the picture back up and looked at the award, one given to Bruno just last year. Had this occurred three years ago, I might've caught it on the news. This wasn't just a meritorious life-saving award; it was a notch up, one of the highest, a county proclamation. My eye jumped to a line that read, "Whereas Bruno Johnson saved a three-year-old's life."

> *On June 5th, BRUNO JOHNSON, who worked for Valiant Security Services, was on routine patrol in the area of Slauson Park at 54th Street and Compton Avenue, when a young mother saw his security vehicle and flagged him down. The mother held a three-year-old child in her arms; the child was turning blue. The panic-stricken mother didn't know the cause of her child's soon-to-be fatal distress. Bruno called for paramedics and then noticed chocolate cookie crumbs stuck to the child's cheeks. He took the child from the mother and administered the Heimlich maneuver, successfully dislodging the chunk of chocolate chip cookie blocking the child's airway. If not for Bruno Johnson's quick and decisive action, the child would not have survived.*

I carried the award over to Marie to read. I felt proud and honored, but something about it bothered me, and I couldn't put my finger on it.

I looked at Bruno. "This is very impressive. Your dad must be proud of you."

He shrugged, his expression without emotion. "I only did what I was trained to do. And as far as my dad being proud, he's in prison. That says it all right there."

He kept his anger and hate bound up tight in his heart. It would strangle him someday if he didn't let go, probably sooner than later. Bruno resented his father being locked up through all of his childhood, missing birthdays and Christmases, proms, and his driver's test, all the firsts a parent wasn't supposed to miss.

What my nephew really meant was, "What did *proud* mean coming from a convict serving a life sentence?"

We stared at each other.

Someone knocked at the door.

CHAPTER TWENTY-EIGHT

BRUNO DIDN'T MOVE. He acted like he knew who'd be out there and wanted to ignore them. I didn't want to answer the door, either, but didn't have any choice. If the cops stood outside on the stoop, they already knew who came and went from the house and they'd have seen us enter. To not answer would only give them reason to come in uninvited and make them even more suspicious. I went to the door, hesitated, and looked back. Bruno and Marie both waited for what I'd do next. Turning back, I saw the chrome-plated nine on the stand by the door. I shoved it in the waistband at the small of my back and pulled my shirt over it.

I flashed on that cold Christmas night when Eli Noble, Johnny Noble's dad, knocked at our door, and Dad looked out the side window first. All those years ago and now I did the same thing, in the same house, at the same door. When Dad opened that door, our lives changed forever.

I pulled the curtain aside and peered out. On the stoop stood a huge man with a head the size of an unshelled coconut, shaved smooth and not large enough for his shoulders. He wore a black suit, tailored too tight, with a white dress shirt and a bolo tie. Behind him, standing in the dirt, stood a cotton-top, the man I'd just seen in the picture, the senior county supervisor, the esteemed

Willy Jessup. In that moment I realized what had been bugging me. Jessup only used my nephew as a poster child to exploit as re-election fodder. Here lived a hero of the neighborhood, who now fell prey to that same neighborhood. What a great opportunity for media exploitation.

I opened the door.

The big man shoved his way in. He took me by the scruff, swung me around, and put me on the wall. I moved with him, helpless to do anything. The man carried every bit of the strength he projected in his size. He also displayed training beyond that of a street-level thug. He patted me down with purpose and imme-diately found the nine. He shoved the gun in his own waistband, took a look at Marie and Bruno, and barked, "Clear." He took me by the belt and swung, then gave me a little shove to propel me to the couch. "Sit," he ordered.

I complied. He had the gun, but it wouldn't have mattered if I still had it. To shoot that rhino with a puny little nine would only serve to make him angry. That man angry could bring the house down all by himself.

Willy Jessup entered with an air of royalty, his nose up slightly as he looked down it at all us peons. He wore a dark-gray silk suit with a bright-yellow shirt and burgundy tie. He must've been col-orblind. When he saw my nephew, his face lit up. "Hey, Bruno, how ya doin', kid?"

Bruno stood and went over, his hand extended. "I'm good, Mr. Jessup." They shook.

Jessup's eyes followed Bruno's with interest, and he didn't let go of his hand. "Any word from those good-for-nothin' sheriffs?"

"That's not fair, Mr. Jessup. I told you, the sheriffs are doing everything possible."

Jessup pulled Bruno to his side, his arm around his shoulder, and gave us his best kiss-the-babies political smile. "Who are these folks? You haven't introduced us."

That smile did it for me, explained the second reason for his presence. Jessup never did anything that didn't benefit him. He'd somehow heard of Noble's white gold, the missing cocaine, and he wanted a piece of it. All that coke on the table would bring out the jackals, and Jessup qualified as the head jackal. Or he wouldn't have stepped this far down from his place in Baldwin Hills to be out on foot in the ghetto, in our little hovel.

Bruno held out his hand. "This is my uncle and his wife. They've come from a long way off to help out."

Jessup let go of Bruno, took a couple of steps over to us, and shook our hands one at a time. "Damn glad to meet you folks. Glad Bruno here has some family support in a time like this." Jessup looked at his thug bodyguard. "Sammy, dial up the sheriff, I'm gonna have another piece of their ass."

"No, don't," Bruno said. "Please, Mr. Jessup, let me handle this."

"How many times I gotta tell ya, you're to call me Willy. And no sir. No, this is unheard of. I don't know why they don't have those children back safe by now. What are they doin'? I don't see 'em set up here with wiretaps and with cars parked at both ends of the street. I know how these things are supposed to work. They're not movin' on this because you live on Nord Avenue in the county. They're not movin' on this because you're black, Son, and I'm gonna fix that problem right now."

"No. I asked you nice. Let me handle it."

Sammy the bodyguard had dialed the phone and now held it out to Jessup. Jessup locked eyes with Bruno for a long second. "You sure about this?"

"I'm sure. Now, please, if you don't mind, could you please leave us?"

"Sure, sure. You need anything, anything at all, you got my number, you don't hesitate to call."

Having a powerful man in his pocket like that could come in handy later on.

Jessup hesitated at the door, looking unsure as to whether or not to leave, but he turned and went out. Sammy took out the nine, pulled the mag, and ejected the round in the chamber, which skittered across the carpet. He set the gun on the stand next to the door and left.

The room fell quiet.

"How'd you meet the honorable Willy Jessup?" I asked.

"I work for Valiant Security Services. Mr. Jessup owns the company. When that happened—" he pointed to the proclamation sitting on the coffee table "—Mr. Jessup came to the office and personally thanked me. He also got that for me. He pushed for it. I didn't deserve it, not really."

"Does he always come over here like this?"

"Why? What are you trying to say?"

"I'm just tryin' to get a feel for the people involved in this thing, that's all."

"I know what you're implying. Mr. Jessup's not using me. We're friends, that's all. I'm not a fool, Uncle Bruno, so don't treat me like one."

"I never said you were." We stared at each other.

CHAPTER TWENTY-NINE

HE BROKE FIRST. He blinked, then dropped the bombshell. "They called just before you walked in."

"Who did? The kidnappers?"

"Yes."

"Why didn't you say something sooner? What did they say? What do they want?"

"Something that's impossible to give."

"What?"

"They want my father busted out of prison."

They wanted the cocaine Noble ripped off. They wanted Noble out so he could lead them to it. But that didn't really make sense, not entirely.

Why now?

And why get him out? He could just as easily pass the information on from inside prison without ever having to leave. Unless they wanted him out for some up close and personal get-even time. That could be, but still, why now?

The young Bruno moved away from the coffee table and walked back and forth in the living room, pacing like a caged animal, a young lion. "What they want is impossible. How can I bust my father out of prison? He isn't in some low mod correctional farm.

They keep him in San Q. He's only down here because of some dumb subpoena a BGF laid on him for a character witness in a jailhouse murder."

The kid spoke with perfect diction without any of the street seeping in. Sasha did a great job raising him, and yet he could also talk like some kind of criminal who'd been immersed in the life. Maybe he got the criminal stuff by visiting Noble in prison.

"Bruno," I said, "what kind of work do you do?"

"Why? What does that have to do with anything?"

The stats didn't fall in his favor. Kids fathered by incarcerated criminals almost always followed in their father's footsteps. Why wouldn't they, with a convicted felon for a role model?

Bruno lived in the ghetto, he dressed like a Crip, and he had a gangster's gun.

"I'm asking, that's why."

"I go to school and I'm an intern at Los Angeles County Sheriff's Department, Lennox Station."

I sat down hard, stunned.

"You see what I mean," he said. "I can't give them what they want. I can't bust my father out. I can't do it, that's flat-out craziness."

Marie gripped my hand. She didn't seem to grasp what he'd just said, or it didn't have the same impact. She said to Bruno, "Do you know who these people are, the ones who have your children?"

"Sure, I've talked to them a couple of times. They won't negotiate. They won't give an inch."

"You know them?" I asked.

"Yeah, that's what I just said. They've been waiting for you to get here. I don't understand why. What can you do about my dad in jail?"

"Me? They told you that? They're waiting for me?"

The phone rang, a cell that sat on the kitchen table. Bruno headed for the kitchen just a few steps away. "That's them. They know you're here. They're watching the house."

"Hold it," I said. "Don't answer that."

He picked the phone up, but didn't answer it. "Why?"

"Where are the police? Noble said that you called the police."

The phone continued to ring. "That's right, I did. Then I found out what these people wanted, and why. I knew the police couldn't do anything, not with these guys. I told the sheriff's detectives it was all a mistake. I told them that the babies' mama took the kids and that they were safe in Texas."

The phone stopped ringing.

"Where's the kids' mom?" Marie asked.

Bruno looked away, lowered his tone, "She's gone."

"Where?"

"The ghetto took her."

"I'm sorry." Marie said.

I got up and walked over to him, held out my hand for the phone.

For a brief moment my eyes tracked to the refrigerator, to the novel on top, and I wondered what the title was, wondered what it would be like to not have the horrible pressure of this problem. To be able to sit down and read for pleasure, in a hammock with our kids playing in the backyard, safe.

He handed me the phone. It rang again. I hit "send" and put it to my ear.

"Nice that you could join us, Bruno The Bad Boy Johnson. Meet us at 913 Prairie Avenue, in one hour."

"No." I hung up.

Bruno stood close enough to hear the exchange. He shoved my chest with both hands. "What did you just do? Are you crazy?"

He moved back in real close, his eyes wide with anger and fear. "Those are my kids you're messing with, not yours. You can't do that, you have no right to."

I put my hand on him and moved him away. "Take it easy. Now tell me who these people are."

He stared me down.

The phone rang again.

"Tell me quick," I said.

"It's the largest cocaine consortium in South Central Los Angeles, in all of LA, for that matter. It's the only one. It's not just one guy like before, it's a group, run by one guy who kind of acts as the president over all these drug lords or whatever you wanna call them. They run all the coke for all the gangs. They don't show any favorites. You have the money, they sell you the dope; white, black, or brown. It doesn't matter to them. They have eyes and ears everywhere, on every street corner. They're in deep with the cops. It's hopeless. There's too much money involved here to do anything other than what they want. That's why I called the sheriff off. You understand now? They'd know if the cops had their nose in this."

My nephew Bruno talked with far more maturity than his young age. Life's lessons came harder and faster when you're raising children. Especially by yourself in the ghetto when you're nothing more than a kid yourself.

I answered the phone. The person on the other end yelled and swore and yelled some more. I waited until he calmed down. I said, "I'll meet you, but at a place of my choosing, not yours. You get to pick the time. I pick the place."

"You gotta set a balls on ya, I'll tell ya that much. I heard that about you. Okay, it doesn't matter, name it." There was no hint of an accent or where he might be from.

"The Santa Monica pier."

"Okay, thirty minutes."

"You obviously know where I am. From here, that drive'll take at least forty-five minutes, probably closer to an hour and ten." I hung up.

Bruno moved to the table next to the door and scooped up the nine, shoved the magazine back in, and racked the slide. He stuck it in his back waistband under his football jersey. "I'm going with you, so don't even try and say different."

I walked up to him and moved in close, inches away from his face. "I wouldn't try and stop you, not for a minute, but you're not goin' carryin' heavy." I reached around, put my hand on the gun. He looked at me as he tried to step away. He didn't try too hard.

"They have my son and daughter."

"Exactly. You take a gun, you might have to use it. If you don't have it, you won't be able to use it."

"That's some kind of Three Stooges logic."

His generation had no idea about the Three Stooges. Noble had always loved them, with their inane comedy. Somehow, through the years, Noble had imparted at least some of his knowledge and experience, even through his prison-visiting window. More of that life that I'd somehow missed.

Bruno held the pressure on the gun a moment longer, then gave it up. I took it from him and, still looking him in the eye, broke the gun down and field-stripped it. I stuck the barrel in my pocket to dispose of later and walked over to the trash can by the refrigerator and threw the rest away. I leaned up to look at the title of the book and couldn't see it.

"I paid good money for that."

I turned. "You bought it on the street. That's a felony. You wanna be a cop?"

He came over to me. "That's none of your damn business. Come on, let's go."

Out front, he automatically got in the back seat. I drove. I didn't want to take him with us. The situation didn't need a hothead. But I knew better than to try and stop him.

I didn't have near enough time on the drive to Santa Monica to talk and get to know him. Not like I should. I should've already known my nephew.

I couldn't stop thinking about what he'd said. *They've been waiting for you to get here.* The words didn't make any sense. No matter how I tried to fit them into the puzzle, those words just didn't make any sense.

CHAPTER THIRTY

MARIE TURNED IN her seat to talk with Bruno. "So, you want to be a deputy sheriff?"

I checked the rearview. Bruno looked out the side window at the passing landscape, not interested in small talk. "Don't be rude," I said. "Marie and I are married and she's your aunt."

"Ooh," she said. "Auntie, that sounds strange, doesn't it?"

I looked in the rearview again. "So you really have no idea why they want me involved in all this?"

He didn't take his eyes off the passing cars. "No."

"If they want your father out of prison so badly, why don't *they* break him out?"

He moved up in the seat and spoke into my right ear. "Why don't *you* tell me the answer to that? You're their star. You're the one they've been waiting for."

His warm, wet breath made me uncomfortable. "Sit back, please."

He complied.

"Tell me," I said. "Where does this group of coke distributors operate? Do the sheriffs or Feds have any intel on them? Do you know any of their names?"

He turned to look back out the side window. "One, just one.

The main guy, he goes by the name of Brodie, Don Brodie. He lives in a bungalow at the Beverly Hills Hotel."

"Where did you find that out?"

"I have friends."

I stuck my hand out to Marie. "Babe, would you dial Mack and hand me the phone."

"You're driving, it's against the law." She said it as she dialed and handed the phone to me. I smiled at her cute comment—talking on the phone, a moving violation, an infraction, as compared to all the felonies I'd been a party to.

Mack picked up. "Yeah, Bruno?"

"I need a favor."

"Really? That's something new."

I chuckled. "I know, I'm sorry. Can you run a guy for me, get all the intel you can? His name is Don Brodie, he lives at the Beverly Hills Hotel."

Mack said nothing.

"Mack?"

"Is this about the thing you have going with your brother?"

"Yeah."

"Don't say anything else on the phone and we'll meet someplace."

"Ah, shit, is it like that?"

"Yeah, it's like that."

"Let me call you back."

"Bruno, don't go sticking your nose in this until we talk."

"I understand. Thanks." I handed the phone to Marie, and she clicked off.

"What did he say?" she asked. Bruno moved up close to hear.

"We're going to have to meet with him."

* * *

An hour later we cruised by the pier and then found a spot to dump the rental in a public parking lot. We didn't know what these criminals looked like, but apparently they had a good handle on what I looked like, so we'd let them make contact.

The sun in the sky moved past noon and started the rest of the journey down to sunset. We stood at the railing overlooking the water and watched the waves roll in, surfers zigzagging across the green faces. Lots of people strolled the beach below, the boardwalk, and the pier, all of them enjoying the sunny day. I watched Bruno watch. He kept his back to the railing and faced the pier side, eyeing everyone. I'd tried to talk with him, and he'd have none of it. His thoughts had to be on his children.

An old man in khaki shirt and pants came to the railing about ten feet away and set down a pail half-filled with dead sardines. He wore his floppy beachcomber hat canted to one side, shading his face from the sun, and making it difficult to get a good look at him. He tinkered with his fishing pole, his hands gnarled with arthritis and scarred from years of hard work. I'd grown up watching *The Rockford Files* and this guy could have doubled as Rocky, Jim Rockford's dad.

I missed my dad.

Bruno turned to face the water and spoke quietly. "Check out this guy's shoes."

I casually looked down. The man wore black lace-up boots, the kind you could buy at any military surplus. Not odd in itself, but he did keep the black leather polished to a high sheen.

I didn't have time to respond. A woman walked up to us, a brunette with a small nose and pretty green eyes. She wore yellow shorts and a kelly-green blouse tailored tight to her body. One pocket of her shorts bulged with something that might've been a small gun. The sheen in her hair glinted in the sun. She looked to be thirty or thirty-five and had the legs of an athletic nineteen-year-old. She held sunglasses in her hand and twirled them. "You're late," she said.

Bruno moved in close to her, not a smart move tactically. "Where are my kids?"

I put a hand on his shoulder, waited a long second, then in a low tone said, "Son, let me handle this, please? You're too emotionally involved."

"Damn right I'm emotionally involved." He jerked away from me and held his ground. Marie stepped in between us and took hold of both his hands. "Come on, let's step over here and let my husband handle this. It's better that way, trust me."

He didn't move at first but then relented. Marie held onto his hand, and they moved down the pier, still watching us.

The woman next to me went up against the rail and faced the water. She put the sunglasses on and looked at me. "Well, are you going to do what we asked?"

"Break my brother out of jail? No way, that's against the law."

"Don't be droll with me. We know your history."

"Who's 'we'?"

"Call us concerned citizens of LA."

"Concerned about letting a half ton of coke hit the streets?"

She smiled. "You've been talking with your brother."

"What you want is impossible."

"No, it's not. Not for a man of your talents."

The fisherman ten feet away wiggled a dead sardine onto his hook and lowered the line to the water. The dead sardine now returned to its home as a turncoat, to spy and lure his friends to their deaths.

"Noble," I said to her, "was stabbed this morning. Last I heard he was in surgery and might not make it."

CHAPTER THIRTY-ONE

THE WOMAN JERKED her glasses off, her smile gone. "What?"

"I guess you're a little behind on the old information pipeline. What difference does it make if Noble tells me where the coke is while he sits in jail or if he's out here when he tells you? That doesn't make any sense."

"No, it doesn't, and it's not for you to try and figure out. There's a lot more in play here, big man. Believe me, more than your chickenshit little part. So do as you're told and we'll get along just fine. You don't, and those kids won't be the *only* losers." She pointed with her sunglasses over at Marie.

My Marie.

I snapped.

Without thinking, I grabbed her by the throat with one hand and shoved her up against the rail. Her eyes bulged. Her mouth made a little "O." Her hands gripped the rail as her feet came off the wooden pier.

"You will leave my wife out of this, you understand?"

The fisherman put his foot up on the lowest rail and looked down into the water. He spoke loud, almost a yell. "Throw the bitch over, save you a lot of trouble in the future. Trust me, I know."

He hadn't been close enough to hear all of our conversation, not in the low tones we'd been talking, and must've thought the woman and I had had a little lover's spat.

Marie started over to us with a concerned expression. I waved her back, still holding on to the crazy extortionist.

"We understand each other?" I asked. I made sure she didn't try and reach for the object in her pocket by holding onto her other hand.

The woman couldn't speak and just nodded.

I let her go. Her feet hit the pier. She bent over and coughed and rubbed her throat. "Are you crazy? Are you outta you mind?" Her voice rasped.

"Yes, I am, when it comes to my wife. You had best keep that in mind. Now, tell me why I'm involved. Tell me why this all started now, twenty-five years after the fact? What's happened to dredge all this mess up?"

She regained her composure and continued to rub her neck as she stared at me. "You lay your dickbeaters on me again, cowboy, and I'll kill you. Do *you* understand? I'm the one callin' the shots here, not you. You play along and you might get the kids back safe."

I nodded. I knew I wouldn't get any additional information, but had to try.

For emphasis, she moved in on me, up close, to show she wasn't afraid of me after I'd taken her to the edge, let her feel her own vulnerability. The woman had grit, or, as Robby Wicks would have said, "Big hairy balls."

"There's a guy with a rifle," she said. "And that black melon of yours is in his sights right now. I could've given him the signal to take you out. You do that again, and I'll do it. I swear to you I will."

I smiled. "Take it easy, babycakes, we're just talkin' here, havin' a nice easy conversation tryin' ta get to know each other a little, that's all. We're gettin' the ground rules laid down so we all know where we're comin' from."

"Don't you ever call me that again. And there's only one set of ground rules, and those are the ones I give you. You understand?"

"I'm beginning to."

Her face, red and bloated from the throttling I'd given her, started to return to normal.

"You have two days, just forty-eight hours from right now, to get that swingin' dick outta jail. Not one minute more, you understand?"

"I understand, but that's not a lot of time. And even if he makes it through surgery at all, he's not going to be walking on his own two feet."

"Again, your problem, not mine. You worked in that same jail, you know its layout, you still have connections there. You can get this done without any problem at all. We have faith in you."

"Are those the reasons why you brought me into this? Is that really the reason why you forwarded those letters from Tommy Tomkins, sent them on to Noble and my father?"

The smile returned, not a pretty one, more the kind you'd see on a psychopath who'd forgotten to take her meds. "You're a lot more dangerous than I gave you credit for. Don Brodie told me to watch out for you."

"The feeling's mutual."

I didn't know that's what they'd done with the letters and had only made a wild guess.

"Any more questions?" She asked. "Your time's up."

"How do I get a hold of you when we do get my brother out?"

"You don't need to worry about that, we'll know."

"Just in case, say we accidently lose you, gimme a number to call."

She reached into her back pocket and came out with a business card with a phone number and *Los Angeles Consolidated Freight and Design* embossed on expensive card stock.

"Thanks. My brother's not in jail, he's in the jail ward at LCMC. I've never worked there."

"Again, not my problem, bro. Deal with it."

I nodded. "Okay, then, I'm going to need proof of life."

"Contrary to what you may think, asshole, we're not in the business of hurting children. They haven't been harmed in any way, and they don't even know they're being held. They think they're just staying with some friends because their daddy had to work. They're so young, they don't know any better."

"I'm supposed to believe you?"

She reached into her shorts for the object. I took hold of her wrist.

"Easy, cowboy."

I held onto her hand in her pocket and stared at her for a moment, then let go.

She brought out a small set of binoculars. "Here, see for yourself. We don't hurt kids, not if we don't have to."

I took the binocs from her. "Where?"

She pointed down the beach. "Two children, down that way, about a hundred yards. They have their shoes off, playing in the sand right at the water's edge. They're building a sandcastle with a friend, my friend. My friend's wearing a pink-and-orange Aloha shirt."

I found them right away with the glasses. Easy with a shirt that bright and obvious. Only the glasses weren't strong enough for me to make them out clearly. I wouldn't have recognized them even if I could. I brought them down and waved to Bruno. He came over. "What?" he asked. He shot the extortionist a scowl.

I handed him the binocs and told him the same information.

He shoved up against the rail, in a hurry, extending out as far as he could to get, a few inches closer, perched precariously over the edge.

"Is it them?" I asked. "Can you make them out?"

He nodded. His Adam's apple rose and fell as he continued to look and swallow hard, swallow down his emotions. The kid didn't want to cry in front of me.

I looked down the beach and watched without the glasses. Her friend in the Aloha shirt rounded up my grandniece and grandnephew and started across the sand toward the parking area. I had not seen the extortionist beside me give any kind of signal to the guy in the Aloha shirt to make the move. That lent credence to her statement about a sniper. These people came organized and ready.

Dangerous people.

The big downside was that I didn't think we'd be able to successfully trade Noble, not without giving Noble to them and letting them walk with him. Once they got the information from Noble, they wouldn't need him anymore. I knew my brother, he'd want to make that kind of sacrifice, make it without a second thought.

Bruno dropped the binocs and ran down the pier, right past the woman, past all the tourists who watched him, as he headed for the beach. He didn't have a chance on getting there in time. I understood how he felt, how he had to try.

I hurried to catch up to the woman, who'd started walking back to the highway.

"Don't follow me. Don't you do it," she said "You have forty-eight hours, don't waste a minute of that time."

"One more question. Only one."

She stopped.

"Why now?" I asked.

"That's a dumb question. Ask your brother. He's the one who wrote this fucked-up playbook."

CHAPTER THIRTY-TWO

WROTE THE PLAYBOOK? A football analogy? Did that mean Noble called the shots, called the plays on this thing?

The extortionist continued on down the pier toward the highway.

Marie caught up to me. She'd stopped and picked up the binoculars from the wooden deck. She took hold of my hand and tugged, halted us. "Don't follow her. I know her type. She's one cold-hearted bitch, and she'll do exactly what she says she'll do."

"What kind of playbook?" I asked of no one.

I looked at her. She'd brought the binoculars up to her eyes and was scanning the terrain. She said, "What did she say about your brother? Oh, shit."

"What?"

"The police, they're comin' fast. Someone must've called 911 when you choked her. You know, for the record, I wasn't too keen on my favorite husband when he put his hands on her like that. She's still a woman."

"She has a foul mouth, she took our grandniece and grandnephew, and she said she was going after you next if I didn't do exactly what she asked."

"She has a foul mouth? You're right, next time throttle the bitch." She smiled.

I took her hand. We had to get off the pier and across the highway before they blocked off our exit. We walked fast and tried not to look out of place. I fought the urge to look down the highway at the approaching cops. "How far away are they?"

"We're not going to make it in time."

"Smile and laugh," I said. I scooped her up, my arm under her legs, and swung her around.

"This is really getting to be a habit," she said. "I like it."

She continued to smile and rub my head and kiss me on the lips as I walked to the end of the pier.

Ahead, the extortionist made it to the end just as a cop car screeched up. The female patrol officer jumped out and confronted her. Whoever called 911 must've given call intake a description of her kelly-green silk blouse. She stood out. A mistake, a bad one for a professional.

I walked on past the cop talking with the extortionist as I carried my wife. The extortionist wore her sunglasses, smiled, and waved a carefree hand at the patrol officer, pretending to be a good citizen just out enjoying the sunny day, and not some lowlife criminal trying to appropriate, by extortion, a half ton of cocaine.

We crossed the street on the green light. "What about Bruno?" Marie asked.

"He's a big boy and street smart. He'll figure it out."

"This isn't the way to the car."

"Look."

Down the highway, more cars came from both directions. Santa Monica fielded a lot of cops and didn't leave us an option.

"Set me down, you big lug."

I set her down. My biceps trembled from curling my wife too many times in the last few hours.

I took her hand.

"Where are we going?" she asked.

I again resisted the urge to look back to see if any of the cops had peeled off to come after us. "We'll go over here to the Third Street Promenade. It's an open-air mall. I know this area a little. Me and Robby once chased a murder suspect to this city."

"I figured it was something like that, or you wouldn't have picked this location so fast when you talked to her on the phone."

The further away from the highway we got, the more I relaxed. When we got to the Promenade, Marie gripped my hand and said, "Oh, goodie, we get to shop for a little while until things cool down."

"Oh, lord."

She jerked on my hand. "What is it with you men that you don't like to shop?"

"We don't shop because we know exactly what we want, go right to it, buy it, and get away from the crowd of women milling about and cackling like a bunch of—"

She jerked on my hand again. "Careful. Don't let that mouth of yours get you in trouble."

I stopped short and froze.

"What is it?" she asked. "What's the matter?"

I slowly walked up to the large window of the bookstore, too stunned to respond.

"What?" Marie asked. "Bruno, you're scaring me."

Unable to form the simplest of words, I held up my arm and pointed.

"What?" she asked. "I don't—Oh, my God!"

Fifty books in the display window rose up waist high. They

stood meticulously stacked, some facing outward for the whole world to see. Their mere presence kept me from talking.

My brother Noble's face appeared on the cover of all of the books, his expression grim, almost menacing. The close-up showed his age and reminded me of all the years I'd missed with him.

The cover said, *A Noble Sacrifice: A Black Man's Journey to a White Man's White Gold.* By Johnny Noble.

Aghast, I moved up to the window and put both hands flat on the glass.

Johnny. He'd used his old name. His name before Dad adopted him.

Marie moved up beside me. "Bruno, *oh, my God.*"

The gift of speech returned. "How did we not know about this?"

"We live in a different country," she said, "whose primary language is Spanish. We also don't have any contact with anyone here in this country. And we don't read any nonfiction. We read Michael Connelly and T. Jefferson Parker."

To the right, taped to the inside of the window, a paper displayed a list of *The Los Angeles Times* bestsellers. *A Noble Sacrifice* came in at number nine out of ten in nonfiction. The next column over said the book had been on the list for fifteen weeks.

My brother had made the LA Times *bestseller list.*

I took Marie's hand and guided her toward the store's front door, just as two bike cops rode down the Promenade, in and out of and around the hundreds of people shopping.

Inside, the air conditioning dried the sweat on my face and went a long way to cool off the shock that tried too hard to anesthetize my body. We moved to the front rack, which held another forty or fifty copies. Marie and I each picked one up.

I opened my copy.

"Dedicated to my Big Bro, Bruno Johnson, who tirelessly fought on the streets of LA to make it a better place to live."

Right there, I eased down to the floor and sat.

"Bruno, are you okay?"

I held the page up for her to see.

"Oh, my God, Bruno." She sat down right next to me. Some patrons stopped to look.

"He's insane. My brother's insane. He put his whole life on display. That's what happened. No wonder. No damn wonder all this went down the way it did. Bad. It went down bad. How could it not? How could he not know what would happen if he did this?"

"I thought you said he dropped out of high school early, as a sophomore or something, right? He couldn't write a pamphlet, let alone an autobiography that hits the lists."

"His senior year. He dropped out the beginning of his senior year. He was eighteen. He worked for Papa Dee for two years. He's been in prison for twenty-five years. You can get a full college education in prison, that's what he said he did, remember? He said he got his degree, remember?"

"So what you're tellin' me is that you can get married, have kids, get a college education, get full and complete medical coverage, which includes dental, all while being in prison? That's bullshit, Bruno. I'm sorry, I gotta say I think that's total and absolute bullshit."

I'd heard her, but couldn't focus on what she was saying. I'd opened to the first page, to the first chapter titled "The Day My House Died."

CHAPTER THIRTY-THREE

NOBLE STARTED THE book with the Christmas morning fire as the inciting incident for his life story. I read quickly, couldn't read it fast enough. Amazing how the prose followed almost exactly how I remembered it. I turned the page and continued to read. Marie didn't press for an answer and started to read as well.

A woman came by. Her low black heels barely registered in my subconscious, I was so intent on the book in my hand.

"I'm sorry," she said, "you're going to have to move. You can't sit here."

"Yeah, yeah, sorry, we'll move," Marie said. "We'll move, sure we will. We'll do it right now." Her words came out distracted, mumbled and without emphasis. Low-Heels moved on.

In the passage describing the fire, I came to something I didn't know, and I'd been there in the front yard, right alongside Noble for that entire incident.

The two firemen came out of the burning house, walked out of the billowing black smoke, right out the front door, a couple of ghastly apparitions in this horrible nightmare that wouldn't end. They wore large yellow air tanks on their backs, their faces covered by oxygen face masks, their eyes an evil red.

I knew they weren't red, but to this day that's how I remembered them. The minute details forever seared into my memory. The names of the firemen, stenciled in black in two places on their turn-out coats, read, "J. Mellor" and "C. Kraig." Their boots dripped with water. They smelled of smoke and sorrow and of death. I didn't know what death smelled like until that day.

They gently set my little brother and sister down at the base of the tree, their bodies wrapped entirely in Flintstone bed sheets. I couldn't see them, but knew. I knew.

I stood off to the side, out of everyone's way, and couldn't take my eyes off of them. My dad and his white whore had moved and now stood over by the same tree, with blankets around their naked bodies, unaware of what lay at their feet. His woman kept saying, "I have to get out of here. I have to go." The deputy said, "Not yet, I need to get your statement first. I'll have a patrol car give you a ride after I get a statement."

"Are you out of your mind?" she half-screeched, then caught herself and lowered her tone. "A black-and-white patrol car taking me home to my neighborhood, with me dressed in only a blanket? Just move those fire trucks, and I'll take my own car."

The irony of her use, her description of the black-and-white patrol car, was not lost to me even at that young age.

"That's not gonna happen," the deputy said. "Not for a couple hours at least."

Down the street, a news van pulled to the curb, the side door slid open, and out jumped an immaculately dressed female field reporter and a cameraman.

My father's whore pulled the blanket over her head like someone from the Middle East. She turned her back to the street and moved to the other side of my father as cover. In so doing, she stumbled over the bundles wrapped in the Flintstone bed sheets.

She had unknowingly stepped on my brother and sister.

The deputy quickly grabbed hold of her and moved her to the side, moved my dad too.

I went to my knees at the sight, the way the woman so casually desecrated the dead. The way she disrespected my little brother and sister was like a kick to the stomach.

I hadn't seen what Noble described in that passage, the children placed at the base of the tree, the woman stepping on them, and I'd been standing right there next to Noble that Christmas morning, my arm around his shoulders. The whole time, sick to death over the pain and sorrow he was going through. I must've seen it. I must've and blocked it out.

Noble didn't block it out.

I skipped on down.

That horrible day, the way those two deputies acted, especially the black deputy as he valiantly attempted to enter the house under great threat and with disregard for his own safety, I believe that event was what inspired my brother Bruno to go into law enforcement. To become a deputy sheriff and work in the same neighborhood where we grew up. To fight tyranny in its most base form, a fight that he did so well taking it to the criminals, fighting them on their own turf. And, as a good friend of Bruno's used to say, "Make the streets safe for women and children."

The clerk in the bookstore returned; at least her shoes did. "If you people don't move right now, I'm going outside to flag down one of the many police officers assigned to this shopping area and have them escort you out."

I waved her off without thought to the consequences. How could I concentrate on anything else? She couldn't possibly mean it anyway, not for sitting on the floor, of all things.

An iron fist had reached into my chest and squeezed my heart, and now it wouldn't let go.

I don't remember ever talking with Noble about why I wanted to be a deputy sheriff. I don't remember telling him the old saying, the one Robby Wicks used to say far too often. But Noble had it wrong. Robby used to say, "Make the streets safe for *white* women and children." I probably *had* told Noble and amended it to protect the innocent. Only Robby wasn't innocent, and I had protected him far too long and never opened my eyes long enough to see him for what he was until it was too late.

I, too, like my brother, remembered names during that incident, but not the names of the firemen. I remembered the patrol deputies. The tall black deputy wore *D.C. Smith* on his nameplate; the other, *J. Humphrey*.

I let the book drop to my lap as I thought about what Noble had written, about my motivation as to why I entered law enforcement. Had that day truly been the catalyst for my motivation? Was it because of D.C. Smith's heroic actions?

Sitting beside me, Marie said, "Uh oh."

I looked up from the book. Two uniformed Santa Monica bike policemen came in the door, taking off their helmets, escorted by Low-Heels. She pointed at us.

I got up, helping Marie. I turned to the police officers who came up to us. "Sorry, officers, we'll move on, we didn't mean to cause a problem."

One officer flanked us; the other stood in a bladed interrogation stance. Both were professionals with excellent tactics.

"Why don't we take this outside?" the policeman in front of us said.

I took Marie's hand. "Sure, sure."

Low-Heels waved her hand. "Wait, wait, they haven't paid for those books."

Marie pulled her thin wallet out and handed the pesky woman a fifty and a twenty.

"I'll get you change."

"Keep it," Marie said. She held the book upside down as she put her wallet back in her pocket. We hadn't yet looked at the back cover of the book. Noble had somehow obtained a photo, probably from Dad. It was an enlarged photo that filled the entire back of the book, one that depicted me and Dad and Noble sitting on the steps leading up to the front door of our house on Nord. A photo Noble's dad had shot not long before the day Noble's house died.

I took the book from Marie and stacked it on top of mine as we followed the cop out, the second one behind us as a rearguard. If the cops saw the picture, even though I couldn't have been more than ten at the time, and they happened to put it together that I was in the book, the forged passport ID I had in my pocket wouldn't match the name in the book.

I subconsciously reached down to feel the passport to make sure it was there and felt something far worse.

The gun barrel to the chrome 9mm that I'd taken from my nephew Bruno.

CHAPTER THIRTY-FOUR

WHY HADN'T I tossed the gun barrel over the side at the pier like I had intended to do? What a perfect place to dispose of it. What a dumbass. I'd been distracted with my newly discovered nephew and then with the extortionist. No excuse, not under the circumstances. Now the cops would find it if they searched me. What were the odds that they wouldn't search?

Zero.

A *DrugFire* test would determine if the gun had been used in any crimes where a slug had been recovered. The *DrugFire* database, though not near as large as fingerprints or DNA, still contained hundreds of thousands of guns, logged by their shell casings, slugs, and their extraction bars and firing pins.

My nephew had bought the gun off the streets of LA, which greatly increased the likelihood of the gun's involvement in a drive-by or an individual killing.

We exited the bookstore out onto the promenade. Marie pasted on a fake smile and tried to step aside, to draw their attention away from me. She couldn't possibly think I'd make a break for it. Could she? I wouldn't leave her. No way.

Didn't matter. The cops corralled her right away and put us both in close to the window, the book display behind us.

Before he asked, I took out my passport and handed it to the shorter cop with the sweat-pasted sandy-brown hair, the one who took the lead.

"Don't you have a driver's license?"

"I lost it," I said.

He nodded. "Why didn't you leave when you were asked?"

Marie handed him her passport and forged driver's license. "Sorry, Officer, we just didn't think it was a big deal, that's all. We were only sitting on the floor reading these books. We weren't causing any kind of problem, really we weren't."

Without warning, the shorter cop handed the license and passport back and put on his helmet. They both ran to their bikes and took off.

Marie walked over to the closest bench and sat down. "That was a close one. Why'd they leave like that without any reason?"

"They were wearing ear jacks so we couldn't hear their radio. They got a hot call. And you're right, that was a close one." I pulled the pistol barrel from my pocket and showed her.

"Ah, Bruno, I'm sorry, but you're a dumbass."

"I know, I know."

I went to the closest trash can and tossed it in. I came back. I wanted to sit there and read the whole book all the way though, cover to cover, without stopping. Not only to find out how the book sparked all the controversy and put this whole mess into play, but also to get a better handle on my brother Noble. This new brother I'd never met before. Sure, some of the prose would be fabricated lies to serve his greater purpose, whatever that purpose might be, but I'd already been given a glimpse of a part of him I didn't know and craved more of. I craved all of it, a desire difficult to resist.

Marie must've had the same urgent need. She opened the book, started reading, and immediately forgot her surroundings.

"Come on, kid," I said, "We gotta roll."

"Yeah, you're right." She closed the book and stood, taking my hand as we jumped into the stream of shoppers. "You know," she said, "we really need to read this whole thing before we make any kind of move."

"I know, but they only gave us forty-eight hours."

She tried to stop midstream. "Really? Two days to bust your brother out?"

I tugged her hand, got her going again. "That's right."

It hurt to think she didn't balk at all over the idea of breaking the law, committing multiple felonies by busting Noble out of the jail ward in the hospital. Our lives had veered out of control three years ago and never returned to a familiar reality, one that was comfortable and safe. I loved her for it.

The stream of people slowed and turned into a clot. I held onto Marie's hand and moved around the lookie-loos. I stood tall enough to see over the crowd. Marie went up on tiptoes to try and see but couldn't. "What's going on?"

"Those two bike cops, they came down here for a window smash. The one cop is holding up a medium-sized ball bearing. The window's made of that safety glass that shattered into a million pieces, that's why we didn't hear anything." I leaned over, lowered my tone. "Lucky for us, huh?"

"Yeah, we should go buy a lotto ticket."

"You know," I said, "sometimes I can't get a good read on your sarcasm."

"Good, keep you on your toes."

We got another ten yards away from the throng before she said, "This—" she held up the book "—is only about a four- or five-hour read."

"For you, maybe. You forget you're married to a knuckle-drag-ging Neanderthal."

"If you're lookin' for an argument there, pal, you're gonna be waitin' a long time."

"Thanks for that. Have you ever stopped to think that if I'm a caveman, what's that make you?"

"Oh, didn't I tell ya? I'm really a psychology major working on my thesis and you've been my subject, my special project for the last three years. All of this here"—she waved her hand around—"has really just been a ruse." She held up her same hand, pretend-ing to hold a digital recorder close to her mouth, and assumed a professional tone. "After a simple pagan ceremony, a mock wed-ding, subject has displayed an abnormal and insatiable sex drive that, in my opinion, and based on previous observations, has been triggered by some sort of misplaced proprietary interest in my fe-male sex parts."

I laughed as I pulled us out of the dwindling stream of peo-ple and headed for the public parking. "If that's the case," I said, "then when this caveman gets his cavewoman back to the cave, he's gonna spank some of those proprietary female sex parts."

She giggled and did a little hop. "Ooh la la."

We rounded the corner to a row of cars. Bruno, my nephew, waited for us at the rental. He leaned against the car, his arms crossed, sporting a scowl visible from a hundred feet away. His somber demeanor reminded us of the dire situation, shut us both up, and wiped away our smiles.

When we got close, I hit the key fob and unlocked the doors. He didn't turn and get in. He continued to watch us as we closed on him. "I don't see anything funny in this situation. Not in the least," he said.

I stopped in front of him. "I'm not gonna start off our relationship by apologizing to you all the time. So here's all you're gonna get. I'm sorry I missed out on your life. And I'm sorry that your two young children have been taken and kept from you. That's it, that's all you're gonna get from me until this thing's over. Now, tell me why you didn't tell us about this book." I held up my copy.

He stared at me for a long moment, turned, got into the back seat of the car, and slammed the door.

I got in on the driver's side, Marie on the front passenger side. I turned in the seat. "I'm waiting for an answer."

He shook his head, "What? Have you been livin' in a cave or something?"

CHAPTER THIRTY-FIVE

WE DROPPED BRUNO at my old house on Nord and then headed back to our hotel to read Noble's book, get something to eat, and make a plan. I told Bruno I'd call him with the time and location where we'd meet Mack, a meeting Bruno insisted on joining. Mack didn't get off shift at the jail until three.

I drove us through Taco Quicky at the corner of Century Boulevard and Atlantic, an old haunt from my patrol days. Marie didn't speak, she just kept her nose buried in the book. I ordered taquitos with guacamole, her favorite, and ate them for her after I finished my burrito. She wouldn't answer whether she wanted them or not. I took her silence as a tacit agreement and knew, when I put the last morsel in my mouth, that I would pay dearly for the error in judgement.

She looked up from the book as we traveled north on Atlantic headed downtown. "This is an amazing story. No wonder it hit the bestseller list."

"Let me just say that a good portion of it could be a fairy tale."

"Don't be a hater, it doesn't become you."

I stopped at a red signal and looked over at her. She smiled and twitched her cute little nose as she sniffed. She glanced down and saw for the first time the wadded-up papers and empty cardboard carrier box from Taco Quicky. "Hey, hey! Where's my lunch?"

"I asked you if you wanted it and you didn't answer. It was getting co—"

She slid over close and took hold of my ear.

I pulled away with nowhere to go. "Not the ear, not the ear. I'm driving, for crying out loud."

She gave it a twist and a yank anyway. Not as hard as she gave the guy in the hallway back at the jail. After all, I was her husband now, but it was still a yank that hurt like hell and turned my ear red hot.

The light changed. I put my hand on her breasts and gently moved her back to her seat. "Take it easy, Tonto, I'll get you something from room service when we get to the hotel."

"Tonto? Now, I'm your Indian sidekick?" She moved her hand up to her mouth and again spoke into the mock digital recorder. "Subject now appears to suffer from some form of testosterone poisoning. He touched my breasts and immediately hallucinated seeing me as an American Indian by the name of Tonto."

"Hey, Professor, why don't you read to me from the book?"

She leaned over and gave my ear a lingering kiss, cool and soothing. "Okay. You want me to start at the beginning or someplace else?"

"Check the table of contents, see if there's a chapter title that sounds like the dope deal with Papa Dee."

"Nope, but here's an interesting one: "A Spook in the Wood Pile." And right below that, "The Double Cross.""

I wanted to hear about the double cross. In all likelihood that one would explain how some historically dormant revenge had been awakened and now reached its long arm into the future to ruin lives. But the setup for the double cross could prove just as important. "Read 'A Spook in the Wood Pile.'"

"Got it." She thumbed through the pages. "Chapter Twenty-Seven. In 1988 Ronald Reagan—"

I interrupted her. "Are you serious, my brother's really going to try and pull the President of the United States into all his mess?"

Marie said nothing. I looked from the street to her. She gave me that expression that telegraphed that, if I wanted to keep my ear attached to the side of my head, I needed to be quiet. "Okay," I said, "I gotcha." I put index finger and thumb up to my lips and mimicked zipping them closed.

She gave me the laser beam a second longer, then looked back at the book. "In 1988 Ronald Reagan tried, without much success at first, to put out the fire *The San Jose Mercury News* had uncovered with the story about guns for the Contras. The CIA had assisted Nicaraguan nationals in smuggling tons of cocaine into the U.S., the profits of which went to buy weapons to fight communism in Central America."

"Are you shittin' me?" I jerked the wheel, pulled over to the side of the road, and grabbed up my copy of the book. "What page are you on?"

She didn't answer. Her eyes moved down the page as she rapidly devoured the words. "Son of a bitch, Bruno, you're not going to believe this."

I checked the table of contents, found the page, and flipped over to it.

. . . smuggling tons of cocaine into the U.S., the profits of which went to buy weapons to fight communism in Central America. Upwards of a billion dollars and maybe more. There are no hard numbers available for how many tons were smuggled in with the help of the CIA. The CIA, with purpose and deceit, introduced the concentrated form of cocaine, "base," or "rock cocaine," the most addictive narcotic on the street today, with only one purpose in mind.

They wanted to hook the blacks in the lower socioeconomic areas in Los Angeles, make them slaves again, slaves to the glass pipe, the most unforgiving master of masters. Harsh and cruel and in most cases, even deadly from the side effects: theft, prostitution, robbery, and violence. Violence against each other, violence against society.

The CIA seeded their little cancer and it grew nationwide. Billions of dollars. I can't imagine they understood the full ramifications of their actions, but maybe they did. Hundreds of thousands of lives were lost to this treacherously evil narcotic. They might as well have unleashed a fatal germ with no possible cure. America lost a generation of its people, a group or class squandered for the 'better good' to protect democracy.

I can't hope to make you believe I knew about what was happening. I didn't, not all of it, anyway. Not at first. I initially got involved for reasons of my own. I did it for a woman. A woman I loved more than life itself, my precious Sasha (God rest her soul).

I went to work for Papa Dee selling the rock. Not for greed or avarice; I did it to work my way up in his organization. I did it with one purpose in mind: to bring Papa Dee down for what he'd done to my precious Sasha.

Once in the upper echelon of his organization, I inadvertently stumbled upon the link to the CIA and the horrible program they had instituted, corrupting and squandering the people I grew up with. So when Papa Dee came to me and asked me to run security on his biggest cocaine deal yet, four hundred and fifty kilos, I said hell yes. From that moment on I started planning to rip off Papa Dee, to save the people from all that cocaine, those four hundred and fifty kilos slated to be sold to them. And more importantly, to expose the federal government that continued to lie and deny to the American people their involvement in their ongoing criminal conspiracy."

I stopped reading, put my hand on Marie's leg.

She looked up at me. "Bruno, this isn't a big complicated dope conspiracy; it's a love story."

I nodded. "Beyond that, I think my brother's grabbed a tiger by the tail, and he's just handed it over to us."

CHAPTER THIRTY-SIX

MACK TURNED PARANOID after I told him about Don Brodie, the guy who ran all the coke in LA. He called the meeting at four in the afternoon, in a public park in Downey with no chance for anyone to listen in or to walk up on us. I called my nephew, who said he'd meet us there. Marie and I read nonstop as we lay on the king-sized bed. I was submerged in my brother's version of 1988 until someone knocked at the hotel room door. "Hey?" I said.

Marie looked up. "What?"

"The door?" I said. "Didn't you hear that? Someone's at the door."

"It's room service, bonehead. Get the door and don't be stingy with the tip."

I hadn't heard her make the call. I had gone back to the beginning of the book and had made it through the first hundred pages, growing more angry by the page that Noble had not told us about *A Noble Sacrifice* when we visited him in the jail. Not a small omission, but one I'm sure he committed because he didn't want to scare us off. Well, stabbed or not, when I saw him next, I intended to make sure he understood just how scared *he* should be.

I got up, went to the door, and checked the peephole. A young man dressed in the gold-with-black piping the hotel service people wore stood behind a cart loaded with plates covered by chrome domes.

Before I opened the door, I said, "Jesus, Marie, did you order enough for an army?" I flipped over the inside-door security latch and put my hand on the knob.

"I know that you're a predatory eater," she said, "and that if I wanted to eat enough to last me to our next meal, I'd need some extra food to distract you. Bruno, you're really not going to believe this. I'm almost done and the dope rip-off that Noble—"

I opened the door.

Two rhinos, men built like football players, rushed in.

Marie screamed and threw her book at them. She jumped on the pile as the men took me to the floor. She kicked and scratched and socked to no avail.

A third man entered and pulled Marie off, lifted her around the waist, and tossed her on the bed. She bounced once, got her legs under her, and came at him again. The man punched my wife square in the face. Marie flew back, her body limp.

I roared and came up off the floor with both of the men. I head butted the closest one and reached down and grabbed onto the second man's crotch and tried my best to rip it from its roots. He screamed.

I extricated myself from under the pile and, with murderous intent, went for the man who'd harmed my Marie.

This same man, dressed in a blue suit, stood by the bed with a gun to the prostrate and unmoving Marie. The gun's ominous black silencer pressing into her forehead made me freeze.

"Good man, don't move."

The two thugs recovered and rose up in front of me. One grabbed me from behind and held my arms; the other, bent at the waist slightly, went to work. His fist hit my face. He stepped into it, put his shoulder and hip into it. The first blow to my right cheekbone shook my world, turned the air in the room into transparent Jell-O, thick, hard-to-breathe air, and just as difficult to see through. That first blow did me a favor: it dulled all the other nerve responses in my entire body, dulled the other blows that rained down as I wilted to the floor. The world tweaked out. Blacks deep enough to blot out the darkest coffin rolled over and engulfed me.

* * *

I came around, my head in Marie's lap, as she gently stroked my hair and cooed. Her tears dripped onto my face.

"Where did they go?" I asked.

"They left."

"What did they want?"

"Hush, I think I need to get you checked out at the hospital."

"I'll be fine." My face throbbed in time with a pulsating pain in my ribs. I tried to get up and she held me down. "Did they hurt you?" I asked.

She shook her head, sniffled, and swiped at her nose. Her left eye had started to swell. When I saw her injury I sat up; she couldn't hold me down.

"Bruno, please."

"I'm all right." I eased her down onto the bed. To the right, the food cart kept the hotel door from closing all the way, the plates jumbled and spilt. I got up, hurried over, and pulled the cart in. I closed the door and flipped on the security latch. I'd been playing this game half-assed, but not anymore. I needed a gun. Maybe two.

I got a towel from the bathroom, poured a glass of ice water on it, and sat on the bed next to Marie. I gently put the cold, wet towel to her eye.

"What did they say? What did they want?"

She tried to take the towel away. "You need this more than I do."

I put it back on her face. "Tell me."

"They said that they would be in touch. They said that they just wanted us to understand what was at stake and that they'd be watching us. Watching us all the time."

"Why? Did they say why?"

"They said—the guy in the suit said—that once we got Noble out of jail, we were to give him over to them. If we didn't, next time we saw them it would be our last. Something hokey like that. Said it like he'd kill us both and not quickly, but slow and torturous. Ah, Bruno, your face is swelling. I don't even recognize you. Come on, let's get you to the hospital."

"I'm fine."

"Did they say who they were?"

"No."

She said it, but her tone trailed off.

"Marie, honey, tell me."

"They didn't tell me who they were."

"You saw something, or you figured something out. Please tell me."

She hesitated for a long moment, her eyes looking into mine. "The guy in the suit, he's a son of a bitch, a real son of a bitch, Bruno." She paused.

I waited for her to tell it.

"He came over to the bed—" Her voice caught a little.

A lump rose in my throat. "What'd he do?"

"The other bastard, the one with the blond hair, held my legs and the one in the suit took hold of my breast with one hand and put his other hand on my throat."

She put her hand to her throat and gently caressed it. "He had his mouth right up close to my cheek. He squeezed with both hands at the same time. He wanted to make his point. He wanted me to believe he'd do what he said he would do if we didn't follow his orders. He squeezed hard and twisted. It hurt. He hurt me, Bruno. And I believe him. I believe he'll do what he says he'll do if we don't go along."

Now she rubbed her neck and her breast at the same time. I pulled her into a hug. Her body shook as she sobbed. No doubt remained, I'd get that gun and if that guy came anywhere close to within range, I'd gut-shoot him.

"Bruno?"

"Yeah, babe."

"When he reached down to twist my breast, his jacket fell open. I saw his shoulder holster. He had a badge clipped to his shoulder holster. He's a cop, Bruno, a sadistic deputy sheriff."

CHAPTER THIRTY-SEVEN

I CALLED DOWNSTAIRS and asked the concierge to call for a cab.

Marie came out of the bathroom with a wet towel filled with ice and applied it to my face. "Why do we need a cab?"

"Those three weren't regular deputies, they weren't street deputies or detectives assigned to a bureau, either. They work on a special team, Major Narcotics, or Crime Impact, something like that. They really know what they're doing, the way they came through that door as a team."

"So you're saying you think our rental car's been bugged and that they probably installed a GPS transmitter? Something like that?"

"It's what I would've done."

She nodded. "Bruno"—She took up my hand—"I don't want you to get sidetracked with these guys. We need to stay focused, get Bruno's kids returned safe, and then get back to our family where we belong. Those men, what they did, they mean nothing, you understand. They're not worth our time."

She read me like Noble's book. I wouldn't leave it alone, no way. I didn't intend to go back to Costa Rica until I had a chance to get up close and personal, whisper in their ears, tell them what a huge mistake they'd made, make them wish they never crossed our paths.

Before we left the room, I took a pair of socks from the dresser drawer and stuck them in my back pocket. Those three came at me again, I'd be ready for all three of 'em.

The cab picked us up out front and drove us to LAX. We entered and walked down the inside, parallel to Terminal Way, watching for a tail. When we reached the end of the terminal, we walked back outside and took the shuttle to the offsite rental car office and picked up a sleek black Cadillac STS.

I continued to fume as I drove us to Downey for the meet. Marie sat quiet and subdued as she read more of *A Noble Sacrifice*. Maybe I'd read into her mood. I didn't think so. I knew her better than anyone in the world. Blue Suit had scared the hell out of her. The look in his eye, the way he'd socked her in the face, a burst of violence she wasn't used to, at least not a violence perpetrated upon her person.

Back in elementary school, in the sand by the monkey bars, Wilfred Simpkins, from the Nasty Simpkins down on 133rd and Wilmington, socked me in the face and gave me my first taste of violence. The person-to-person violence didn't hurt as much as the idea another human could perpetrate it with such cold and callous efficiency, without guilt or remorse. I remember it like it was yesterday.

Add in the way Blue Suit looked Marie in the eye, tweaked her breast, and threatened her life and . . . oh, I looked forward to meeting that bastard again.

I cruised Wilderness Park once, early by forty-five minutes, made sure no one stood out of place, clocked who stood where and their activity, and then drove to a convenience store. I left Marie in the car, her nose still in the book. I bought a couple packs of Sno Balls, some chocolate milks, and Marie's favorite, a Chick-O-Stick. The kid rang up the sale as I continued to watch the window, watch the rental with my precious cargo. I turned back. "Hey, let me have some of those D-Cell batteries."

The kid turned and reached back. "How many?"

"Six or eight. Go ahead and make it eight."

He tossed the batteries in the bag.

I drove us back to Wilderness Park and backed into the most strategic spot possible, where I had an advance view of anyone coming into the park and, at the same time, could keep an eye on the folks already there. No one looked out of place. I wouldn't be caught unaware again.

We waited. I wanted to read some more, needed to, but couldn't, not with the ugly revenge festering in my belly. I unwrapped the Chick-O-Stick and touched the end to Marie's lips. The touch startled her. She saw the candy, looked up, and smiled. "Thank you, babe." She took it, sucked on it, and went right back to reading the last few pages.

I opened the Sno Balls and ate one with some chocolate milk. The sugar rush surged through my body and, for a time, sharpened my mind. I unwrapped the batteries from the bubble packaging one at a time and let them rattle loose in the bottom of the bag, all eight of them.

Marie closed the book. "Amazing. If half of this stuff is real, it's an amazing story. Bruno, the whole thing is a love story. He did it all for the love of Sasha, got caught, and paid the price. He's still paying the price."

He got caught all right. I caught him when he worked as a clerk in the convenience store. And he may have been right, he might've walked away clean had I not put it together.

"What happened in the dope deal?" I asked. "Where's the four hundred and fifty kilos? Does he tell that much in the book? Did he at least put forward some sort of half-assed opinion?"

"He says that the deal was set, that it was supposed to go down at nine o'clock at night on a pier in San Pedro. The Nicaraguans kept the coke loaded in the hull of a ship."

"But?"

"Noble played it smart. He wanted to get his girl Sasha away from Papa Dee and, at the same time, get his stake for them to go off and live together. He must've loved her a lot, Bruno. He ran security for Papa Dee on this deal. He was supposed to, anyway. He checked out the pier ahead of time. He hired some of his cronies he could trust and bought the guns. He was going to take down the dope and the money at the same time."

"What happened?"

Back in the day, after Noble left our house and started slingin' his dope, he and I never spoke again. We inhabited different sides of the street. I just hadn't been aware at the time of Noble's motivation for his abrupt moral decline, enrolling into the largest criminal enterprise in Los Angeles. No motivation other than greed ever came to mind.

Well, unless Sasha truly did motivate him.

But I'd met Sasha back when I was a street cop, back when Grover Porter brought her to me to do something about the injuries Papa Dee inflicted upon her. At the time I didn't know she was linked to Noble. She'd become the common denominator who brought all of us together. Noble and I almost came together over it. So close, but without touching or seeing one another's involvement, linked without our knowledge, almost as if on purpose. Did she know?

Yeah, sure, I knew Sasha. Knew what she was capable of. She knew her weapons, her sexual allure, the reaction all men had toward her.

Marie shrugged. "It's a helluva thing, Bruno. There was a

shootout like something right out of a Bruce Willis movie or, or like that last scene in *L.A. Confidential,* at the abandoned motel, you remember that one? Papa Dee showed up to the meet with Del Fawlkes and . . . well, you just have to read it for yourself. Here . . ." She handed me the copy of *A Noble Sacrifice.*

I took the book from her. "What's he say happened with that nine million in cash? Do you know how much room that kind of money needs? How much it weighs? I did a deal once where we seized four million in cash. They'd stored the money in cowboy boot boxes, fifties, twenties, and hundreds. The boxes filled a standard hall closet from floor to ceiling." I started to ramble as I suppressed my guilt for arresting Noble and not listening to him that night in the Stop and Go, the night he'd shot up armed robbers who weren't there to rob the store after all. They'd come at Noble for the dope and/or the money.

"It wasn't in cash," Marie said.

"What? What are you talking about?"

"It's just like you said. That much cash was too hard to deal with, to transport and to exchange. So according to what Papa Dee told Noble, the CIA wanted payment for the coke in diamonds. That way the CIA could transport that kind of wealth in a diplomatic pouch."

My head whipped around all on its own. "What?"

"What's the matter?" Marie asked.

"You said diamonds? You sure it says diamonds?" I grabbed up the book from my lap and thumbed through it. "Show me where? How many diamonds? What would the container for that amount of diamonds look like? Those would be real easy to hide for twenty-five years. You could hide 'em anywhere."

"I don't know. You're going to have to ask your brother. He didn't describe it in his book, not in the aftermath of that big mess. Read, you're gonna have to read it. He said he thought Papa Dee probably got spooked with the CIA being involved. Noble postulates that Papa Dee just cut his losses after the shootout and scrammed down to Rio. That he wanted nothing more to do with dope dealing. Maybe even Costa Rica. Noble actually mentioned Costa Rica. Wouldn't that be something if right now, Papa Dee lived down in Costa Rica?"

Her last few words didn't fully penetrate into my thought process. I'd opened the book to read a story I'd come to dread. I really didn't want to know the truth. Not this truth. Had I been so wrong about my brother, my best friend?

I found the chapter titled "Ghettocide" and started reading.

CHAPTER THIRTY-EIGHT

FROM *A NOBLE SACRIFICE*
BY JOHNNY NOBLE

Chapter Twenty-Nine
Ghettocide

I met Sasha for the last time, the last time while I could still breathe free air. I didn't know that would be the case or I would've held her longer. Much longer. Hugged her so tight and never let her go. I would've kissed her long and deep and said that final good-bye, that missing good-bye I regret to this day.

We met at Grover Porter's place, the abandoned red brick library at Century Boulevard and Bullis where Grover lived. He let us in and left us to it.

The library didn't have any electricity. The drafty air managed to weasel in from someplace in a high-low whistle. On that cool December evening, the ten or twelve guttering candles heated the crisp air and made our shadows jump and waver and dance on the partitioned walls. I held both her hands in mine and let my eyes soak her up.

I know this sounds more like a crazed teen crushing on his first high school sweetheart, but I'm not a poet, not by any stretch, and can't express myself well enough to describe the emotions that gripped me whenever I came around her. Not what this twenty-four-year-old woman did to a twenty-year-old kid in love for the first time.

She looked as if she couldn't hold it in any longer and spoke first. "I saw them. I saw the diamonds."

"What?" This wasn't what I expected her to say.

"The diamonds, silly, I saw them. Papa keeps them in one of those purple Crown Royal bags. Seven hundred and fifty two-carat diamonds, twelve thousand dollars apiece, nine million dollars' worth. All of them, the whole bunch are no bigger than this—" She held up both her cupped, delicately boned hands. Can you believe it, nine million dollars' worth?" Her manicured fingernails were painted with Matrimonial Red. *I know because I painted them for her the last time we'd seen each other not two days before. Met her in that very same broken-down, rickety library.*

What a wonderful and magical place.

She'd shaken the bottle of polish and held it out for me to see the name, smiled at me with that coy, 'come hither,' look that I'd never seen from any other woman. And she looked at me like that all the time. She loved me like I loved her.

I digress. I do that when I think back, remember how she looked, how she smelled, the touch of her skin, the sheen in her brown hair.

"He's so arrogant," she said. "Proud of his precious

little rocks. He keeps the purple Crown Royal bag in his pocket, right here." She pointed to the area on her hip where her pocket would be if she'd been wearing any clothes. I'd untied her dress straps as she spoke and let the dress slip down past her curves to lay at her feet. She never wore a bra or panties. Papa wouldn't let her. I hated that bastard.

She stood there unabashed, vulnerable yet unafraid.

I led her over to Grover's cot and kissed her on the lips, kissed her ear, kissed her neck. She groaned.

I won't go any further here; it wouldn't be gentlemanly and would be terribly unfair to her memory.

Afterward, we lay on the cot, our naked bodies clinging to each other for heat as the sweat cooled on our skin.

"It's tonight," she said.

I jerked up and looked down at her. "Tonight? You sure?"

Like I stated earlier, I'd been asked to run the security for Papa Dee's deal, but he'd found out about us and beat Sasha yet again, worse this time. Papa Dee needed killing and I intended to take care of that pressing issue at the conclusion of his upcoming and grandiose dope deal.

Grover, as always, had been called in to fix her up. That'd been two months ago. I'd been on the outs with Papa, who had every hype, coke fiend, pimp, and thug out lookin' to cash in on the contract he'd put on my ass. I'd been on the dodge big-time, watching over my shoulder, never getting a good night's sleep, just short catnaps. Two months of that shit wears on the body.

The only thing kept me going was the thought of taking out the fat man and stealing away with my woman.

I didn't know the date until right at that moment when she told me.

"What?" she asked, "What's the matter? You scared, baby? Don't be scared, you've got it all planned out. You're so much smarter than those people. You can do this."

"Let's go," I said. "Leave right now, run off and live in Madrid. You said you wanted to live in Madrid, right? Let's go then, right now."

She eased me back down on the cot and edged over until she could get on top, her soft breasts resting on my chest, her chin resting on mine. When she spoke, I not only heard her words but felt them as well, the vibration from chin to chin. "I would love to do that, go right now," she said. "Go this very minute. But you know Papa, he won't stop until he finds us. He'll spend tens of thousands of dollars to do it. You know that. You know Papa, you worked for him. He'll hunt us both down, not because he loves me, because he doesn't. I told you that. You've seen firsthand how he treats me.

"He'd run us down because we'd embarrassed him by taking off. It would show him as weak. And that's the last thing Papa wants, to be shown up in front of his peoples." She made her voice deep when she said "his peoples."

"No," she said. "If it wasn't for Papa, it wouldn't matter what kind of job you had. I told you that. You could be the postman, a waiter, you could be the night clerk at an all-night liquor store. It wouldn't matter,

because I love you that much. You understand. I really
need you to understand how much I love you. Tell me
you understand, Johnny, please?"

I nodded. Her words got to me, made a lump rise in
my throat. This beautiful woman loved me like no one
else in the world ever had.

"So you see," she said, "we can't live like that. We
can't have regular jobs. We have to run, and run hard,
disappear. And to do that we need money, Johnny.
We've talked about all of this. But if you're scared,
really, baby, we can find another way. I don't want
you to do it if you think it's not going to work like we
planned. The last thing I want is for you to get hurt."

DOWNEY, WILDERNESS PARK
CURRENT DAY

I LOOKED UP from the text. I didn't want to be a cynic but
couldn't help it. I couldn't help thinking Sasha wound up Noble
like some kind of toy soldier and sent him off to war. Knowing
that any outcome other than what she had in her current
situation, that of being sexually indentured to Papa Dee, would
be acceptable to her. Best case, Noble could come away with the
dope and the diamonds, and they'd run off as planned. Worst
case, the dope rip got botched, people died, and if she came out
of it real lucky, Papa Dee would've been wiped off the big board
and sent where he belonged: the morgue. We'd had a saying for

that in the Violent Crimes Team: "Case cleared by exceptional means."

I put the book down to check the environment around me, sitting in the car with Marie. Over by the entrance, Mack arrived at the park.

CHAPTER THIRTY-NINE

MACK DROVE INTO the park in his older model navy-blue Ford Ranger. He, too, cruised through once, getting the lay of the land, and then drove over to us. He parked his car like cops tend to do, driver's window to driver's window, before he shut it down. Over at that same entrance, still a long way off, my nephew Bruno came into the park on foot, moving along the tree line beside the asphalt drive.

Mack's window whirred down. "Holy shit, Bruno, what the hell happened to your face? That didn't happen at the jail. You didn't look that bad." He leaned forward in his seat to see Marie. "Ah, man, what happened to you two?"

"We were up at the hotel in the room when these three thugs burst in. They jumped me and attacked Marie."

Mack tried to look around me to get a better look at Marie. "She okay? You okay, Marie?"

She waved. "I'm fine."

"Who were they? I told you not ta mess with Don Brodie. Man, he's bad news. They're already calling him 'Don the Don.'"

"Mack, they were deputies. All three of 'em were from a special team."

His eyes went large, his mouth dropped open. "Are you shittin' me? How do you know? Did they identify themselves?"

"No. When the leader got up close and personal with my wife, she got a look at his star clipped to his shoulder holster."

"Sons a bitches. Dirty-assed, corrupt cops. What'd they want?"

"They want Noble."

"What's that supposed to mean? He's in the can for the rest of . . . Oh, no, no, no, they wanna bust him out, don't they?"

"Yeah. You seen this?"

Marie handed me a copy of *A Noble Sacrifice,* and I handed it to Mack through the windows.

The way I handed the book to him, the first thing he saw was the back cover. "Well, I'll be a son of a bitch, is that you, Bruno? You were cute as the dickens, weren't you? What happened, man, you turned ugly. Sorry, Marie, no offense." He held the book picture up for comparison.

"None taken," she said.

"Hey, I'm sittin' right here."

He turned the book around, looked it over. "Your brother wrote a book?" He opened it and thumbed through it.

"Yeah, you didn't know about it?"

"Nope."

"Mack, it's on the *LA Times* bestseller list for nonfiction."

He held up the book. "No way can this be nonfiction, not if *your* brother wrote it. And *I* probably missed it because I don't read much, and I've been on graves until just recently."

I liked Mack a lot, more so than my brother, but his disparaging remark cut me close to the quick, and I suppressed the urge to say something rude. I said nothing instead.

"Besides," Mack said, "the name Johnson's like Jones and

Smith. And look, he used Johnny as a first name. I wouldn't have recognized the name even if I were a big reader." Mack lost his smile. "You're not gonna bust Noble out, are you, Bruno?"

My nephew caught up to us and got in the backseat without being asked.

"Johnny Mack," I said, "this is my nephew, Bruno Johnson."

"The hell you say." He started his car and jerked the gearshift in reverse. Then he backed up, got out, and came around to the passenger side. I didn't know his intent and jumped out of the car.

Mack opened Bruno's door and stuck out his hand. "I'll be a son of a bitch, another Bruno Johnson, ain't that somethin'?"

My nephew shook hands with him. Bruno didn't smile.

"That's right," I said. "And he's an intern over at Lennox Station."

Mack took a step back. "Well, I'll be damned. I got a good friend works Lennox, Pete Sommers."

Bruno slid out of the backseat displaying a rare smile. "Really? You know Lieutenant Sommers?"

"Yep, got some shit on him, too, so if he ever gives you a hard time, tell him you know all about that shift-run to Vegas. He'll shit his pants."

Marie got out and stood with us, her smile not as bright as usual. She carried what Blue Suit did to her on her shoulders like a smothering weight.

Mack sobered. "Sorry to hear about your kids. We'll get 'em back. You have the great Bruno *the Bad Boy Johnson* on your team, you can't lose."

I took a step closer. "Mack, you're not in this. You can't be."

"Don't start up on that tired old tune. It won't do you any good, and you know that. Let's get on past it and get this thing goin', so

Bruno junior here can get his kids back."

"I'm not a junior."

"I know that, but hey, you could do worse, kid."

"I don't think he feels that way," I said. "Come on, we can talk about all that mess later. We need to get Noble out."

Mack nodded, "First tell me what you got goin' with Don Brodie."

"He's the one who has the two children."

Mack's expression turned grave. "You sure?"

"It's the LACF and D that has them," my nephew said.

"Shit." Mack turned to my nephew. "How do you know? Are you sure?"

"Lieutenant Sommers told me."

"Who are they?" Marie asked.

Mack said, "Los Angeles Consolidated Freight and Design. It's a cocaine distribution network, pure and simple, with a bullshit name. They're just trying to make a Gucci purse out of a pig's ear. That name's their cover, their brand. On the street, they call 'em the Coffin Dancers, which is more appropriate with the way they deal with malcontents, competition, and people who get in their way. They're low profile, ghosts, until they need to take care of business and put someone in the ground. They know how to drop bodies without witnesses or physical evidence. At least so far. One day the midlevel crook tryin' to move in on the business is there, the next he's gone and no one knows what happened to him. It's a missing person case without the body.

"They're bad news, Bruno. They run all the coke in LA. There's a joint task force; LASD, LAPD, State DOJ, and the FBI, are up and running with fifty investigators working on this group exclusively for the last eighteen months. Wire taps, pin registers, the works, and they never seem to get a handle on 'em, not so much as a foothold. This group is that good. The task force even has a mobile command post they use full time and move around as needed." Mack looked back at me. "This is serious shit. Every time they think they've cut off the head of the snake, the snake grows a new one, comes right back stronger than before."

"And this guy Don Brodie?"

"He's just recently been identified, new info within the last couple of weeks. Now they're thinkin' that he calls all the shots. I'm surprised Sommers even let that out. I'm surprised Sommers even knows about it. The task force only just got a whiff of this guy Brodie, and that was nothing but luck, buddy boy. They got him through GPS on an associate's car. And if Brodie's half as bad as the talk on the street, then you better watch your back. Seriously."

"What kind of background does he have? Where did he rise up, what neighborhood?" I asked.

"That's just it, the guy's a ghost, just like his organization. They have ten investigators on Brodie, just on him, ten of their best. He rarely leaves that bungalow in Beverly Hills. He eats room service and, twice a week, he has a high-dollar escort come visit, a redhead each time. They got his prints and he comes back with nothin', not so much as a birth certificate, not a piece of property in his name, no relation to any corporations or shell companies, no family, I mean zilch."

"That's not possible," I said. "Not with today's information highway."

"I know."

"You get a look at him?"

"No. Wong's on the task force, on the FBI contingent, and we stay in touch. This guy Brodie looks like some kind of nerd. I seen a photo. He wears glasses and sweaters like he's some kind of yuppie trapped in the seventies. He has twenty-four-seven security all around his bungalow, must cost a fortune."

"If he doesn't use a phone, get around the money or dope, they're never gonna get him."

"That's right. Why does the LAFC and D want your brother out?"

Marie held up the book. "This caused the whole mess. Noble wrote about a dope deal that went down twenty-five years ago. A half ton of coke went missing, and Papa Dee and his lieutenant disappeared with nine million dollars in diamonds."

Mack gave a long whistle. "Nine million in diamonds. Those are probably worth even more in today's market." He paused, shook his head. "I'm not buyin' the coke, though. Diamonds like that would probably fit in the palm of your hand, a half ton of powder, no way. Someone would've found it. That's a lot of blow."

My nephew said, "I don't care about the diamonds or the dope. I just want my kids back."

We discussed the plan, to spring Noble, set the time, and disbanded. Mack insisted on being involved, and since he worked at the sheriff's department, I got overruled. We'd use his plan, also against my better judgment. A plan that, on its face, appeared beyond ridiculous. Mostly because it called for me to ride a wheelchair right into the lion's den. Mack said for his plan to work we needed only to "pretend you know what you're doing. It's just that simple."

When we left, I let Marie drive, which rarely happened. I had to get back to the book, back to the "Ghettocide" chapter to find out what happened.

CHAPTER FORTY

A NOBLE SACRIFICE

Chapter Twenty-Nine
Ghettocide

With great difficulty, I left my love Sasha in that drafty red-brick library, lying naked on the cot with candle flames of hope flickering in her brown eyes, and headed off to meet up with my boys. I paged all three to a pay phone on Willowbrook Avenue. We met at Stops on Imperial Highway across the street from Nickerson Gardens.

Now it's okay to name names; they're all gone. They went the way of the ghetto gunfighter, the way they wanted to go.

Life on the street.

Much later, though, after I'd gone to the joint, I heard about each one, got the news while at Chino and in The Q. Their families should be proud; at least pride was what I felt at the time. Not so much anymore. What a terrible waste of human life. Now, as a keeper of the word, I covet life as a sacred gift.

For the job, I decided to stick with friends whom I could trust beyond question. For those of you who live in Willowbrook and might have known them, they were legends, they were closer than brothers: Conard, Little Boom, and Alpo. Conard, because he could drive the hell out of anything with wheels. Little Boom, the same but with guns—he could drop a Blood running down the street from a moving vehicle. And then there was Alpo. Well, Alpo just because, when it came right down to it, I didn't know if I could do what had to be done. I knew I could tell Alpo the plan, and he'd stick to it no matter how bloody a road we traveled.

The caper turned simple with diamonds involved and without all of that bulky money to lug. The plan—not well wrought, but everyone agreed to it—hatched right there in the parking lot of Stops over a hot link smothered in barbeque sauce.

We'd all take separate cars, G-rides. Conard took care of that. He didn't need much notice. He had the cars scoped out already. Took him less than an hour to grab all four.

The plan? We'd pick up Delbert Fawlkes and Papa Dee as they left the safe house in Compton headed for the deal in San Pedro. We'd follow them to a location that looked good to Conard. Conard would give us the signal: flash his headlights off and on twice. And then, before the next intersection, we'd box Del and Papa in. We'd get all around their car with our cars as we approached the traffic signal, one of our cars for each side of their car. We'd move in tight so they couldn't open their doors or drive forward or backward, not so much

*as an inch. Mash right up into the grill and trunk. They
wouldn't suspect a thing, not until we made our move
and closed the trap on them. We'd have the element
of surprise on our side. Then I'd ask . . . no, I'd order
that woman-beating bastard to toss over the diamonds.
Simple. Keep it simple and nothing could go wrong.*

The best laid plans of mice and men, right?

The first part came off without a hitch.

*We set up at eight thirty, only three hours after I'd
left Sasha. Her kiss, her scent, lingered like a physical
presence.*

*Del walked out of the house on Aranbe at eight for-
ty-five, right on the nose, and looked around. He kept
his hand under his navy peacoat, ready for action. He
favored two customized Colt Combat Commanders
with satin finishes. Everyone knew about those guns,
some more intimately than others. Not that they could
ever talk about them again.*

*I'd parked closest, insisted on it; everyone else laid
off a little.*

*Del stood in the shadows under the tree, away from
the streetlight. Once he nodded, out popped Papa Dee
and they made for his car—a big Cadillac El Dorado,
gray with a black landau top—got in and took off. I
dropped in behind until the first turn. Conard took
over, driving a one-ton flatbed with tall tires. The
backup plan, if they tumbled to us, Conard would put
an end to their escape by ramming the life out of that
beautiful car. Come in from the side and hit it right in
the center.*

Conard stayed with them for less than a mile, until

the first signal at Compton Avenue, and peeled off, his truck too memorable. Next, Little Boom took up the tail. Conard came back in off a side street and stayed third in line to wait for the right time to give the signal, and if necessary to leave enough running room to ram. He wouldn't wait too long. The longer it went, the better chance they had of spotting us. I'd take the right side, Conard the back, Little Boom the left, and Alpo the front. That's how we planned it, anyway.

Del made a left onto Wilmington heading south. The streets were wet from a passing rain. Houses lit up the night with red and green Christmas lights. All the lights reflected off the wet black asphalt.

Nine o'clock at night Wilmington still ran heavy with traffic, too many people out doing their Christmas shopping. That many people made our play that much more difficult. With each passing minute, Del drove closer and closer to San Pedro. My nerves had started out frayed; now they screamed for relief from the awful tension. And the game had only been in play a few minutes, less than five.

Conard flashed his lights. He'd made his choice.

Too soon. Too soon. We were still in our own hood. He must've felt the same pressure.

The intersection he chose, Wilmington and Greenleaf, didn't leave enough time. Not enough for all of us to get into position. The distance between all the cars southbound on Wilmington started to compress as we approached the red signal at Greenleaf, making the maneuver to get up beside or in front of the Eldo next to impossible.

No chance. We didn't even have one side of the box.

We'd have to wait for another opportunity. Right? We'd have to wait. Please, Conard, wait.

We didn't have cell phones back then to communicate, so you just had to roll with whatever went down.

Wilmington and Greenleaf wouldn't work for us. The Eldo came to a stop grouped in the middle of uninvolved people—civilians unaware of the major coke traffickers, Del and Papa Dee, sitting amongst them, predators amongst the lambs.

I held my breath for one long half second, wishing for the light to change, wishing for none of the boys to jump the mark at this inopportune time.

Damn, wishing didn't work.

Alpo jumped out and ran down the row between the cars, his big .45 plainly visible under the bright streetlights.

Conard popped out of the truck next, then Little Boom. Nobody wanted to miss out on the action. I got out fast, my limbs not moving like they should, moving as if at half-speed, although, I knew they weren't.

Alpo made it to the Eldo, the driver's window. That's when everything slowed to a crawl, everyone's movements shifted into slow motion.

Alpo yelled, "Hands up, motherfucker." He didn't wait for compliance. He opened up point blank right into the closed window. Right on top of Delbert Fawlkes.

The big .45 boomed.

Conard came up at the same time and started to pass in between the back of the Eldo, headed for the passenger side to cover Alpo.

Del must've seen Alpo coming up. He fired, and Alpo

crumpled. His one arm came up to hold his belly in, but Alpo kept firing with the other hand.

Under withering fire, Del shifted in reverse, the white backup lights coming on. Conard saw the threat as he passed between the cars. He flipped backward on top of the hood of a Toyota Camry just as Del backed into it, tires spinning for traction. The Eldo would've taken Conard's legs off.

Del put it in drive and rammed the car in front, Papa Dee yelling now, in between the gunfire, "Get the hell outta here. Get me the hell outta here."

Little Boom made it up, stopped behind the Eldo, raised his hands, a nine in each, and fired.

And fired.

And fired.

Fifteen rounds in each gun. The brass shell casings flicked out over his shoulders and tinkled down on the wet asphalt.

The Eldo continued to ram cars, backward then forward and backward.

All the windows to the Eldo shattered as bullets flicked through them. The red brake lights blinked out. The trunk was pocked with multiple holes.

Alpo held his gut, dropped his mag, and reloaded. He went at the inside of the car again, his arm extended. He unleashed hell from two feet away. Conard, from the hood of the Camry, let go with his .357, much louder than the rest. The muzzle flash lit up the night, each shot freeze-framed the action, as his face contorted in fear and anger.

Me? I stood in place, too stunned to participate, the gun, a big Ruger Redhawk .44, limp in my hand.

With the first rounds fired and the ramming of the cars, the civilians took off.

The guns went silent.

The signal changed from red to green. That's how long death and mayhem had taken, the time in between the red and green signal. A minute to a minute and a half, no more.

White cordite hung in the air, thick and acrid, tinted yellow by the streetlights. Papa Dee and Del no longer sat upright in the car. The Eldo, now a ghost ride, slowly drifted off all on its own.

None of my guys moved. Alpo was bent over at the waist, the .45 in his hand almost touching the street. Blood dripped down his hand, onto the gun and the street.

I took a breath, sucked in a large one. I hadn't realized I'd been holding it.

Then, without warning, Del sat up in the Eldo and stuck his foot down flat on the gas. The Eldo leaped forward into the night. The silver car flashed in and out of the streetlights, growing smaller.

Del made the first quick turn and was gone.

CHAPTER FORTY-ONE

I SAT IN a wheelchair, pushed by Mack, dressed in his Class B, Los Angeles County Sheriff's uniform and escorted by Marie clad in blue doctor scrubs purchased ahead of time for our little operation. I didn't want Marie along, but Noble needed constant medical attention so soon after traumatic surgery for the stab wounds inflicted by the Sons of Satan. Wounds intended for me.

Mack wheeled me in the emergency door, past all the chairs filled to capacity with the maimed, the sick, and the hurting, past the reception counter, and right over to the elevator that said "Law enforcement only." Like any deputy in the county, Mack knew the way. The place smelled of body odor mixed with disinfectant. The people paid us no mind, too caught up in their lives of pain and illness.

Getting into the facility wasn't the problem. Getting out with an unconscious patient, a prisoner from state prison serving a life sentence, now that wouldn't be a cakewalk, no matter what Mack wanted to believe.

In the elevator, all three of us looked straight ahead at the stainless-steel doors when they closed. The booth bitch, up on the fourth floor, monitored the camera in our elevator car, and I fought the urge to look up at the camera.

All three of us stayed in character. I tried to keep my knees from shaking. I shouldn't have been so scared, but our failed little foray into MCJ weighed heavy on my mind. Piled on top of that was the insane plan that Mack had concocted. All that stress combined gave me a headache, a grinding stomach, and the shakes.

"Hey, just act like you know what you're doin'," Mack said again, once too often in fact, until I wanted to smack him. "It's as easy as that."

Out of the corner of my mouth, I barely moved my lips. "Hey, Mack, there's going to be a video record of you being here."

"Buddy boy, you take care of your end of this thing. I'll worry about mine. And hey, thanks for burning me down with my girl."

"What are you talking about?"

"Barbara went through my pants like a sketchin' dope fiend looking for a penny. She knew what she was looking for and found it. The ring. You're the only one who knew about it. Thanks a million, pal."

I looked up from the wheelchair at Marie and didn't say anything, not wanting to burn her. I gave her the look that said we'd discuss this one later, little girl, and there'd be a spanking involved. She didn't seem to care. She shrugged and fell on the sword. "Us women need to stick together." She smiled. "So, did you pop the question?"

"What choice did I have?"

Marie giggled, the first real emotion since Blue Suit attacked her. She went up on tiptoes and kissed Mack on the cheek. He blushed bright red.

The elevator door opened.

My brother Noble stood there right out in the open. Unescorted, unfettered.

He stood right there in front of us, swaying on his feet, sweat beading and running in rivulets down his too-pale face. He wore the uniform of a Valiant Security officer, complete with a plastic sheriff's security badge clipped to his pocket. The blue uniform blouse was speckled with blood over the wound on his abdomen where it had started to bleed through.

The sheriff contracted with Valiant for the lower-level security jobs. Noble had somehow appropriated a uniform and had already made it past the most difficult part, the double-gate sally port that led out of the hospital ward.

Of course, sure, my nephew Bruno worked for Valiant Security. Now it all made sense. But why hadn't Bruno told me about helping his father with his escape?

Marie moved first to catch him as he wilted. "Oh, my God," she whispered.

I jumped out of the chair and helped ease him down into it. He looked horrible.

That could've been me if he hadn't jumped in front of that shank.

He'd made it past the sally port out of the jail ward all on his own. If we hadn't been there, he wouldn't have made it another foot. He would've collapsed to the floor and the deputies would've fallen to the ruse. Nabbed his sorry ass, added an attempted escape charge. Worse though, they'd have then made him a red suit, an escape risk, escort only. A red suit would cut his chances of escape down below nil.

Now we just needed to get past the elevator camera, out past the ER, and then the parking lot, and he'd be home free. Nothing to it.

Mack hit the door to close it and then pressed the lobby button. Noble, his voice weak, said, "I told you I had a foolproof plan."

"You're not out of the woods yet, fool."

"I'm the fool? What kinda plan are you brain-trusts working from?"

"Take it easy, you two," Marie said. She touched my hand, I hoped out of view of the elevator camera.

"Looks like we got here just in time. You were about to DFO." Ghetto for *"done fell out."*

"Get a life. You just can't admit that I did something spectacular without you."

Mack moved over close to me as the elevator dropped us fast to the lobby. He pulled my hands behind my back and cuffed me.

"Hey, what the hell?"

"Noble's got the wheelchair. He obviously can't walk out under his own power. The wheelchair was your cover. Someone sees *you,* they might take a second look. You're too well known and might be recognized. Cops don't look twice at the fish already caught. They won't see you even if they look you in the face, not with these cuffs on."

I hated it when he was right.

Noble's head lolled to the side; his eyes rolled until only the whites showed.

The elevator dinged. The door opened. Marie pushed the wheelchair out, and Mack and I followed back out into the free world, the one still looking to put us back in the cage.

I didn't like the cuffs, not one damn bit.

Out in the parking lot, my young nephew Bruno pulled up in an ambulance, one misappropriated that would go right back where it came from as soon as we finished with it. We didn't bother with taking out the gurney. We opened the rear doors, helped Noble in, climbed in behind him, and took off. I couldn't believe the caper came off that easily. Marie gently eased Noble down on the gurney. The man still possessed bulk, jailhouse muscle from working the weight piles and doing push-ups every day in the slam. What else did one do? I'd been there, did two years of my own.

Marie put on latex gloves and went to work on my brother. Bruno kept looking back, trying to see what was going on. "Boy, pay attention to your driving or you're going to pile us up," I said.

He shot me a scowl, held it for a long moment to prove a point, then went back to steering the ambulance. I spun in my seat so my cuffed hands faced Mack, who sat next to me. He didn't move.

"Hey, come on man, I hate these things."

He grinned and looked at Marie, who'd paused to watch. Marie smiled and said to me, "Ah, I guess you shouldn't have told me about the ring, huh?"

CHAPTER FORTY-TWO

WE DROVE IN and out of traffic, watching for a tail, and then into the back parking areas of two hospitals. Each time, we backed into the ER loading docks to mix with the other ambulances. Both times we let Mack off on foot, wearing his t-shirt and uniform pants, to lurk in the parking lot and again checked for a tail. Satisfied, we drove to our prearranged fleabag motel, Le Ménage, on a side street off Sunset Boulevard. The bed covers hung off the caved-in mattresses, their colors faded and the material worn. The cheap owners had spray painted the carpet blue, the over-spray evident on the baseboards. The tacky paint made the carpet crunch underfoot. Still, the place looked like the Taj Mahal compared to an eight-by-eight prison cell with bars.

Noble had used every bit of his strength to make his break from a prison and jail system that had been a part of his life for the last twenty-five years. Now he lay asleep or unconscious. I didn't know which and could only hope he hadn't drifted into a coma.

Either way, I couldn't talk with him, but wanted to, needed to in the worst way.

"It's best for him to sleep right now," Marie said as she tinkered with the IV she'd started.

"Is it just sleep?" young Bruno asked.

"Yes." Marie put her hand on my nephew's shoulder. "He's going to be fine. He just needs some time for his body to heal. Why don't you boys take the ambulance back and get something to eat?"

"I'm not leaving you alone," I said. "Not until we're safely back home."

"Come on, kid," Mack said. "Let's go."

My nephew sat at Noble's side, staring at his face and holding his hand. Bruno was seeing his dad for the first time out in the open, free and not restricted by bars or reinforced glass. It must've been a strange feeling.

Mack nudged him.

"Huh?"

"Come on, kid, let's take the ambulance back."

"Oh, yeah, right, sure."

They left. The room went quiet. I sat next to Marie on the bed and held her hand. "You okay?" I asked.

"Whatta you mean?"

"You know what I mean."

She tried to hold my gaze but then looked away. "I'm fine. I just need to work through it. You buggin' me about it all the time's not gonna help." She turned back, put her warm hand on my face. "Sorry, didn't mean to snap like that. Just give me a little room, and I'll be fine, really. Not a big deal."

"It is too a big deal. It's never gonna happen again. Take my word on that. No one's gonna get close enough to hurt you ever again."

I kissed her. And kissed her some more. I eased her back on the bed. I hugged her tight. I never wanted to let her go. She sensed my need and clung to me, held on, her fingers dug into my back as the kiss turned more intense.

Noble's voice croaked, "Hey, I'm laying right here. Can you resist your animal instincts just this once? Or at least take it into the bathroom."

Marie and I sat bolt upright. Marie went over to him, took up his wrist, and checked his pulse.

I took his other hand and held it. "Good to see you, little bro. Thought I lost you back there in that jail hallway. Thank you for that. I owe you big."

Marie said, "Yes, thank you for saving my lughead husband."

"Can I get some water here? I'm parched. And you don't owe me a thing. You just being here is all I could ever ask for." His voice clogged up a little at the end and his eyes filled with tears.

"I'll get that water." I swiped at my eyes on the way to the bathroom. I wasn't ready for such strong emotions. I hadn't thought of Noble for years, had put him out of my head for good when I never should have. What a fool I'd been.

Behind me, Marie asked, "I don't know if you can have any water orally yet. What did the surgeon tell you? Did he say the intestines were compromised?"

"I think I'm okay with water. They gave me some in the ward before I jammed out of there."

I came back with the water. Marie took it from me. "Here," she said, "help me sit him up. I wish we had his medical chart. I'm flying blind without it."

We scooted him up. He groaned and grunted. I held him forward while she stuffed some pillows behind him. "There." She took up the water and put it to his lips. He reached for the glass. "I'm feelin' better now. I can do it."

He started to drink and kept going. Marie put her hand on his and stopped him. "That's enough for now. If you throw it up, that action is a little too violent for you right now. The movement could pull your sutures loose. I don't know what they repaired on the inside. You can have some more in a few minutes, okay?"

He nodded. "You a doc or something?" He looked at me. "You got yourself a doctor, big brother?"

"I'm not a doctor, I'm a physician's assistant. And your brother hasn't 'got' anything. We're husband and wife, we're partners and good friends."

"Same damn thing. As far as I'm concerned, you're a doc."

Oddly, I glowed with pride over my brother's words, and I'd never been like that toward him before. Well, maybe a little.

"I got a bone to pick with you, little brother," I said.

CHAPTER FORTY-THREE

HE LOOKED AT the nightstand and the two copies of his book. A book I hoped stayed classified as nonfiction and didn't turn out to be a novel. He smiled, showing all his teeth. "You found my book. Ain't it somethin'? I mean, no way did I think anyone would want to read that sorry excuse for the written word. Amazing, ain't it?"

"Why didn't you tell us about the book when we came to visit you?"

"You have time to read it yet? Whatta ya think?"

"I think it could easily be a movie," Marie said.

"Oh, don't do that," I said. "His head is large enough as it is."

"You read it, Bruno?"

"Not all of it, not yet. I've been a little busy pullin' your cookies outta the fire."

"And I can't thank you enough for that, truly. Did they make contact with you or Little Bruno about my grandbabies?"

"Did you write that book just to stir all of this up?" I asked. "Because it worked."

"You read a lot of the book, I can tell. What about my grandbabies?"

"Is it bullshit or is it true?" I asked. "I mean the thing about the shooting, the one at Wilmington and Greenleaf? I was working the streets back then. That was our area, and I don't remember any calls or bodies hitting the ground."

"Can I have some more water, please?"

Marie gave him the water but held the glass and limited his intake.

"I have a number," I said, "to call when we're ready to make the trade for your grandchildren. Now tell me about Wilmington and Greenleaf."

"Take it easy, Bruno." Marie said.

"Yeah, listen to your wife. Take it easy, Bruno."

"Noble?"

"Okay, okay. Yes, it's all true. I did write the book to spark some interest to help get me the hell outta the can. I can't begin to tell you how tired I am of livin' that prison life." His expression turned grim, the smile gone. "You gotta believe me, though, I had no idea someone would snatch my grandbabies. If I had, I wouldn't of done it. You believe me, right, Bruno? You believe me, right?"

I really wanted to believe him. I did. But couldn't, not with his priors for lying. I squeezed his hand. "Of course I do."

"Thank you for that. It was a dumb move, like you said. What did I expect was gonna happen? Huh? What a dumb-assed move."

"Why now, brother? Why after all this time did you choose this moment in your life to do this?"

"I told ya, I got tired of bein' locked down."

"So you decide to write a book?" Marie asked. "That doesn't make any sense at all."

"I know, it's kinda crazy, me of all people. Crazy, huh, Bruno?"

"Yeah, I'm still trying to wrap my head around it. So you don't have the diamonds or the dope?"

"Come on, man, I told you, it happened just like in the book.

We shot the hell outta that Eldo and it drove off. It just drove off into the night like some kinda stupid, freaky horror movie. Just gone. Poof."

I shook my head. "How could anyone live through that kind of barrage, the way you described it?"

"I know, huh? It was really something. I couldn't believe it the way that car was shot to hell. It looked like the Bonnie and Clyde car. I'm not kiddin' either."

"You didn't follow the Eldorado?"

"No, I didn't say it in the book, but we had to get Alpo to the doc, you know, Grover Porter, that guy who lived in that broken-down library at Century and Bullis. The guy who fixed up Sasha after Papa beat the hell outta her."

Noble pointed to his pelvic area on the right side. "Alpo took one right here and right here." He moved his finger up higher indicating his right abdomen. "Didn't think he'd make it. Ol' Grover worked one of his miracles."

"You never heard on the street what happened to Del or Papa Dee?"

He shook his head. "Like I said, that car was shot to hell, and they shouldn't have walked away from it but—"

"But what? Spill it, Noble."

"Well, they didn't survive, at least Del didn't. Del drove off and crashed a little while later, probably not five minutes after the shooting. Made it down to LAPD's Harbor district. Head-on right into a telephone pole, sheared the mother off at sixty-plus miles per hour."

"How do you know that?" I asked as my mind shot out ahead of him, trying to figure what had changed all these years later for him to uncover that new piece of information. And how he came by it.

"I didn't find that out, that part of this whole screwed-up mess, until recently. I mean, I could've used the information for the book. I mean that shit's really important. Right now that part of the story in the book just hangs out there without any type of conclusion. And you gotta have a conclusion, my editor said. But I told her no, no, this is the way it happened and it's the way it's gonna be."

"How did you find out?" I asked. "How'd you just now find out about the crash?

"Can you believe it, that fat bastard Papa Dee just walked away from that Eldo? He left his friend Del behind, left him right there lying across the seat to bleed out."

"Noble, tell me. Quit avoiding the question. What do you mean you found out last week? What happened?"

He paused, looked at Marie, then back at me. "The District Attorney investigators came into the jail and booked me for murder. Add charged me for 187."

Now it made sense, the part about the new information at least. But something still didn't quite sound right, and I couldn't put my finger on it.

"For murder?" Marie said. "What murder?"

I held up the book, *A Noble Sacrifice*. "Noble, here, ratted himself out by writing a confession. There isn't any statute of limitations on murder. They're going after him for the murder of Delbert Fawlkes."

Noble nodded. "Yeah, and that ain't right."

CHAPTER FORTY-FOUR

MARIE'S MOUTH DROPPED open. "They can't do that, can they? You said in your book you didn't pull the trigger, that you couldn't."

"Felony murder rule," I said. "If someone dies during the commission of a felony, doesn't matter if you pulled the trigger, crashed the car, or slipped the knife between a guy's ribs. If you so much as drive the getaway car, it's still considered murder."

Noble nodded his agreement. "And it doesn't matter if the guy's a POS, non-taxpaying asshole like Del or Papa Dee, either."

"POS?" Marie asked.

"Watch your mouth, little brother," I said to Noble. I told Marie, "It means piece of shit."

"So," I said, "you think Papa Dee crawled off and died?"

"No," Marie answered for Noble. "Noble thinks Papa fled to Costa Rica, remember? We had this conversation, old man." She smiled at me, that cutesy smart-assed one she liked to flash when she wanted to goad me a little in a friendly, spousal way.

"That's right," Noble said after a sip of water. "When I wrote the book, at that time I thought, by some miracle or the grace of the devil, himself, they somehow both escaped. I didn't want them dead. Hurt bad, maybe, but not dead. I thought I did, but found I didn't much have the stomach for it. Not in cold blood, not in ambush like the one we'd set up.

"I didn't know Del died until the DA filed that 187 on me. Not that I cared as far as a new case was concerned. I wasn't ever gettin' out. Go ahead, I told 'em, pile up those years. Twenty-five more years on top of life, what did it matter? In prison, you only ever do two days, the day you go in and the day you get out. Only they'd slated me for never having that second day. Ever."

"That's why you got that job in the Stop and Go," I said. "Because you thought the threat had passed and you wanted to show Sasha you could be an everyday Joe and not a dope-dealing criminal."

He looked at me, his expression serious. "Yes, that's exactly right. Without the diamonds or the dope, I needed a working stiff's kinda job to support us." He drank some more water.

"Dad's a working stiff. He did all right."

"You know what I mean."

Now Noble's motivation made more sense. But at the same time, it heaped more guilt on top of the pile already smothering me. Further confirmation that those three gangsters who came into the store hadn't gone there to rob him. They went there to fulfill the contract put on the street by Papa Dee, and at the time they just hadn't yet gotten the word that Papa Dee went belly up. Or they went there to coerce the location of the diamonds and dope out of Noble. Diamonds and dope he didn't have.

"If you didn't have the stomach for it, little brother," I said, "you sure did a good job going to guns on those three outside the Stop and Go."

"That was different." His eyes went wide a little, and he sat forward as much as his wounded body allowed. "Come on, man, you of all people can see that. Those three in the store, *they* came for *me.* I didn't have a choice. Don't get me wrong. I'm not tryin' ta justify taking a life. I mean I'm not tryin' ta throw a good excuse at you all, 'cause there ain't one. I'll tell ya the truth, what went through my mind. At the time, all I could think about was the 'what if.' What if these three assholes came up on me as I walked down the street with my girl? Would Sasha ever be safe with me? Right at that moment I realized the plain and simple truth. No. She'd never be safe with me. It hurt, I'm tellin' ya, boy did it hurt. And I turned mad over it. Just like that—" he snapped his fingers "—that quick. And then I wasn't thinkin' straight. I'll admit it right here to you.

"Sure, I shot their sorry asses, and I regret the day that I did, but truth be told, I'd do it all over again. If pushed in that same corner like that, I'd do it. They were armed and came for me."

He shook his head and took a long breath. "The irony of it is, I got into the life to get close to Sasha, and that one stupid decision ended up being what pushed her farther away. Hell, she was safer with me bein' in prison than if I was out."

"Did she believe that?" Marie asked.

"No. My incarceration tore her up. And it tore me up just watchin' her live with it."

His last few words diffused into a blur as that night when I confronted Noble at the counter in that Stop and Go came flooding back on me hard and fast.

We called them *Stop and Robs,* a violent and dangerous job, especially on graveyard shift. He'd taken that job for gallant reasons. Why had I not seen it?

The sights and smells returned in distinct colors and scents in only the way post-traumatic stress can do for you.

The look in his eyes.

That horrible look of betrayal in his eyes. My betrayal.

The event hadn't been physically traumatic to me, but I guess when you pistol-whip your own brother and then arrest him, send him on his way to a lifetime in prison, that qualifies and moves the emotional stress to the top of the scale. That night, he shot at all three and hit two, shot them in the back. Later, both of them, the one in the backseat and the one in the front with his leg blown off, died.

I didn't want to put too heavy a point on it, but that night Noble also tried to hide his crime. He didn't come forward to tell Deputy Wilson what he'd done. He stuck to his story that the three came in, took two cases of beer, and fled. Said he didn't know what happened after the three had left the store. Like a lot of folks in the ghetto, Noble didn't trust the police. Noble not saying what really happened did show a consciousness of guilt. He'd been wrong. He broke the law.

But he was also my brother, and now after all these years, when the law I'd so avidly enforced had let me down when Derek Sams killed my grandson, I could see my error. Maybe I should've given him a pass that night.

"Bruno?" Noble said.

I returned to reality. "Yeah?"

"I don't want my son involved in this. I don't want him there when we make the exchange."

"I understand."

"Wait." Marie said. "Why? What am I missing here? Oh, no, no, no, we're not going to just let them take you off. We get the kids back, we get you back, too, right then. No, no, we're not going to let them walk with you. No way. Right? Tell me that's right, Bruno. We're not going to—"

She saw the answer in my eyes.

CHAPTER FORTY-FIVE

I PUT A hand on each of her shoulders and looked her in the eye. "Noble's correct. There's no way to get the kids and keep them from taking him. Not unless the cops get involved, and that can't happen. Noble's wanted and so are we. We're all alone in this thing. We don't have the resources or the manpower. You understand? We have to get those children back, priority one."

Her chin trembled as she fought the tears. She nodded. And then shook her head, refusing to accept the painful truth.

Noble gave a weak try at a chuckle. "Trust me on this. Those bastards, whoever they are, ain't gonna get blood from this turnip. I can't tell 'em something I don't know. Right?"

"Right," I said, only with even less of his weak enthusiasm.

In his case, though, it didn't mean those guys wouldn't try their best to get it out of him. That part of it went unsaid and sat in that motel room between us like a fat gray elephant no one wanted to look at.

I took the card out of my pocket, the one the crazy woman on the pier gave me. "I'll make the call."

"Wait, before you do that, I gotta do something first."

"What's that? We really don't have the time to do anything.

They're gonna know you busted out. We don't want them to think we're playing games, not when they have the kids."

Marie moved over and turned on the television and said, "I hadn't thought about the news."

"I need to go the cemetery to see my Sasha," Noble said. "I have to do that before . . . we do this."

I understood his desire to say good-bye to Sasha but, weighed against the safety of the children, it didn't make good sense. He was the one who had to stand up against the real-world, finger-nail-pulling, knee-busting, toe-crushing interrogation, so how could I begrudge him a last request?

The old tube television came to life. Marie flipped through the channels. We'd left the jail part of the hospital about three hours ago, not enough time for news to tumble to the story. Not when the sheriff would do everything in his power to suppress the em-barrassment of an escape.

"You sure about this cemetery thing?" I asked.

Noble nodded. Some of the color had returned to his face. I took two bottles of water out of the banged-up mini-fridge along with two pink coconut-covered Sno Ball cupcakes and handed him one set—forgetting he wasn't supposed to eat anything—keeping the other for myself. My stomach growled at the thought.

I dialed the number on the card. After one ring, the woman said, "Good, you got him."

I couldn't focus my full attention on the call, not a good thing with the children at stake. Marie stood by the television and watched the news story unfold. They broke into the cheesy reality court show for the breaking news.

Willy Jessup and his cotton-top never let grass grow under his feet when he could stand in front of the cameras and rant. He stood out in front of LCMC at the exact spot where we'd parked the ambulance to load up Noble. The scene of the crime.

The woman on the phone said, "We'll make the trade out in Lancaster, way out in the desert so you can't pull any of your bull-shit. Brodie says you're real good with the bullshit. I'm runnin' this op and I won't put up with it. You understand me, cowboy? We get your asshole brother and you get the kids. Any other variation and the sniper takes care of business. And he goes at it for real. You understand? I mean everyone out there gets tagged with a hundred-and-fifty-eight-grain boat-tail .308. And I mean everyone."

She'd just indirectly threatened to shoot the kids if it went down wrong.

The news director cut from Willy Jessup's rant to a more faded color image pulled from a different source. Marie backed up and sat on the bed as she watched. The surveillance cameras had caught us coming out of LCMC wheeling Noble. Caught all three of us with our hands in the cookie jar.

Not Mack, though. He'd somehow stayed out of the frame, the video camera catching only his body. Mack had known ex-actly where to stand. He, too, had been trained by Robby Wicks. Wicks taught everyone on the team to "be aware of your envi-ronment; that includes cameras. These days cameras are the same as guns, and they'll do you in just as fast." I hadn't been looking for cameras, hadn't looked for them in a long time. Once already wanted, what did it matter? Good for Mack.

Marie and I wouldn't be able to just hop on a flight to go back to Costa Rica, not now. All the cops in Southern California would be looking for me—for us—again.

I sat down next to Marie and took her hand. "You okay?"

"Sure. I just can't believe how fat I look on television, that's all."

I kissed her ear. "You don't make a very good liar."

The woman on the phone said, "Hey, asshole, you hear me? In Pear Blossom, at 116th Street and Fort Tejon Road. You got it? Two hours. Be there."

"Huh? What? No, you get the location this time; that means we get the time."

"No chance," she yelled. "No way, asshole, no way do we—"

I hung up on her.

From over at the bed, Noble said, "Hey, I look pretty good on TV, don't I? Look at that uniform, I should've been a cop. Hey, Bruno, I should've been a cop like you. Huh? Whatta think?"

I looked over at him. He reminded me of the kid I used to know, the return of that sparkle in his eyes, dreaming dreams that didn't have one chance in hell to work out no matter how hard he tried. Not when you rise up out of a burning house like he did. Not with a burnt family to drag around with you forever and ever.

The phone rang. I answered it as the TV played the surveillance-camera feed again. This time they froze our images, blew them up, made our faces huge on the screen.

Beside me, Marie brought the back of her free hand up and tapped under her chin, checking the nonexistent fat. She did it to throw me off her fear of every cop in the state after us. I knew her that well. I smiled.

Noble needed to see the grave of his loved one, and I wouldn't deny him that, not with the stakes he chose to play. I said, "Three hours," to the crazy woman.

I hung up.

CHAPTER FORTY-SIX

"Where's the cemetery?" I asked Noble. I turned to Marie. "Let's get him ready. I want to get out of here before Bruno and Mack get back."

"It's Forest Lawn in Hollywood, not far from here," Noble said.

Marie got up and shut off the television, then went over and pulled the IV from his arm, taped it, and checked his pulse and blood pressure.

Noble watched her with great interest, watched her every move. I watched Noble.

She finished. Looked up at me.

"Well?" I asked.

"I wouldn't recommend that he leave this bed for at least two weeks, but I guess we don't have that luxury, do we?"

"Not hardly," Noble said. He tossed off the blankets and swung his legs over the side as if nothing ailed him at all. "Hand me those pants, please."

Marie got his pants. I helped him stand by holding onto his arm. Up close, the gray in his hair showed. In another year or two he'd look like Dad, he'd look like Willy Jessup, a cotton-top. My hair didn't have as much. Prison life could do that to a person.

He got his pants on and his shoes. The little bit of physical exertion stressed his body and showed by the sweat on his face and his labored breathing. We helped him out to the rental, the sleek black Cadillac STS parked at the fleabag motel conspicuous among all the beater cars driven by sketchers and thieves and people of the night.

We put Noble in the back. Marie got in the front, and I drove. I started up and looked around again for Mack and Bruno, hoping they wouldn't happen in before we got away.

I flipped on the turn signal and waited for westbound traffic before pulling out to make a left.

"Bruno?" Noble said from behind me.

The way he said it, I looked around for my nephew. I continued to pull out across the westbound lanes, waiting for the last few cars to go by eastbound before completing my turn.

Noble yelled, "Bruno!"

Marie yelped like a puppy a split second before I looked to the right where the westbound lanes should've been empty.

The huge truck hit us broadside on Marie's door. Traveling fast. Traveling far too fast.

The whole world exploded.

The airbag deployed and slapped my face. Broke my nose. The big Caddy spun. The powder from the airbag shoved out all the oxygen and made it impossible to breathe.

In the same instant:

Glass shattered.

Tires screeched.

The sound of rending metal on asphalt pierced the havoc.

I fought the airbag, shoved it down in time to see through Marie's mangled side window. This time a second, smaller truck, still a full-sized half ton, smashed into Marie's door. The intrusion from the already damaged door shoved her all the way over into my lap.

The Caddy spun again.

"*Marie? Marie?*" I spoke the words in my head. They wouldn't come out audibly no matter how hard I pushed on them.

How could she be all the way over on me? What happened to her seatbelt? What happened to her airbag? My head lolled to the side. I tried my best to stay conscious and failed.

* * *

"Bruno? Bruno?"

I rose up out of the blue-black darkness to find Mack's face close to mine. My head hurt something fierce. I'd banged it good on the support beam during the impact from the second truck. My ears rang and I could hardly hear Mack at first. The bright blue sky haloed his head. The siren in the background grew louder, then faded away.

I tried to sit up. A hand on each shoulder pushed me back down on the gurney. I grabbed Mack's hand. "Marie?"

"Bruno. Bruno, listen to me, they transported her to the school. That was her ambulance that just left."

"Huh? Her ambulance. To a school? What're you talkin' about?"

But I knew. I'd been a street cop too long. I knew how all this worked.

"They're taking her to an airship. They cleared the school grounds for an airship. They're airlifting her to the hospital."

My adrenaline surged. I tried to rise up. Mack and the paramedic leaned in, put all their weight on me. "Take it easy," Mack said.

"Sir, I think you have a concussion," the black-haired paramedic said. "You need to lie perfectly still. We need to immobilize your neck."

I grabbed him by the throat. "Let me up, now."

He choked and clawed at my hand.

"Better do what he says," Mack said. "I've seen him like this before. We let him up or he'll take us all on. And the bad part is that he'll probably win even in his condition."

I let go.

The paramedic choked and coughed. "Bullshit. Bullshit. I'm filing charges. He can't do that."

Mack whispered in his ear.

"All right," the paramedic said, "but he's gonna sign off AMA, against medical advice." The paramedic's features smeared together in a mess of eyes, a nose, and a mouth and then returned to focus.

"I'll sign and take full responsibility," Mack said. He showed him his sheriff's star, the gold blurred in my vision. I did have a concussion, no doubt about it.

Mack sighed and helped me to my feet. The world swirled out of control in an unholy vortex that threatened to pull me down to the earth's core. I didn't have time for the out-of-control part. I needed full control to get to Marie. I had to get to Marie.

Mack put my arm over his shoulder. I closed my eyes tight for a long minute and then opened them. It helped. We moved through the people, the LAPD officers, the firemen, and around the tow truck backing to hook up to the wreck.

I froze, stopped us dead.

The wreck sat a few feet away. Not one square inch of smooth metal remained on the sleek new Cadillac that we'd only minutes before been riding in. The passenger-side intrusion—Marie's side—reached across almost to the inside of the driver's door. How could that be? That had been where Marie sat.

"Mack, where's Marie?"

"I told ya, pal, she's on her way to the hospital."

Nausea rose up. I couldn't hold it. I threw up. Sno Ball and chocolate milk spattered the glass-strewn asphalt. My knees went weak. I wilted to the ground. Mack eased me down.

"Get that gurney back over here, now."

They lifted me onto the gurney, immobilized my neck with sandbags on each side, my forehead taped, my arms and chest strapped down. Someone started an IV.

"Mack?" My voice came out in a horse rasp. My eyelids screwed down tight to keep out the violent spinning world.

"I'm here, buddy."

"Come closer."

I opened my eyes. He came into view, his face close to mine.

"Don't let them . . . I mean, I don't care about me, but don't let them figure out who Marie is, how she's—"

"You trust me, Bruno?"

I tried to nod and couldn't. "You know I do," I said.

His lips close to my eyes, he said, "Then listen to me when I say, you have nothing to worry about. No one, I mean no one, is going to get at Marie, not the bad guys and not the good guys, no one. You hear me? You rest easy, pal, I got this."

They put me in the ambulance, slammed the doors, and turned on the siren.

"Mack," I said over the siren.

"I'm here, Bruno." Mack came back in my field of view.

"Noble? What happened to Noble?"

"They got him, buddy. They got your brother."

CHAPTER FORTY-SEVEN

THE HOSPITAL PERSONNEL checked and rechecked my vitals, shipped me down to x-ray, and brought me back to the ER. Wires ran out from my open shirt to a machine that beeped in time with my heart. The IV helped clear away the nausea and bring back a semblance of control. I wouldn't regain complete control until they unstrapped me and took off the tape binding my head to the board. The headache remained constant and began to feel as if I'd always had it, a resident now not easily evicted.

They dumped me in a curtained ER slot and left me, pending the x-ray results. I couldn't let up on my focus, and kept Marie's smile, the twinkle in her eyes during our wedding, foremost in my mind so the ringing headache wouldn't take over the world.

Maybe being strapped and taped worked in my favor; it suppressed the overwhelming anxiety, the need to be with Marie, and kept me from causing a scene. The image of the crumpled Cadillac wouldn't leave me alone. All of that force, all of that energy directed at Marie's door caused me to shiver. Grief and worry started to take a backseat to anger, and worse, the need to get even. I tried to justify the thoughts of revenge by masking them in the pretense of protecting my wife from further hazard. You cut off the head of a snake and the snake dies. Some snakes would lose their heads over this. I knew that much for damn sure.

I couldn't see anything but the ceiling. My nose throbbed and, from what I could see of it, had swollen up double, making it more difficult to breathe.

A police radio moved down the long room, coming closer. I tried to thrash about to force some wiggle room, to loosen the bindings, but it was useless. The police radio came in close, stopped not ten feet away, and stayed.

Maybe the cop wasn't there for me. Maybe he had brought in a drunk driver. Maybe—ah hell, who was I trying to kid?

A voice said, "Hold it right there, kid. What business do you have here?"

A guard. The cop stood guard at my bed. Now it no longer mattered whether I got loose or not.

"It's okay, I'm this guy's nephew."

"Sorry, my orders are no one gets close to him."

From off down the way, Mack yelled, "He's okay." His voice was a welcome comfort.

What the hell? Mack knew about the police guard and he could dictate to the cop who gets to have access and who doesn't?

The curtain rustled.

"Is that you, Bruno?" I couldn't see. "Come closer."

Bruno's face came into view over the top of my broken nose.

"How's Marie? Did they tell you how Marie's doing?"

"I'm sorry, Uncle, about the accident. Aunt Marie, I think—"

"What? Tell me."

He took a step back. "Take it easy. They won't say anything. I don't think it's that bad, though."

"How do you know? Wait, do you have a knife?"

"Yeah, sure."

"Cut me loose."

"Not a good idea, Uncle, not until they get the x-ray back. You could have a broken neck or something."

"Cut me loose, damn you."

"No."

I took deep breaths to calm down.

"What about my kids?" Bruno asked. "I'm scared. What's going to happen to my kids?"

What an insensitive ass, not thinking about his awful situation. "I'm sorry. I'm just worried about Marie and didn't think about the other problem. It was stupid of me."

The kids—they needed to come first.

"What are we going to do?" he asked.

"They have Noble now, so I don't know what's gonna happen. We lost what we had to negotiate when they took him." Even that sounded insensitive, poor Noble. Noble, this kid's father.

"What do you think's going to happen?"

"I don't know," I lied. I had a pretty good idea. "Come on," I said, in a lower tone so the cop couldn't hear. "Cut me loose."

"Not gonna happen."

"I have the card from the lady on the pier. Cut me loose, and I'll call her, and we'll see what's going on."

Bruno came closer. Nothing wrong with my hearing—his footsteps, the light swooshes of his clothing, came in loud and clear. His hands went in my pockets, searching for the card.

"Hey? Hey?"

He found it.

"Don't," I said. "Don't *you* call them."

"Why?"

"Think about this, Bruno. Who's better qualified to talk to these people, me or you?"

His hands went to work and freed my left hand from the soft restraints. With a snick of his knife, he cut the tape binding my head as I untied my other hand. I sat up, taking it slow and easy. I didn't want the nausea to return. My swollen nose forced pressure up into my face. The tube for the IV snaked over to the IV tree. I'd leave that for now. I plucked off the EKG leads and let the wires hang off the bed. My head pounded worse in the sitting position.

The nurse, a harried Hispanic gal, came in to check on the alert from the EKG going silent. "You shouldn't be sitting up." She scowled at Bruno for releasing me. She took hold of my shoulder and tried to ease me back down. I didn't let her move me an inch. "You have something for this headache?"

She gave up and took a step back. "I can give you some aspirin, but you're not going to get a painkiller until the doctor sees the x-rays." She turned and left to get the aspirin.

My nephew had changed his clothes. He no longer wore the gangster attire familiar on the street where he lived, clothes he wore to blend in, to not draw undue attention. Now he dressed like a yuppie college student with bleach-faded denim pants and an in-style button-up shirt cut to fit tight. He looked good this way, like someone who had his life together. And he did, until his father decided to intervene with one of the dumbest moves I'd ever heard of.

I stuck out my hand. He handed me the card. I no longer needed the card; I'd memorized the number. I just didn't want him to have continued access. He gave me his phone.

I dialed.

Bruno moved in closer and put his head next to the phone.

The woman picked up on the first ring. She spoke cool and collected. "Hey, you've got a big problem, ass-wipe, and it's too late to come sniveling to me about it. You had your chance."

She hung up.

I sat there, stunned.

What would happen to Rebecca and Ricardo now?

CHAPTER FORTY-EIGHT

I REDIALED AS I watched Bruno. His expression showed no emotion until I looked in his eyes; they pleaded for relief from his agony.

I'd never met the children, but felt as if I knew them just from visiting their home. Seeing the pictures Bruno had framed and spread about the house. Seeing their toys and the Crayola drawings on the wall, drawings of stick figures and dinosaurs and trees and of the house they lived in. The same house I grew up in. And of course, the cotton-top picture of Dad.

How had this whole mess gotten so screwed up?

The woman answered and said nothing.

"You have my brother," I said. "Now do what's right and give me the kids."

Saying the words helped their meaning to sink in even more. Noble, at that moment, sat before tormentors, strapped to a chair as they tried to get *blood from this turnip*. Noble's own words.

She didn't answer for a long beat. "What are you talking about? We don't have your brother. You no-showed in Lancaster, in Pear Blossom. You're in deep shit, my ape-brained friend."

My breath caught for a moment and then I realized: of course they would deny it. They planned to bury Noble out in the desert after they got the information, or tortured him to death trying. The end result was the same. They just wanted to cover their tracks now for limited liability in future death-penalty charges—kidnap, torture, and murder.

"You didn't show up to the meet. You're not a man of your word. And now you're trying to delay by saying you no longer have your brother."

"Don't play games with me. You rammed our car on Sunset out in front of our motel *and* you took Noble."

She said nothing.

"Come on," I said. "Quit yankin' my chain. We're in the hospital right now. And you're the ones who put us here. You don't believe me, you can check it out. I know you have your informants in the police, so check it. Check out the accident, too, you'll see I'm tellin' the truth."

I had to play their game, pretend they didn't take Noble until I had a chance to figure the angles. There had to be an angle here; I just couldn't get at it through this ringing headache. And if by some unfortunate circumstance, if fate had intervened unannounced and "The Don" Brodie and the crazy woman didn't have Noble, then once they checked out the story, they'd know we didn't show up in Lancaster for good cause.

I couldn't think of any other reason why they'd say they didn't have Noble.

I slid off the edge of the bed and stood.

I hadn't been thinking clearly. The three cops, the deputies who came into the hotel room, had wanted Noble as well. Would they go as far as ramming a car with two separate trucks? Risk killing the occupants, one of whom was the target they'd come for? I needed time to ponder it.

"Well," she said, "if you don't have your brother, then there isn't anything else to talk about, is there?"

Bruno leaned away and took the phone with a yank. "Wait. Wait, I have the diamonds," he said into the phone. "Don't hurt my father. You can have the diamonds, I don't want 'em. I want my family back safe. I'll give 'em to you for my kids and for my father."

I looked on, my mouth sagging open. I didn't know which would be worse—if he really had the diamonds, or if he had the guts to bluff like that. He did have my brother's blood, but still . . . he'd just thought awful fast and made a dangerous play without considering the fallout. I moved over to listen. Bruno let me and didn't even flinch.

The woman said nothing for a long moment, then, "Who is this?"

"Bruno Johnson. You have my father. You have my children, Ricardo and Rebecca."

"Why should I believe you?"

"My dad told me where the diamonds were hidden. He told me in case something happened to him. I guess he was right—something did happen to him. You happened to him. I got 'em and don't want 'em, not if I can trade them for my family."

"Prove it. Give me some details, tell me where you got them from."

"My dad hid them in a green Folgers coffee can that was rusted through when I dug it up from under the porch at our house on Nord."

"How many are there?"

"I don't know."

"You're lying."

"Seven hundred and fifty two-carat diamonds in a purple Crown Royal sack in a rusted-out Folgers coffee can under the porch."

How did my nephew have all of that detailed information? My mind spun around the pain and locked in all on its own. When Marie and I first entered my old house on Nord, Bruno stopped reading a novel, walked in the kitchen, and put the book on top of the old Amana refrigerator. And this was before I knew of the existence of *A Noble Sacrifice*.

The crazy woman on the phone hesitated. "Okay, I'll call you back with the location—"

"No," my nephew said. "No more bullshit. If you want the diamonds, if you really want them, you bring me my family right now. Same place as before. In two hours." He clicked off and put the phone in his pocket.

He picked up on things quickly, handled the call like a pro.

He looked at me, his expression still blank. "You coming, Uncle?"

"I have to find out about my wife," I said. "Bruno, do you have the diamonds?"

"Hell, no. What, you fall down and hit your head or something?" He grinned at his inappropriate joke. "No, I don't have them," he said. "The conversation you had with that crazy woman wasn't going anywhere. I thought I'd give them something to think about and at the same time give us some wiggle room."

Man, this kid even talked like me. "You really only twenty years old?"

"Twenty-one next March, and in June I want to attend the Sheriff's Academy."

"Come closer and let me look in your eyes when you say it."

"If you knew me better, you'd know I never lie."

He did as he was asked and came closer. His eyes were green, unlike Noble's brown.

"I swear to Pete I don't have them," he said. "Never did."

His words shook me a little. That was Dad's expression: "Swear to Pete." My nephew could only know the words and syntax from contact with my father, Bruno's grandfather. Bruno's words reminded me that Dad had known all along about Noble and his family outside prison, a secret that hurt. Why had he not told me? Why didn't anyone tell me?

Sure, why would they tell me? I'd been the one who didn't believe in my own brother. I'd also been the guy who pistol-whipped him and sent him to prison for the rest of his natural life. It made perfect sense. Why would they want me around?

CHAPTER FORTY-NINE

BRUNO EASED OFF his intensity. "So," he said, "if these guys want something we don't have, then there's nothing we can do but bluff. It wasn't that big of a leap. You would've done the same if you hadn't been in that car accident and if you weren't so worried about Aunt Marie."

His words made a hell of a lot of sense.

He watched me close and said, "What do you think?"

"I think that woman on the phone didn't deny having your dad and tacitly agreed to return him. I think your story, all those details, convinced her. You did a great job, kid."

I pulled out the IV and bent my arm up in case of a bleeder.

"What are we going to do next?" he asked. "We have two hours."

On the other side of the curtain, Mack came up and spoke to the uniformed LAPD officer standing guard. "Hey, man, could you go down there and stand by that doorway?"

"Sure."

"Thanks. Keep your eyes open, these guys are highly motivated."

What guys? What kind of scam had he set in play? Mack could never play by the rules. He'd been thoroughly corrupted by Robby Wicks and sometimes preferred to play in the gray area even when it was unnecessary. He liked the added threat level.

Mack pulled the curtain aside, entered, and pulled the curtain closed, as if the thin material had the ability to muffle all sound to those who wanted to listen. He'd changed out of his uniform pants and black work boots and now wore denim pants, a long-sleeve blue chambray shirt—his favorite look—and dark-brown leather boots. His blond hair, cut in a flattop, was two weeks overdue for a tune up. Not like him to look scruffy, but working the jail—a concrete cave with the six percent of the country's antisocial population—tended to wear away self-discipline.

"Looks like you're feeling better," Mack said. "Ooh, that nose looks like it hurts."

"How's Marie? Is she in surgery?"

Mack looked uncomfortable. "Bruno?"

"Mack, tell me."

"She's fine."

"Bullshit, you're lying. How can she be fine? I saw the car. You saw the car. How can she be fine? They airlifted her. So don't bullshit me. Give it to me straight."

"They airlifted her as a precaution. And as for the car, sure, now it's nothing but a hunk of scrap. It used to be a top-of-the-line, late-model Caddy. That car had state-of-the art crumple zones to absorb the transferred energy from the impact. It had side airbags and seatbelts. No, she's shook up, no doubt about that, but she's gonna be fine. I swear to you, she's gonna be fine. She can't be moved for a while, though. Maybe not even for a couple a weeks."

I wanted to believe him, I did. I just couldn't get the image of the Cadillac out of my head, all of that twisted metal. The thought of how my wonderfully soft Marie came in violent contact with her door and the huge truck on the other side of it traveling at high speed—that's what scared the hell outta me.

I missed her.

The anger returned, stronger now. I started to believe Mack a little at a time, which automatically moved me on to what needed to be done next. I'd get the children back first then—

"Wait," I said. "What are you talking about? You said she couldn't be moved for a while. *Two weeks*? If she's okay, why can't she be moved? What's going on, Mack? Tell me now."

"Take it easy, Bruno."

More of his words flooded back. "Airlifted as a precaution? Come on, Mack?"

He took a step back, pulled the curtain open. "Hey, Doc, can you help me out here?"

We waited. I tried to control my rapid breathing. The pounding headache ramped up a notch. Why call a doctor? What could the doctor tell me that Mack couldn't? He wanted the doctor to give me a sedative to calm me down. A sedative meant bad news, the worst. I stepped over to him, grabbed his shirt, and yanked him in close as my anger continued to rise.

He smiled. He shouldn't have smiled. I punched him in his lying, smug face. He stumbled backward and regained his balance before he fell all the way to the floor. The blue-uniformed LAPD officer ran in, baton out and at the ready.

Mack held up his hand. "Hold it, hold it. It's okay. I got this. Go back to your post." He swiped at his bloodied mouth with the back of his hand.

The officer hesitated. He looked at me standing feet spread, hands balled into fists, ready to go to war, then looked back at Mack.

"I said it's okay," Mack said again.

The officer turned and went back to the doorway where he'd been standing watch. From behind him came a large black woman dressed in blue scrubs too tight for her legs. She had a round, flat face and sympathetic brown eyes. "What in the world's going on here? This is a hospital, not some sort of gladiator school."

Mack again wiped the blood from the corner of his mouth. "Bruno, I didn't tell you because I didn't think you'd believe me. Go ahead, Doc."

The doctor came up close, put a hand on my arm. "Come on now, honey, you need to be lying down. It's confirmed: you have a mild concussion and that nose of yours needs to be set."

"No, tell me. What's he talking about?"

"I just walked in here. I have no idea what you all are talking about."

"My wife's condition. How is she? Why does she have to stay in the hospital if she's all right? What's wrong?"

"Bruno?"

I looked over at Mack.

"She's pregnant, you big lummox."

"Pregnant?"

My head whipped around back to the doctor, who nodded. She held onto my arm as I slowly backed up to the gurney and sat on the edge before my knees gave out entirely. "Pregnant?"

"That's right," the doctor said. "And all of the tests we were worried about came back negative. The baby's fine. We want to keep her in the hospital because of the severity of the accident. Just to be sure, you understand."

Mack came over to the gurney, his fingers gently probing his split lip. "Marie told me that you didn't know. She made me promise that I wouldn't tell you. I promised her, Bruno. She said *she* wanted to tell you." His voice started to rise. He pointed his finger at me. "But, oh no, you wouldn't just take it easy until we could get you in there to see her. No, no, Bruno the Bad Boy Johnson was going to bring the whole place down, stick by stick."

That's why he'd called the doctor in to tell me, so he could keep his promise to my wife. And my boneheadedness forced him to tell me anyway.

"Pregnant? She's really pregnant?" The word turned alien in my mouth. I'd not thought about starting a family with Marie—not ever. Stupid, though, why wouldn't I? At the wrong end of forty, almost fifty, with Marie twelve years younger, I'd just taken it for granted that a family at my age never entered the equation. I shivered. And loved her all the more, if that were possible.

"That's right, buddy boy." Mack held out his hand. I took it and shook. He pulled me into a hug so hard I couldn't breathe. "Congratulations."

He let go.

"I need to see her, Mack. I need to see my wife right now."

CHAPTER FIFTY

WITH THE CONCUSSION, the doctor wouldn't let me move around unless I traveled in a wheelchair; she insisted on it. She'd have preferred that I stayed in bed. No chance on that happening.

Mack relieved the orderly of wheelchair duty. Bruno followed behind, along with the rookie LAPD cop. Bruno quizzed him on the difficulty of getting through the LAPD Academy. Once Bruno told the cop he worked at the Lennox Sheriff's Station, and that he planned to attend the Los Angeles County Sheriff's Academy in Whittier, the cop opened up and they talked non-stop. Bruno reminded me of the excitement and the adventure of looking forward to a career in law enforcement. I only hoped he never ran into a supervisor like Robby Wicks.

Mack moved us down the long hall toward the elevator. "Sorry," I said, "about the lip."

"You really have trust issues, pal, you know that? You always have."

"That little love tap I gave you wasn't a trust issue. It was paranoia and fear that the worst had happened." I lowered my tone. "Hey, what the hell's going on? Is that cop here as a custody officer so, once I'm cleared medically, he's gonna transport me to the jail ward?"

We came to the elevator and stopped. With the cop so close, Mack said nothing. We waited for the car. The doors slid open.

Mack held up his hand. "Can you guys take the next one? I need to talk to my witness." Bruno and the cop didn't seem bothered by the request and continued their conversation. Mack wheeled me in. The doors closed. He pressed 4.

"Your witness?" I said.

"Yeah, it was a little dicey there on the timing, with Marie en route to the hospital by air and me on the ground keeping you from assaulting the paramedic. The paramedic, I might add, who was only trying to help you. But I pulled it off. And I don't mind saying I'm kinda proud of my little caper."

"Pulled what off? What little caper?"

"I managed to get a call into Wong before the traffic investigators and the hospital needed your names."

"What's Wong have to do with this?"

"I told you, he's working the Coffin Dancer investigation on that task force. I told him I came across two very important witnesses in that investigation."

"The Coffin Dancer investigation?" The name sounded familiar, but the headache kept me from pulling it up.

"Come on, old man, you're better than this."

I smiled. "Just tell me, asshole."

"You know, the Los Angeles Consolidated Freight and Design, the LACF and D. The case agent on the task force about pissed himself when I told 'em I had two wits that could bring down the entire organization."

"You did what? We can't do that. I mean Marie and I don't know a thing about that investigation." I put my hand to my head. The pain worsened as I tried to wrap my brain around what he'd just said. What would happen once the case agent found out Mack lied? Mack's little house of cards would implode, with Marie and me on the inside. We'd catch the brunt of the fallout from the angry investigators.

"Of all the dumbassed things to do," I said.

The elevator dinged far too loud. The doors opened. Mack wheeled me out.

"Not really," he said. "You're now both in the witness protection program under John and Jane Doe."

"Mack, that can't work for very long, and when the wheels come off this little plan of yours, you're gonna be in the grease again."

He pushed me down the hall. "You're not thinking this thing through," he said. "Sure, there's some risk, but we've been there before and in a lot worse. This isn't as bad as you think it is. Once the whole thing works out, you and Marie just melt into the background and disappear. Everyone will be too interested in the big fish we caught and not even think about you two."

"Enlighten me, please. Not as bad as I think, what the hell? How much worse could it be?"

"Hey, you and your pregnant wife aren't in custody, are you?"

"I'm sorry, yes, thank you for that. I should be more grateful. It's just this damn headache. Go on, tell me the rest."

We passed nurses and a janitor in the immaculate white hallway.

"Bruno junior's kids got snatched and you shouldn't be working this without the help of law enforcement. You know that."

He was right, of course. I'd put Marie's safety above the kids' and shouldn't have. What had I been thinking? What he said now made so much more sense. If it worked.

Wait. I'd missed something, a key piece hiding back under the throbbing pain. There had been a reason, a contributing factor not to bring in the cops. Yes, yes, Bruno said the LACF and

D had influence with the cops. The three deputies who'd given us the bum's rush back in the hotel room proved it. Unless, of course, those three had been bought off by Don the Don Brodie. Nine million could buy a lot of folks—even a lot of cops. Sure, that made sense. Those three, which included Blue Suit, could be working for the crazy woman from the Santa Monica pier.

"This isn't such a good idea," I said.

"Just listen a minute, would ya? The LACF and D task force has been up on these guys for months now, spent tens of thousands of dollars in man hours. They've identified some of the players, but haven't been able to hang a predicate crime on them, at least not one to support a 182, a conspiracy indictment. From the mid-level up, no one touches the dope or the money. It goes against every other dope conspiracy I've ever been involved in. No one understands how it's really working, and they're scared to death this method's going to spread throughout the U.S. They have the street-level guys doing all the handling. Those street guys screw up, they get taken outta the box, sent to the can, and replaced. It's as simple as that. Normally you can grab the midlevel guys and at least have a chance at flipping them for one of the top, if not the top guy. Not now, not the way this thing is set up. They even have cutouts like spies use."

"And we're working a kidnap," I said, "that involves narcotics and big money."

"Exactly."

The fog cleared a little more, the pain eased up. "Wait, wait, they've been on them for months now, right? Do they have video of the kids? Do they know where the kids are?"

He stopped at room 410. Another blue uniform stood watch outside Marie's door, a young kid without much experience. Probably a nice guy, but he didn't inspire confidence, not with

Marie's safety involved. Even so, I never thought I'd take comfort again in a cop being so close by.

"Wong's getting with the case agent as we speak," Mack said, "to go over the surveillance notes. What are the odds, though? Probably not very good, but there's still a chance. We'll know in another thirty minutes or so. The best part about this whole thing . . . go on and guess what the best part about this whole mess is."

Based on his huge smile, I said, "You've been transferred from the jail TDY to the task force."

"Bingo, buddy boy. All because of you. I owe you for that."

He seemed to forget that I'd been the one to get him busted back from detective on the Violent Crimes Team to jail deputy working graveyard at MCJ. He also got the hell kicked out of him and spent four weeks in the hospital because of my last little caper. No, we weren't even, not by a damn sight. I still owed him big.

"Here, help me up. I can't be wheeled in to see my wife, not like this. I gotta go in standing on my own two feet."

CHAPTER FIFTY-ONE

I EASED THE door open, half-afraid of what I'd see, and at the same time I wanted to rush in and scoop her up in my arms.

Marie sat propped up in bed, her eyes closed. The right side of her face bulged with a white bandage. Her right arm lay across her chest in a cast. The doctor said nothing about a broken arm. I ached inside over her injuries. I'd been the cause of this.

She looked like a bird with a broken wing. A large lump rose up in my throat and tears burned my eyes.

I wanted to hold her, protect her, something I'd failed to do even after my promise in the motel room. The anger returned and tried its best to chase out the tenderness. I gritted my teeth and walked over to the bed. Who'd done this to her, done this to our unborn child?

I stood at the edge of the bed and looked down at her, the way her chest gently rose and fell. Her beauty radiated no matter what the environment, no matter what the circumstance. Not even a semitruck broadside on her car door could subdue beauty like this.

Her eyes opened. She smiled, a weak, semi-sedated one, but still a smile just for me, a smile that warmed me all over.

She raised her good arm and extended her hand. I made the final step forward and took her hand.

"Hey, baby?" she said, her voice little more than a rasp. "Ah, Bruno, your poor nose."

I waved my hand. "It's just a nose. "You though, scared the hell outta me. Look at you. Jeez, Marie . . . I thought . . . I thought I'd lost you."

"Don't be silly, I got hurt worse when I fell off Alonzo's skateboard." She smiled again at her little white lie, her voice getting stronger as she shook off the sedative.

I moved in closer and glanced down at her tummy. She caught the look and lost her smile.

"I guess they told you, then? I'm sorry. I wanted it to be a special time for us. I didn't know, Bruno, not until they told me here at the hospital. I guess I shouldn't have been drinking. Who would've thought, huh? Babe, you're going to be a father." She scooted to the side and patted the bed. "Come on, big fella, climb on up here."

I didn't think it a good idea, but what she wanted overrode all good sense. I'd do anything for this woman, anything she asked of me and without hesitation. I gently crawled up in the bed beside her. "I don't want to hurt you."

"Don't be silly."

She tried to hide a grimace as I scooted in between her and the bedrail. Her body radiated a heat I'd never experienced coming from another person, and in a strange way I craved it.

I hoped she'd not taken a fever, contracted some kind of infection in the hospital. I gently kissed her cheek, the side without the bandage, and her neck and her ear. "I'm sorry," I said. "I didn't see the truck."

"Shush. No harm done."

"No harm done? What about that poor car?"

She giggled. It warmed my heart.

"I can't stay long, I have something I have to do."

Marie came out of the violent assault on the car well enough, better than expected under the circumstances. Thanks to the great design and engineering of American-made cars. Now she'd be safe in the hospital with a cop standing guard outside her door. And I could go do what had to be done without worrying about her.

We lay silent for a long few minutes.

"I need to look at you," she said.

I moved around to look her in the eyes. "How are you with this?" she asked. "I mean, with the baby? I didn't want it to be this way. I didn't."

She didn't wait for my answer. I knew her well enough. She was hesitant to tell me right off about the baby out of an unwarranted fear I wouldn't want a child.

"I wanted us to go for a long walk on the beach when I told you," she said, trying to keep the sob out of her voice. "I'm sorry it didn't work out that way. I know you're concerned about your age, Bruno, and you shouldn't be. I know we never really talked about this. Bruno, darling, tell me honestly, how you feel about this? Please tell me."

"You can't be serious. You honestly don't know how I feel about this? Marie, this is the happiest day of my life. Having a child with you . . . I can't begin to describe the joy it brings." This time I had difficulty getting the words out, as they clogged up in my throat and got choked off.

Her chin quivered. Tears welled in her eyes and spilled down her cheeks.

"You sure, Bruno? You really sure?"

I leaned over and kissed her long and deep. Her good arm came up around my neck. She pulled me down in a hug that I wanted never to end. She tried her best to pull me right into her, to meld us into one person.

We broke only to come up for air. She laughed and laughed, her total relief evident. My poor sweet little girl had worried about me, what I'd think.

I took up the sleeve to her hospital gown and wiped my eyes. "I don't know why you put up with me," I said. "I've turned into some kind of weepy old man."

Marie nodded. "Yes, you have, but you're my weepy old man."

"Thanks. This was the moment when you're supposed to lie to me about being old."

She brought her hand up to her mouth to speak into the mock recorder. "Subject continues to need constant reinforcement to bolster his . . ." She turned the mock recorder my way for me to speak. " . . . his what?"

"Oh, you want to play doctor now?"

She held up her finger. "Bruno—" She tried and failed to keep from smiling. "Now, I've just been through a serious accident."

I raised my hands in the air like claws of a monster. "Suddenly, I'm feeling kinda hungry."

She shrieked like a child and I gently tickled her. We enjoyed the moment, the pure release with nothing at all left to interfere.

Then it ended and I froze. An ugly image crept in unbidden to ruin the happy moment. I tried to keep it out and couldn't. The cop in me wouldn't let me keep it out. The image of Blue Suit in our hotel room, groping and threatening my wife, my wife who carried our child—the image wouldn't leave me alone. He still lurked somewhere out there, still a threat, his act unanswered. And it needed to be answered.

"Bruno? What's the matter? You just went someplace."

"No, I'm right here."

"What were you just thinking about?"

I pasted on my biggest smile. "With ten children at home," I patted her tummy, "this little girl's going to make eleven. I think we'll call her Marjory, if it's okay. Marjory, after my mother."

"Is that right? So you've already decided this child's gender?"

"Yes, a beautiful little girl who'll most definitely take after her beautiful mother."

"I don't mean to be contrary, but this boy's father is so virile there isn't any chance at all for a girl. And we shall name him after your father, no arguments."

I started to get up.

"Where are you going?"

"Rebecca and Ricardo."

"Right now? You're going to meet with those people right now?"

I slid off the bed, stood at the edge. "That's right."

She held up her hand. I took it. "Bruno?"

"Yes, my love."

"I know that look in your eyes, that place you just went to in your mind, and it's not one that I like. You know that. That look says you're going to burn down the world. Please tell me that you're not going to burn down the world, please. Promise me, Bruno."

"I promise I won't burn down the world."

"Bruno Johnson, you're going to be a father and our son's going to need his father to stick around. You get those two poor little children back safe, and then you get your ass back here, you understand?"

"Yes, dear."

CHAPTER FIFTY-TWO

MACK WAITED FOR me outside Marie's room. "You ready?" he asked.

I put a hand on his shoulder and pulled him away from the blue-uniformed LAPD officer. "You sure you're okay with this cop here watching over Marie while we're gone?"

"What kinda paranoid are you, buddy? This isn't some kinda cheap horror movie. These guys are pros. Relax, would ya? Come on, I sent your nephew down to wait for us by the car."

"What about those three deputies that assaulted us back at the hotel? Do you call them professionals, too? What if one of them comes here and flashes a badge, says he's the relief for this guy's shift, just to get at Marie?"

Mack lost his smile and walked back to the door, with me close on his heels. "Listen," he said to the cop, "no one, and I mean no one, is to go in there without my approval. You understand?"

"Yes, sir."

"And no one is to relieve you except me and I mean no one, not even your supervisor. You have my number. If your supervisor wants you somewhere else, you call me, and I'll get right back here. Do not leave that woman in there unprotected."

"Yes, sir."

We walked away, headed toward the elevator. "You feel better now?" he said, taking out his cell phone.

"Yeah, thanks, I do. What are you doing? Who are you calling?" We stopped at the elevator to wait for the car.

"You and your damn paranoia. Now you gave it to me like some kinda virus. I'm calling Barbara to come sit with Marie until we finish this thing."

The elevator doors opened and out stepped Barbara Wicks, the chief of police of the Montclair Police Department, Mack's fiancée.

"That was fast." I said.

She wore a brown suit coat over a beige silk blouse and denim pants. She carried a radio in her left hand, leaving her gun hand available. She'd been married to Robby Wicks for years and knew how to handle herself. Soon she'd be married to my friend Mack, an absolutely honorable man and an exact opposite of Robby. I took at least a little comfort in their relationship, their age difference not all that different from Marie's and mine.

Along with Barbara, two Hispanic men dressed in nice suits stepped out.

Mack punched off his cell. "I was calling you. What're you doing here?"

She gave Mack a peck on the cheek. "Marie called me, told me what was going on, said you two boys were off on some sort of chest-thumping expedition. I'm guessing it's to get those two little kids back." She said to Mack, "You should've called me, babe, told me about the accident."

Mack nodded. "I've been a little busy. Ask Bruno, I was just going to call you." He tried to change the subject. "You brought help?" indicating the two Montclair detectives, who'd yet to speak and stood off to the side awaiting assignment.

She pointed a finger up in Mack's face. "You think after only being engaged to you one day, I'm going to let you go off with this bozo"—she hooked a thumb my way—"and get yourself all broken up again? No chance, my friend. I'm goin' with you. I brought my guys, who I trust with my life, to stay with Marie. No arguments." She moved over closer to me. "You got something to say about this, Bruno?"

I held up my hands and took a step back. "No, not a peep. I'm glad you're here."

* * *

With less than an hour left, the four of us met down in the parking lot by the two cars Mack and Barbara had brought, an early model blue Honda Accord and a black Dodge Charger.

We didn't have much time; the drive to Santa Monica Pier would take thirty minutes.

Mack looked right at me when he spoke. "I called in the task force. They're already set up based on the way you said it went down the last time, with you on the pier and the kids down the beach about a hundred yards. We have forty-five detectives and agents on this and have both sides of the pier covered in case these guys decide to get smart and do a change-up." He handed my nephew a purple Crown Royal bag, the bottom rounded with fake glass diamonds.

"Everything looks good," Mack said, his eyes still on me.

I read his demeanor, his tone, and asked, "With one exception, right?"

"Ah, yeah, that's right," Mack said.

"What's wrong?" Bruno asked.

Barbara also watched my expression.

I broke eye contact with Mack and looked at my nephew. "I can only guess, but with all the cops involved, someone's sure to recognize me. So what my good friend here is trying to say is that I have to stay in the car when we get there."

Mack nodded.

Bruno shook the Crown Royal bag, anxious to get moving, anxious to get his children back. "Is that a problem, Uncle? I don't see that as a problem."

"Oh, it's not as far as I'm concerned." I looked from my nephew back to Mack. "This wouldn't also be because you don't want me involved in the takedown, would it? This is my grandniece and nephew who are in jeopardy here."

Barbara smirked. "Bruno, every time you take a hand in something like this, the odds of someone getting shot, run over, or beat to within an inch of their life increases exponentially."

"Hey, come on, that's not true at all." My mind spun back on past capers to offer up an example and couldn't find even one that didn't fit her description. "Dad always said you lay down with dogs, you're gonna get fleas."

"Bruno?" Barbara said.

"Okay, but that's not necessarily a bad thing, right?" I said. I held up my hand to stop them before they could answer in protest. "I have no problem sitting this one out."

It hurt to say it, but the look in Marie's eyes not ten minutes before, when she asked that I not burn down the world, carried too much weight.

Burn down the world, of all things. I never for a moment thought of it that way. When you dealt with violent suspects, what did people think would happen?

My Marie should take up writing like my brother, with those kinds of exaggerations. *Burn down the world.*

"Gimme the rest of it," I said. "The intel you got from the surveillance notes."

Mack looked at my nephew and hesitated, then said, "The task force has video of some of the midlevel guys chauffeuring around two kids. They treated them like their own kids, so they didn't think anything about it. Taking them to McDonald's, the park, that sort of thing. We'll need you to ID the kids in the video, later on for the case prosecution. They also have audio on a conversation with Brodie talking in code. The task force now believes, after finding out the kids were kidnapped, the code links Brodie to these kids. Now they can take the whole top end of the organization down. That is, once we recover the kids and make the arrests."

"Did they take the kids back and forth to any one residence in particular?" I asked. "Did they see Noble?"

"They took them to a motel in Inglewood, by Hollywood Park. No sign of Noble, but it's only been about four hours since the accident when they grabbed him. They're gonna have him in a safe house. Once we take everyone down, someone will roll and tell us where he is. You know how that works. With that much time hanging over their heads, they always roll."

The way Mack talked about the kids—again more his tone than anything else—hit a wrong note with me. I knew Mack too well. "What's going on? What's happened?"

Mack visibly squirmed a little.

"Spill it, Mack."

"Okay, okay, once I told them about what we had going on—"

I cut him off. "Ah, hell, they shortcut it, didn't they?"

"What?" my nephew asked. "What's going on?"

I looked at my nephew. "You don't need a search warrant if there's an exigent circumstance, and kidnapping's the very definition of exigent circumstance."

I looked back at Mack for confirmation.

"Yeah," he said, "the team tried to shortcut this thing to avoid the hostage exchange, and came up empty."

"Ah, shit," I said. "You've got to be kiddin' me."

CHAPTER FIFTY-THREE

"Okay, I don't understand, we're still going to the pier right?" my nephew asked.

"Yes, *you* are. Gimme your car keys."

He didn't argue and handed over his keys. "It's that beat-up gray Toyota Corolla, right over there. Where are you going? What's the matter? Tell me what's going on."

"The task force got greedy," I said. "They wanted to close their case the fast, simple way. They jumped the gun and hit the motel. They came up empty and didn't get the kids. Now that crazy woman with her sniper knows the cops are onto her. That's information they didn't have before. They're gonna change up their game based on that information."

"How do you know that?"

I started walking toward the Toyota. "Because given the same information, that's what I'd do."

He followed along with Mack and Barbara in tow. "You still haven't told me where you're going."

I stopped. "*You* have to play this thing out. You have to go to the pier just like the plan and show yourself." I looked at Mack. "You have your own counter-snipers set up, right?"

He nodded. "Trust me, we're good."

"This is really bullshit, Mack, and you know it." I took a step over, poked him in the chest. "You better take good care of my nephew."

Barbara shoved in between us and stuck her own finger up in my face. "Don't you dare talk to him like that."

I took a breath and tried to calm down. "I'm sorry, you're right. I'm sorry, Mack. You're not the one that screwed this up."

"Uncle, where are *you* going?"

"To get your children back."

"I'm going with you."

"No, kid, you can't, you have to play this thing out. These people have to see you on the pier. It'll give me the time I'll need."

I turned to Mack. "I need a gun."

Before Mack could reply, Bruno reached behind and pulled a blue-steel automatic from his rear waistband. "Take mine."

I took it from him. "After this is over, we're gonna talk about your illegal gun possession." The gun, a Sig Sauer model 226, fit in my hand like an old friend, the same as a hammer would a carpenter. I pulled the mag and checked the slide to make sure a round sat in the chamber. I picked my shirt up and stuck it in my waistband, the metal cold against my belly.

"See what I mean," Barbara said. "No good's going to come from you having that gun."

Barbara leaned up and kissed Mack on the cheek. "I'm going with Bruno."

"What? Just like that, you jump ship?"

"If something happens to him," she said, "do you want to be the one to have to tell Marie about it?"

"You're right. Go."

Barbara and I headed for the car, with Mack and my nephew close behind, going to another car.

Mack said, "Keep in touch by cell."

Barbara grabbed my sleeve. "Come on, let's take mine." I veered toward the Honda and tossed Bruno's keys back to him.

"Not the Honda, this one." She keyed the fob, and the door locks popped on the black Dodge Charger.

I went around the other side and said over the top of the car, "Now, see, I would've thought you'd be driving—"

"I never took you for being gender biased. This is my car, so get over yourself." She got in and started it up. "Where we goin'?"

"Head toward Inglewood."

I punched an address—913 South Prairie Avenue, Inglewood—into the onboard GPS.

Barbara watched as she drove, and she drove fast. The big engine rumbled. "What's that address have to do with this?"

"When I first talked with these people, they tried to set this location as the place for the hostage exchange. Then I changed it to the pier to take away some of their advantage."

"What makes you think this location's gonna have anything to do with it now?"

"Two things. First, Mack said the task force followed these guys to a motel in Inglewood by Hollywood Park. Look . . ." I pointed at the GPS screen "Hollywood Park isn't that far from this address."

"Okay, and second?"

"The woman I spoke to on the pier came off as a solid professional, ice cold, and a psycho for sure, but still in complete control at all times. I don't think she was bluffing about anything. She said she had us all covered with a sniper."

"So then you think this location isn't where the kids are, but it's a location close enough to the kids and close enough to cover the exchange in the parking lot with a sniper, right?"

"It's just an educated guess. Robby would call it a WAG."

Invoking Robby's name around Barbara didn't sit right. It came attached with a big dollop of guilt.

"Yeah," she said, "It's definitely a wild-ass guess, but I'll buy it. What else do we got?" She put her foot on the accelerator and the muscle car shoved me back in the seat.

"We'll have to get there and find this place before the meet on the pier goes down," she said. "What do you think's going to happen at the pier? Why do you think the kids will be at this place in Inglewood and not at the pier?"

"Like I said, it's just a hunch. If I were in their shoes, and knew the cops hit the motel I used to be in, then I'd also know that the cops were going to be all over the meet at the pier. They won't risk taking the kids there. The kids are evidence that proves kidnapping."

"So you think they're going to go through with the meet because, why?"

"They might not show at all. Or they just might lay back and see how the game plays out, how many cops and what kind of cops—county, state, or federal. Information is king, and these guys really know how to use it to their benefit. They have their ace in the hole. They have Noble, who can give them the diamonds, if they push him to push his son. That's what I think's gonna happen if we don't get lucky and find this place first. That's the only reason why I think Noble's still alive."

* * *

Thirty minutes later, we drove past Hollywood Park, or at least where Hollywood Park used to be. I couldn't believe it; the racetrack, a large part of history in the Los Angeles area for the last seventy-five years, no longer existed. I moved to Central America for a couple of years and the world kept on moving along, continuing to evolve, stopping for no one and destroying historical landmarks.

Many years ago, in happier times, Dad took Noble and me to Hollywood Park to watch the horses run. Dad knew a guy who'd let us in through the paddock. A wondrous time of family and friendship, and chili dogs with onion rings and chocolate malts. I'd never lose those great memories, even if the racetrack had disappeared.

I'd also, after my childhood visit, returned once, later in life, chasing the murderer Dewayne Simpkins. Robby and I traced him to the racetrack, where he liked to burn money betting on the ponies—money he attained selling rock cocaine as a midlevel dealer.

"What happened to the track?"

"Boy, you've been out of touch. They closed it and mowed it down. There's going to be houses, a shopping center, and a park. Two hundred and sixty acres of prime real estate. They're going to leave the casino, though, and renovate it.

"Remember that night Robby shot Simpkins right there at the track? Right in the middle of the crowd, no concern at all for his backdrop. Jesus, what a dick. Remember that one?"

"Yes, I do."

She let her eyes leave the road to look over. "That's right, you *were* there." She looked back. "That night, Robby celebrated, drank too much tequila, cooked shark steaks on the barbeque. He always cooked shark steaks after a kill. You weren't there that night at that barbeque. And you were always there, at least for most of those shark nights." She paused, checked the road, and said, "Some of those shark nights were yours." She looked from the road back to me, expecting a reaction.

I didn't oblige her.

"You wanna know what he said that night?" she asked. "He said, 'I gunned that poor slob Simpkins. He died in a *dead heat*. Dead from the heat, get it?' The bastard actually laughed at his own stupid joke over the death of a human being." She shivered. "What a fool I was. What the hell was I thinking? What does that say about me staying so long with that callous, cynical son of a bitch?"

Barbara was obviously dealing with her own ghosts.

I didn't want to defend Robby, not to Barbara. I wanted the conversation just to die all on its own. But that night at Hollywood Park, Simpkins got the drop on me right in the middle of all the folks waiting in the lines at the windows to make their last-minute bets. Simpkins felt no moral obligation for innocent bystanders.

Simpkins grew up in my neighborhood, a bully for sure, but we'd played together just the same.

That night, I spotted him first. He recognized me, knew I'd joined up with the cops. Knew I'd come looking for him for the brutal murder of his girlfriend. I froze for just a second. Not long, just for one second, enough time to remember in a flash our childhood together, the warm days on the swings and then later on the basketball courts. I hesitated long enough for him to grin and pull his gun. I didn't drop the hammer on him, Robby did. Even so, I still felt obligated to make the notification to his parents, one of the hardest things I'd ever done. No shark for me that night.

CHAPTER FIFTY-FOUR

"LOOK," BARBARA SAID. "913 Prairie Avenue is a 7-Eleven. They wanted to make the meet in that shopping center parking lot, right? That wouldn't have been my first choice."

I came out of my funk. "Take a left here on Arbor Vitae. Look, right there, that two-story apartment building, the Langston Arms. Those two-story apartments look right down into the 7-Eleven parking lot at what, about four or five hundred feet away? Those apartments are going to be where they'd have watched the exchange, from that high point, that position of advantage. I don't see anything else close that fits the bill. Yeah, that's going to be it.

"Go down, turn around, come back up, and park on Prairie. We'll walk in." She didn't comment or complain, an ex-felon telling a chief what to do. We parked on Prairie and walked back. I stopped and checked out the back of The Langston. Up top, on the second story in the back, looked like the bedrooms for the units cantilevered over the parking stalls. The stalls were numbered for each apartment, starting with 101. The two hundreds for the upstairs must be around the front. I stopped and looked back down Prairie to get my bearings.

"What?" Barbara asked.

"This is it. Now I'm sure of it. The Lennox Sheriff Station is less than two miles from here. And these guys are smart and would know that if we had to, we'd check every hotel and motel in the area. An apartment is a great idea. It's close to where my nephew Bruno works at Lennox Station, if they wanted to keep a closer eye on him. Yeah, this is it." I adjusted the gun in my belt under my shirt, the metal warmed now, making the weapon a part of me.

We went around to the front. The place looked like an old motel converted to small apartments. Tall wrought iron surrounded the front with two openings for the occupants and visitors to enter and exit. An exterior walkway for the second floor ran the length of the building, with the front doors looking down on the parking area.

"What a great defensive position," Barbara said. "I see what you mean. How are we going to handle it?"

"You're the chief of police, you call the play."

"Don't yank on my dick, Bruno. I'm a desk jockey. It's been years since I played on the street. Throw me out some options here. You've had to have run into something like this in the past."

"I have, and they didn't turn out as well as they should've."

"Shark for dinner?"

"Yeah."

Not so many months ago, Barbara went with me to a door to recover three children—Eddie Crane, Elena Cortez, Sandy Williams—and Marie, who were held against their will. I kicked the door and got a chest-load of buckshot for my trouble. Laid me out flat, knocked the wind out me. The body armor saved my life. The FBI agent with us went next and fell to multiple gunshot wounds. He never made it across the threshold. Barbara, third in our entry stick, did not hesitate. She stepped right into the kill zone and continued to advance as she fired, taking out the suspect, Jonas Mabry. She should've been awarded the medal of valor for her actions, but as chief, the citizens expected nothing less.

No way did she qualify as merely a desk jockey. She possessed that innate street sense that great cops take years to hone to a fine edge. I'd go through a door with her anytime.

"I got an idea," I said. "Come on." I led the way to the end unit. Over the door, a cheap metal sign read "The Manager."

Overhead, a naked yellow bulb illuminated us. I knocked. I didn't have to tell Barbara; she got out her flat badge wallet and had it ready. The door opened. The manager stood back in the shadow created by the rusted-out screen door. "Yeah?" the woman said.

"Police, ma'am. Can we come in and talk with you?"

"Hell, no." She slammed the wood door.

I pulled open the screen.

"Bruno, don't."

I tried the knob. It turned. I barged in.

"Bruno!"

The rail-thin woman had a mop of gray hair. She was dressed in men's pants and a blouse that hung off her boney frame. She backed up, her eyes large. "Wait, wait. You're not cops. Cops don't act like that. I'm calling the real cops right now." She recovered some of her moxie and headed to the old rotary-dial phone on the end table next to her recliner.

I took two long steps over to her, grabbed the phone from her hand, and slammed it down. "Sit." I used two fingers pressed to her forehead to ease her into the recliner.

"You can't do this. I'm reporting you."

"That's fine," I said. "I'll even dial the phone for you after we're done with our business here."

"What is it you want?"

"We *are* the police, and we're here on a life-and-death matter. Two small children have been kidnapped."

She lost her scowl and her expression turned to one of care and concern. She could've almost been someone's grandmother. Almost.

My eyes adjusted to the gloom. The place reeked with five decades of tar from cigarettes. Tar impregnated the walls and curtains and carpet. The walls carried a yellowish tint over the old beige paint. On the end table next to the phone sat three opened Old Milwaukee cans of beer, the tall, 16-ounce cans. Next to the beer sat an overflowing ashtray with ash and butts piled high. Next to that, an open carton of Virginia Slims. Now up close, I smelled the alcohol on her breath and emitting from her pores.

"It's those people in 207, isn't it?"

"I'm afraid so," I said, trying to keep the momentum going with a bluff. "How long have they been renting from you?"

"About two months now. I knew something was fishy with them."

"Why?" Barbara asked.

The woman looked at Barbara. "I guess 'cause I never had problem one out of 'em. Everyone else, they make too much noise. The women use the place as a hot-pillow joint. And damn near all of 'em are late on the rent. Not those folks in 207. They keep to themselves and paid the rent up three months in advance, said they didn't want to be bothered with it every month."

"What do the children look like?"

Her face lit up. "Cute little boy and girl, nice and polite, brought up real good."

"How long have they been here?"

"The children?"

"Yeah, the children."

"No more than a week, I wouldn't think. No, no, maybe four days, now that I think about." She picked up the Old Milwaukie and took a long chug, her throat working hard to carry the load. She brought down the can. "Now that I think about it, there is something strange about 'em."

"What?" Barbara asked.

"Yeah, yeah, I only seen three men with those children, never any women. Never thought about that until just now. That's awfully odd, don't you think?"

I looked at Barbara. "You satisfied?"

"I'm good with it. How we going to do this?"

"By that clock"—I pointed to the wall—"we have about ten minutes before the meet on the pier. We have to hustle before they confirm the cops are involved and make a phone call that will surely cause them to move the kids."

"Why move the kids?"

"Just to be safe. If the cops are involved, they wouldn't leave them in any one place too long. You good with a cold knock?"

"Sure."

"I can't go up there with you." I said. "They've had a look at me already. You get the door open and I'll come runnin'."

"I'll tell them I'm with Social Services and need to get a count on how many are living in their section-eight housing."

"I'll be up on the landing down at this end. You get the door open and give me the signal."

Barbara headed for the door.

"Thanks, ma'am," I said. "Please stay off the phone until we leave the premises."

She nodded as she took another chug of her beer.

I walked out the door, the shopping center in plain view across the street. The layout in relation to The Langston Arms struck me as odd. Outside, I looked down the side along the concrete path in front of all the apartment doors and then looked back at the parking lot to the strip center across the street. I tried to imagine the point of view ten feet up on the second level. I turned and stepped back into the manager's apartment. Barbara stayed right with me and stopped at the threshold.

"Hey," I said, "put that phone down. What'd we just tell you?" The woman had not even waited until her door closed with us outside before she'd started to dial. She fumbled the phone back into the cradle.

"Do the people in 207 have more than one apartment?"

"Ah, yeah, sure, I don't know why I didn't think of that. Forgot all about it. I guess I'm getting old."

I turned back to Barbara. "Come back in and close the door."

CHAPTER FIFTY-FIVE

"Hand me your cuffs," I said to Barbara. She didn't question the reason and gave them to me. I stepped over to the woman. "Turn around and put your hands behind your back."

She turned around. "You can't do this to me. I haven't done anything wrong."

"You sure thought about it, though, didn't you?" I ratcheted the cuffs closed on her wrists, wrists almost too narrow for the cuffs. If she worked at it, she could slip them.

"California Penal Code section 32, aiding and abetting a felony. To wit, kidnapping," Barbara said. "If you'd completed that call, you'd have been exposed to a lot of years in the joint."

"Now, which other apartment did they rent?" I asked.

"207 and 208."

Barbara looked at me. "What if's she's lying?"

I picked up my shirt, showed the woman the Sig nine. "I'm going up there to apartment 208 to kick the door in. If it's the wrong apartment and I shoot the wrong people, or if the crooks we're looking for, tumble to what we're doing because I hit the wrong apartment and someone, anyone, gets hurt, you become an accessory just like my partner explained. You understand?"

"Okay, okay, it's 211. The other one is 207. They offered me a butt-load of cash if I'd call and warn them if the cops came sniffing around. I didn't mean anything by it. I could use the cash, you understand, don't you? I'm justa broken-down old woman living on a pension."

"Now what?" Barbara asked. "We call in a SWAT team?"

I took the woman by the arm and sat her down in the recliner. "What's your name?"

"My friends call me Millie, but you can call me Mrs. Jenks."

"Mrs. Jenks, have you seen an older black man like me go to either one of those apartments? He might be walking kinda funny from an injury."

"No."

"What cars down in the front lot belong to 207 and 211?"

"You can figure that out easy enough. They don't fit in."

"What kind of cars?" Barbara yelled, getting tired of the delay as the clock continued to tick down.

"Take it easy. What a witch, huh?"

"Please tell us," I said.

"It's a gold Lexus and a black Suburban. My old man was in the car business until he fell off the roof drunk one Christmas putting up those damn Christmas lights. I told him, too. I said, 'Herb, we don't need none of those shitty-ass Christmas lights.' He went ahead and put 'em up anyway. The dumbass. God rest his soul."

"What now?" Barbara asked.

"You have a contract tow service to tow unwanted cars in your lot?" I asked Mrs. Jenks.

"Yeah, Bernie's, the number's over there on the wall."

Barbara caught on, went to the wall, taking her cell phone out. She dialed, spoke, told them she needed a Lexus and Suburban towed right away, gave them the address and clicked off. "They're in the area and less than five minutes out."

"Okay, these guys are organized. They won't come out of both apartments, not at the same time. I'm guessing only one guy outta one apartment," I said. "I'll take down the guy who comes out and then clear the apartment he came out of."

"Right. Then I'll take the other one."

"Hopefully, I'll have my guy down and the apartment cleared in time to be right behind you," I said.

Barbara took hold of Mrs. Jenks's phone and ripped the line from the wall. "Sit right there and do not move. You understand me?"

Mrs. Jenks nodded.

We went out the door and over to the stairs that led to the second level, walked halfway up the steps, and waited for the tow trucks.

Barbara reached inside her coat. She pulled her Glock .40 from her shoulder holster and held it down by her leg out of view. "Fell from the roof, my ass," she said. "That woman's poor husband jumped."

Barbara's phone rang. She answered it with her free hand. "Yeah. Yeah," she said. "We're there now and about to find out. We're across the street from, and catty-corner to, 913 Prairie, in Inglewood. Yeah, if you want to start this way. Love you, babe." She clicked off.

"It was a no-show?" I asked.

She nodded, too intent on watching the upper landing to answer verbally.

"If the crazy woman no-showed at the pier," I said, "they could just walk out of these apartments all on their own without the tow truck ruse. Or worse, they might not be in there at all."

"That's the way to think positive."

Minutes later, two tow trucks chugged into the lot, swung

around, and backed right up to the Lexus and Suburban, making plenty of the normal noises associated with snatching a car. I moved up past Barbara and onto the exterior walkway.

Three-quarters of the way down the walkway, the door opened, right about where I'd guess number 211 would be. Out popped the crazy woman from the pier, a towel in her hands, her hair flopping wet against her shoulders, turning her blouse dark. She went to the rail. "Hey, hey, you two fucks get the fuck away from our cars."

I started moving at a fast walk right toward her.

The drivers, having dealt enough times with irate car owners, ignored her and worked faster.

"Did you hear me, you dickwads, leave the cars there. If I have to come down there I'm gonna—"

That lizard part of her brain must've kicked in, told her to look to the side.

She saw me. She didn't look the least bit startled or scared. She sneered at me, then turned and fled into the room to arm herself.

I ran.

Her reaction, the lack of fear, and that sneer scared the hell out of me. This woman could handle herself. My big size-elevens pounded the walkway as I poured on the speed. One second. Two seconds. I reached the open door and went through, diving to the side. Wood from the door frame splintered as slugs thumped into it. A silencer. She used a silenced weapon. I rose up, my gun over the bed.

The woman stood with her feet apart, her arms extended as she brought the gun down to bear.

I fired.

The round caught her in the naval. Probably took out her spine. She wilted to the floor, her eyes still angry. The gun fell and thunked on the cheap linoleum. Her body twitched. She moaned.

No time for anything else. No children in 211. I backed out to the walkway. Two doors down, in apartment 207, Barbara yelled, "Put the kid down. Do it now."

CHAPTER FIFTY-SIX

I DID A quick peek into the apartment and caught a glimpse of Barbara's back in a slight profile, her gun extended, pointed at a man who held a small child. His gun was touching the child's head, Barbara not more than ten feet away.

I stood with my back to the wall, trying to control my rapid breath. Someone would've heard my shot and called the cops. We didn't have much time. I said, loud enough for them to hear, "I'm comin' in." I entered, the gun down by my side.

"Put the child down," Barbara said again.

The man was of average height and weight, with jet-black hair down to his shoulders and intense blue eyes. He held an expensive H&K automatic to Rebecca's head, my grandniece. The man kept his finger on the trigger, the hammer back on the gun, ready to fire. A pound-and-a-half trigger pull, that's all that remained between life and death. A dangerous situation. The worst kind.

"I'm walking out of here," the man yelled. "You're both going to put your guns down and you're going to do it right now."

Ricardo sat on the bed closest to the man and cried.

"Mrs. Wicks," I said to Barbara, "this isn't at all what we thought it was going to be."

She started to turn her head and caught herself. "What the hell are you talking about, Bruno?"

"They're not your standard, everyday dope dealers."

"Drop the guns," the man said. "Now!"

"Bruno, talk to me."

"The Suburban with the tinted windows, the sniper, and the woman in the next apartment, the way she acts and talks. She had a silenced weapon."

"What are you trying to say?"

"They're pros, Barbara, professional operators. This isn't what we thought it was. There's no way out, none."

"Bruno?"

"It's shark for dinner tonight."

She didn't hesitate. She took the shot. The gunshot filled the room with noise and a billow of white cordite.

The man's head kicked backward. The round hit him solid on the cheek just below the right eye, a brain shot. She'd hit him exactly right and shut down all of his motor coordination.

On the way down, the gun came off target, off Rebecca's head, and flopped to the man's right as he wilted dead. His finger remained inside the trigger guard.

The gun in his hand hit the floor.

The gun discharged.

Barbara grunted.

She spun around. I caught her.

"No. No. No," I said. "Barbara? Barbara." I scooped her up and laid her on the bed. The children screamed in terror.

"Bruno," Barbara said, "Get the kids out of here. I'm okay, I'm okay, just get the kids away from all this."

I pulled her jacket open. Her blouse blossomed with red. A

small black hole high on the left abdomen, just below the rib cage, oozed dark blood. Her hand grabbed my shirt. "Get 'em outta of here."

"Stop it and lie still." I applied pressure to the wound with one hand. She groaned. With the other I searched her coat pockets and found her phone and car keys just as the phone rang. I checked the screen.

Mack.

Shit.

I answered it. "Mack."

"Yeah, buddy, you get the kids, okay?" He heard the kids screaming in the background. "What's going on?"

"Mack, I'm sorry, it went down bad, real bad."

"Barbara? Where's Barbara? Let me talk to Barbara."

"Gimme the phone, you horse's ass."

I handed her the phone and, still holding pressure, reached for the landline phone. I dialed 911.

The operator came on. "Police emergency, what are you reporting?"

"Shots fired, officer down. Officer down." I dropped the phone on the nightstand.

Barbara's eyes rolled up and her hand dropped the phone. I picked it up.

"Barbara? Barbara?" Mack yelled into the phone.

"It's me again. I have help responding."

"How bad, Bruno? How bad, damn you."

"Mack, you're going to have to hurry." A lump rose up in my throat and choked me. "Hurry, Mack."

Two cops ran in, guns drawn, blue uniforms from Inglewood who'd been dispatched to the first shot in the other apartment. I dropped the cell phone. "This is the chief of police for Montclair.

She's hit hard." I picked Barbara up, an arm under her legs, and one under her arms. "We need to do a scoop and run if she's gonna make it."

One cop said, "I'll drive." He yelled at his partner, "Stay with these kids, contain the crime scene, and call Centinela hospital, tell em' we're rollin' in hot with an officer down."

He led the way out the door and down the walk. Time ticked by too quickly for Barbara and too slow for us.

"How far is it?"

"We're good, it's only two blocks, not even half a mile. We're good. We're good. Two minutes. We'll have her there in two minutes."

He opened the back door. I got in with her as best I could, my leg half out, the space too tight to do anything about it. "Go. Go. Go."

He took off, driving crazy. The centrifugal force on the first turn leaving the parking area as we entered Arbor Vitae almost pulled us both out the open door. The Inglewood cop spoke on his radio. Two more quick turns, and we entered the driveway to the hospital. He hadn't exaggerated about the distance. He pulled up on the sidewalk, right up to the emergency room door, got out and came around. He helped me get her out. Her head lolled back, her eyes rolled up, only the whites of her eyes visible. Blood soaked her clothes and mine. Lots of blood. Too much blood.

The automatic doors swung open when we approached, just as the nurses came on the run with the gurney. We set her down, too rough, the gurney already moving back the way it had come.

I bent over, hands on my knees, and tried to focus on breathing.

CHAPTER FIFTY-SEVEN

THE INGLEWOOD COP put his hand on my shoulder. "You good here? I have to get back and maintain that crime scene."

"Yeah. Thanks man, you did great."

The young cop smiled, got in his car, backed up, and left. Had he been more experienced, he wouldn't have left me; he'd have secured me as a witness or an involved party.

Down the long drive to the hospital entrance, at the driveway to the street, Mack's midnight-blue Honda skidded, the tires roiled with white smoke. He let off the brake and hit the gas as he made the turn. The Honda bounced violently, its headlights shooting skyward and then back down. The undercarriage banged and sparked. Two LAPD patrol cars in pursuit of him bounced the same way right on his tail. He'd picked up the cop cars in his head-long race from Santa Monica. They thought he was a vehicle-code violator who wouldn't yield.

I stepped out a little from the building to let him see me and waved. He skidded to a stop, got out, and ran up. His eyes took me in, all the blood. I didn't know what to say. I couldn't speak if I wanted to. I pointed to the door to the emergency room as the patrol cars stopped and the uniforms got out, guns drawn. They yelled at Mack to freeze. Mack ran into the emergency room.

The cops came around the open car doors to give chase. I held up my hands, but not too high to raise my shirt to expose the Sig in my waistband. "It's okay, he's a cop. He's a cop. His wife's been shot."

They shouldn't have believed me, but they did. They stopped by me and lowered their weapons. Barbara's blood all over me, my clothes, my hands, some on my face, all of it gave my statement credibility.

The lead cop with sandy-brown hair and wire-framed glasses said, "Is that what that mess is back on the corner?"

"Yeah, it's an OIS, and Mack"—I pointed to the Honda—"that's his wife. She's the chief of police for Montclair. She was working a kidnap. The suspects had one of the children with a gun to her head. His wife took the shot. Took out the suspect, but she caught one too."

"No shit. Is she going to make it?"

I couldn't answer and just shrugged.

They holstered their weapons. Their bodies, pumped up with adrenaline, started to calm down.

"You want me to go in and get his ID for your report?" I asked.

"No, man, he's got enough to worry about." He took out his notepad. "What's his name and where's he work?"

"His name's John Mack, he's a detective with LASO. That's his car, the Honda, and it's registered to him and or his wife, Barbara Wicks."

He finished writing. "Hope it works out for him. Tell him our thoughts are with him."

"I will, thanks. I'd shake your hand but—" I held up my hand, let him get a better look at the blood.

"I understand. You take it easy." They got in their cars and left.

The license plate on Mack's car, once they ran it, would confirm everything I told them.

I didn't like being alone. I sat down on the asphalt with my back to the wall. More cars arrived. Uniformed cops and plain-clothes detectives ran into the ER. I should've gone in as well but couldn't face Mack.

A few minutes later, the double doors to the ER wheezed open. Out came Mack with a stunned expression.

I stood, brushed my hands off. "How's she doin'?"

His eyes refocused on me. "Emergency surgery. They won't tell me anything. What the hell happened, Bruno?"

"They're professionals, John."

"What are you talking about?"

"These aren't street-thug dope dealers we're dealing with. These guys are professionals, probably ex-military, Special Forces or something like that. It doesn't make any sense, but that's the way it is."

"I don't care about all that shit. She was with you, Bruno. What the hell happened? Tell me."

"I am, that's what I'm trying to tell you. Look at their tactics, the sniper, the Suburban, and the silenced weapon. And—"

He grabbed a hold of my shirt and yanked me up close to his face, his breath humid on my skin. "Tell me." His emotions were boiling up and he didn't know which way to turn, what he should do, who to blame.

All of a sudden I wanted him to hit me. I wanted him to put the boot to me and spit on me. I deserved every bit of it. Instead, my old training kicked in, and I gave him the official report. "Barbara and I tracked the children to a possible location, two blocks from here, just down from the corner of Arbor Vitae at Prairie. We believed the suspects would be moving the children at any time and wanted to take them down before they did. We didn't believe there was time to wait for backup. We created a ruse to draw them out. I took one apartment and confronted the suspect I recognized from my prior contact with her on the pier. She fired a silenced handgun at me, and I was forced to shoot her. Barbara—"

"Chief Wicks to you."

"That's right, Chief Wicks went to the second apartment and made contact with a second suspect who had both children. The suspect had a gun to the head of one of the victims. Chief Wicks, fearing for the safety of the children, took the shot. The suspect's gun fell to the floor and discharged, striking Chief Wicks."

"Where were you? Where were *you*, Bruno, exactly?"

"Behind her."

He pulled back and slugged me. I caught it just below the eye. My world lit up. I bounced off the wall. My knees turned weak and I sagged. I kept my hands down at my side. I deserved it and a lot more.

Mack grabbed hold of me and propped me up. "I'm sorry, Bruno. I don't know what's wrong with me."

His emotions bled off just that fast.

"I know you did what you could, you did what was right. I'm sorry," he said. "You got the kids back, that's what counts. That's what Barbara would say. Right? That's what she would say."

I held my hand over my eye. "I don't know how to express how sorry I am."

"I know." He pulled me into a hug. "Come on inside. Let's wait inside."

"I'm good. I think I'll stay out here for a few more minutes. I'll be in. You go."

"You sure?"

"Yeah, I'm sure. Go."

He backed up, watching me, then turned and disappeared into the hospital to wait word on his fiancée. My good friend.

I put my back to the wall and slid down until I sat on the ground. In a gradual shift, my grief and guilt turned to anger, building steam without a place to vent. Those people shot a good friend of mine. Those people kidnapped my grandniece and nephew. Those people groped and menaced my wife, rammed our car, jeopardized the welfare of our unborn child. Those people still had my brother. I stood and brushed my hands together, knocking off the grit. I pulled the keys to Barbara's Dodge Charger out of my pocket.

I started to run.

CHAPTER FIFTY-EIGHT

MY LUNGS ACHED and my heart pounded by the time I made it to the corner of Arbor Vitae and Prairie. I stayed to the opposite side of the street to The Langston Arms as I huffed and puffed. I made a promise to start up running again if I made it back to Costa Rica.

I went right to the side of the 7-Eleven and, in the recessed shadow, used the spigot to rinse off my hands and arms and face. The blood on my clothes had started to dry and without the wetness, blended in better with the dark colors.

Lots of emergency vehicles jammed into the narrow parking area to The Langston. The red-and-blue rotators lit up the neighborhood. Cars on Prairie in both directions slowed to look. Gawkers stood out in front of the 7-Eleven, the closest place to stand without getting shooed away by cops guarding the crime scene behind their yellow police line tape. I blended in with these folks to get a longer look without being noticed. The police had to be looking for me by now.

Minnie Jenks stood out in front of her manager's apartment talking with two plainclothes detectives, a Virginia Slim in one hand and a tall boy, Old Milwaukee, in the other. She waved her arms as she spoke with great animation, the star of the hour, enjoying every second of it. I could only imagine the lies she spun.

After all the excitement, the post-adrenaline symptoms hit my nervous system hard and gave me the shakes. I went into the store. The pink coconut cake of a pair of Sno Balls caught my eye. I bought them along with a carton of chocolate milk, eight Eveready D batteries, and three burner phones. I went back outside to wait for my chance to cross Arbor Vitae. I needed to get farther west on Prairie to where we'd parked the Charger. I didn't have much time; the task force would be writing warrants to swoop in and pick up the rest of the co-conspirators. They wouldn't care about Noble, an escapee from state prison. He didn't pay taxes, he didn't vote. They'd want him only to throw his skinny ass back in the can to finish wasting away the rest of his life. I needed to find him first.

And I needed a little alone time with the guy responsible before the cops got to them. I wanted to put the hurt on them—*whisper in their ears.* That's what Robby used to say when he severely counseled a crook.

My nephew pulled up in his old Toyota Corolla. He stopped at the yellow tape, parked illegally right in the middle of the street just as the coroner's wagon arrived. From the passenger seat, a young and pretty Hispanic girl wearing a pink angora sweater—obviously his girlfriend—also got out. The Inglewood cop on scene security yelled, "Hey, hey, you can't park there."

Bruno and the girl ran up to him. Bruno flashed him something and spoke low enough that I couldn't hear from where I stood. Rebecca and Ricardo, who stood over by the manager's open door, saw their father and started crying, "Daddy. Daddy. Daddy."

The Inglewood cop jacking Bruno up over the parking job now waved him on. Bruno ran to his kids. All the personnel at the scene stopped and watched the reunion. I fought the strong urge to go over there and join in the group hug. My turn would come later, I hoped. I also looked forward to Marie's expression when she saw them for the first time.

I took the opportunity to cross the street and move past the corner and down Prairie to the Dodge Charger. I got in and started her up. The car rumbled at idle like a big mountain cat. Of course Bruno would have a girlfriend. Good-looking kid like that with his life wrapped tight, of course he'd have a nice girlfriend.

I opened the burner phone and dialed my nephew.

"Hello?"

"It's me, your Uncle Bruno."

"Uncle." He said it too loud, then lowered his voice. "Where are you? I want to thank you in person for what you've done." His voice caught as he tried not to cry. "I want to shake your hand. You have no idea . . . I mean I can't tell you how scared I've been and—"

"Kid, I'm glad it worked out."

Saving the kids had come at a heavy price.

"I know you can't come back here," my nephew said. "Where are you? I'll come to you. I have some things I need to say."

"I know, and we'll get together soon, but right now I have something I have to do."

His tone changed. "What? You're going after my father, aren't you?"

I said nothing.

"I'm going with you."

"You need to take care of your family."

"Carmen's here. I have to go with you, Uncle; he's my father."

I hesitated, my mind running through all the options. I would need someone to create some sort of a distraction if I wanted to have any chance at all. And Bruno did have the right to be involved.

Then I thought of what had happened to Barbara. Her words rang harsh and loud in my head. They made me sick to my stomach, made the Sno Balls and chocolate milk roil and threaten to come up. *Bruno, every time you take a hand in something like this, the odds of someone getting shot, run over, or beat to within an inch of their life increases exponentially.*

"Please, Uncle. I need to do this."

"Okay, I'm down the street, to the west of you."

"I'll be there in two minutes. I need to get the kids in the car with Carmen."

"Bruno?" I said.

"Yeah, Uncle?"

"Bring your girlfriend's sweater with you."

"Huh? What? Ah, yeah, sure." He clicked off.

He didn't wait for a reason, he just trusted me. I liked the kid more and more.

Three minutes later, he jogged around the corner. The pink sweater in hand pulled in every bit of the ambient light and all but glowed. He recognized the Dodge. He got in and, before his door closed, he offered me his hand. I took it and shook.

He closed his door. "Thank you."

"You don't need to thank me, we're family. That's what families do."

I put her in gear and pulled a U-turn.

We drove in silence for a few miles. The thought that this new caper we were headed to was a bad idea wouldn't leave me alone. If something happened to my nephew, my brother Noble's son, I'd never forgive myself.

Bruno broke the silence and spoke as he watched the scenery go by. Something was eating at him. I wished we had the time to go somewhere to sit and watch the ocean or the moon rise in a park and let it come out naturally.

I waited for him and let him take his time.

"You know, I have hated you all my life," he finally said. "I never told anyone, but I have always hated you."

I looked from the road to him and back. "I can understand that. You had no reason, otherwise."

He turned from the window. "You put my father in prison for the rest of his life."

I said nothing.

I didn't want to argue with him, but what he said wasn't entirely true. Noble shot and killed two people. I only detained him. Did my job. Though that lame excuse no longer held up. I'd done worse, a lot worse, since that night I arrested him. Not always legal, but definitely morally correct.

I should've listened to Noble that night, heard him out. But would it have made a difference? Not legally. But morally? Without a doubt it would have.

"My father," Bruno said, "he never held it against you. He always, *always* said nice things about you."

He started to choke up and passed that emotion onto me. "Okay, kid, thanks, that's enough, please."

"No, wait, now I understand. I've gotten older. I work at Lennox, and I understand the job and the responsibility. I feel bad about hating you all that time. I was wrong and want to apologize."

"Thanks, kid. Now quit talking or I'm gonna pull over and let you out."

He complied, but not for very long.

"Where we going?"

"Beverly Hills."

He nodded.

CHAPTER FIFTY-NINE

I CRUISED BY the Beverly Hills Hotel, down the long drive, around the half circle where the valets waited to take the patrons' cars. Lots of people moved about, all dressed a lot better than me, which made our infiltration all the more difficult.

My nephew watched out the window as I tried to decide the best way to get in and to finesse Don the Don Brodie's bungalow number from the front desk personnel.

Bruno turned to look at me as I pulled back down the driveway, headed back to the street. "It's Bungalow 135."

"What? How do you know that?"

He shrugged.

This kid really had it going on. If he didn't get caught up in my caper to get Noble back, and thrown in prison, he'd make a hell of a street cop.

"Make a left right here," he said, "and then a right on the first street. We're going to have to walk back."

I did as he said and parked in the dark shadows. The black Dodge Charger all but disappeared as it blended in.

"You scouted this place, didn't you?"

He said nothing and only peered through the dark at me.

"You were going to come here on your own. That's why you had this Sig on you, isn't it?"

"They had my family, Uncle. They had my kids. I wasn't going to let them get away with it. Now they have my father. Are we going to talk all night or are we going to make our move?"

Our move. The words sounded bad and reminded me I shouldn't be involving him. What would Marie say about it? *Bruno, come here and let me slap you upside the head.* I missed her something fierce.

I watched his eyes, his face in dark relief, and couldn't see them. "Gimme your socks," I said.

"My socks?"

I snapped my fingers. "Come on man, we don't have all night."

He took off his shoes and tugged off his socks as I opened the bubble pack to the eight Eveready D-Cell batteries. I put one sock inside the other while Bruno watched and added the batteries. "Oh," he said, "12020."

I stopped, stunned. "That's right. Kid, you just keep amazing me." He smiled. His teeth glowed.

I tied a knot close to the batteries, forcing them down snug, and then two more knots higher up to act as a handle. I handed it to him.

"I've read about these but never saw one or learned how to use it. PC 12020, possession of a deadly weapon; to wit, a slungshot, felony, sixteen months, two years or three years with a ten-thou-sand-dollar fine."

"You're gonna have to be the one to use it," I said. "I'm too old and look too much like a threat to get in close enough. You think you can handle it?"

"Sure, just tell me what to do."

He had too much false bravado that came with youth.

"We're going to walk in together," I said. "This Brodie has se-curity outside his bungalow, and from what I understand, it's not some fly-by-night operation, it's top-drawer professional.

"When we approach, we'll separate. I'll draw his attention, and you keep the battery end of the sock in your back pocket with the other two knots hanging out. Once I distract him, you grab the two knots and swing it around and upward, aim for the back of his head. Don't put everything you have into it or you'll kill him. You understand?"

"Sure, I got it."

"You think you can pull this off?"

"No problem. But what makes you think this guy's going to let us get close enough to him for me to use this?"

"You're going to wear the sweater."

"What?"

I watched his eyes as his mind processed what I'd said.

"Ah, man," he said as he figured out the play.

We got out of the Charger. I held up the pink fuzzy sweater.

"Why me? Let's flip for it."

"Come on, look at this thing." I held it up to my chest. "No way's this gonna fit me."

He took it and put it on. Carmen wore a few sizes smaller than Bruno. The sweater fit tight and gave off the desired effect. I put my arm around him as we walked. "You're going to have to pretend we're lovers or this isn't gonna work."

"Uncle, I like you and all but—"

"Funny. Keep moving."

"You really think we look like that, I mean—"

"This is LA, where anything's possible as long as we own it in our own minds. You look cute, sugar."

"Oh come on, Uncle Bruno."

"Which way?"

"Down this path," he said. "And when we come to the fork, we go right. This is a big place, we got a little ways to go."

Plants and shrubs and trees decorated the smooth concrete path, illuminated every ten feet by subdued landscape lights alternating yellow, blue, and green.

Up ahead, a golf cart loaded with two hotel security officers dressed in suits and ties came right at us. "Remember what I said, we gotta own it."

My nephew said nothing and added a sway to his hips. Just enough.

The cart slowed as it approached. I stepped to one side and pulled Bruno into a hug, chest to chest, and put my hand on his butt. "Come on, sugar, let the nice men pass."

He whispered, "Oh, come on, Uncle Bruno. Really?"

The cart sped up. The men made some inaudible derogatory comment and sped off. When they rounded the first corner, Bruno pushed me off. "I think *you* liked that a little too much." He grinned.

I took his hand. He didn't resist.

"Listen," I said. "If you have to go hands on with one of these guys, or even later on as a cop with a suspect, you take him fast, down and dirty. You don't mess around. Forget the sheriff's policy. Forget using the escalation of force that they're going to teach you in the academy. You understand what I'm telling you here?"

"Yes, I think I do."

"Good. Okay, now, let's say you go hands on with one of these guys we're about to confront. You go hands on and try and take him down and dirty, like I just explained to you in how to use the slungshot, but for whatever reason it doesn't work 'cause he's a bad ass. And you have to fight him. What are you going to do?"

"I'll take him, Uncle, don't worry about me. Okay?"

Ah, the wonders of youth, and again with the false bravado.

"No, this is important. Say you're goin' all out for sixty seconds and you're not getting the better of him, what do you do?"

"Well, if for some reason something like that does happen, given the circumstances you described, I would disengage and run. He who lives to fight another day lives to fight another day."

"That's exactly right." He'd surprised me again.

We came to a fork in the path and went right.

"Up ahead," he said, "there's a bottlebrush and a big bird of paradise. The first security officer will be standing back in the shadows between both of those bushes."

"We can handle one, maybe two, but if there are three, we're gonna have a problem."

"Then I guess we're going to have a problem, Uncle."

"Ah shit, you're kiddin' me."

CHAPTER SIXTY

"ARE THERE THREE of them, really? You know this for sure? We have to back off and think about another approach. We can't take three." My whispered tone turned more desperate toward the end of my rant.

"Here we go," my nephew said. "Twenty feet. Ten—"

He didn't say the next number; I did. "Five."

Out stepped a large man, ex-military, in great shape, wearing a blue blazer and gray slacks, his hair cut close to his scalp. "Hold it right there," he said.

This guy was going to hand us both of our asses and laugh about it.

Bruno broke away, not like the plan. I was supposed to, not him. He took two more steps, with a pronounced sway in his gait, before the security officer grabbed his shoulder and spun him around.

Bruno used the man's own momentum and stepped in close. He slugged the guy in the throat with a strike so fast I almost missed it. The man bent over, gasping and choking. Bruno took a half step back and kicked him in the groin. He gave him a third blow, a side kick to the knee. The man went down.

The second man jumped Bruno from out of the dark. Bruno

sidestepped and gave him a palm strike to the face just to get the guy off him. The second man recovered fast and came right back in. Bruno swung the slungshot and caught the man behind the head. The strike thunked like a watermelon hitting the ground. The second man went down, lights out.

The third man hit me from behind. The blow rocked my world. I flew face first and slapped the concrete walk in a belly flop.

"You okay, Uncle?" Bruno helped me up.

"What happened to the third guy?" I looked around; all three men had disappeared.

"I dragged them into the brush." He held up the slungshot. "Man, this thing really works. I like it."

I rubbed my head where a goose egg was already starting to rise. The guy had hit me with something. "You didn't tell me you've been training. What is that, jujitsu, karate, what?"

"Aikido."

"Black belt?"

"Come on, I got the key." He held up the card key he must've taken from the lead security officer.

I pointed my finger at him, "You're dangerous, you know that? You're dangerous. Twenty years old and you can do that. That's just not normal. That's weird."

"Twenty-one in three months, Uncle, then I'm in the Sheriff's Academy."

He moved away. I hurried to catch up. "Hey, hey?" I said. "Let's talk about what we're going to do." I caught up to him as he entered a recessed entry to the bungalow.

"What's to talk about?" He swiped the card key, his hand on the door handle.

"Talk, as in is there anyone else in there with Brodie?"

He shrugged and pushed his way in. I pulled the Sig nine and followed. As I crossed the threshold into the building, I looked up and caught a small camera pointed at the door. Brodie knew we were coming. "Bruno?"

I went deeper into the lush bungalow. The thick carpet underfoot dampened all sound of movement. I passed Carmen's pink angora sweater on the floor as I entered the main living area.

Across the huge living room, Brodie sat on a couch, clad in a maroon satin robe with black lapels. He had his legs up on the low living room table, unconcerned by the intruders who'd just taken out his security and entered his lodging without permission or authority. His hands rested across his stomach, his eyes on us. Every hair on his head was in place and perfectly coifed. His skin tanned brown to leather. I put him at about sixty-five, maybe seventy.

Off to the right, a leggy redhead shimmied into her thong, unhurried and unabashed. She picked up her black-lace bra and slipped into it in one of the most sexy moves I'd ever seen. She finished dressing, picked up her black heels, and walked by us as if we'd never existed. Her scent, feminine and exotic, followed after her. The door opened and closed behind us.

"Sit," the man said, "please."

I looked around and didn't see anyone lurking in the corners or over by the bar.

Brodie held up his hand. "Please, make yourselves at home, have a drink."

"Where's my father?"

The smile left Brodie's face and, when it did, I recognized him. "I don't have your father," he said.

"Don't play games with us," I said. "Too much has happened, too many people have been hurt, and if you don't tell us you're going to be next. And please don't take that as a threat; it's a fact." The anger over what this man had caused rose up and threatened to flip that switch inside me that I hated. I gripped the gun tighter and resisted pointing it at him. Not yet.

"Listen, I openly admit to borrowing your kids for a time, but that was just business. You have your children back safe, and I'm out two of my best operators. If anything, you came out ahead in this botched little fiasco. And let me give credit where credit is due. I definitely underestimated you, both of you. But I'm telling you as a businessman that I do not and never did have your father."

My nephew stood two steps closer to Brodie and one step to the right. He looked back at me for help. Tactically, he shouldn't have taken his eyes of his opponent. He didn't know what to do. I stepped forward, brought the Sig up, and shot the lying bastard in the foot.

CHAPTER SIXTY-ONE

BRODIE YELPED, GRABBED his foot, and leaned over on his side. He gritted his teeth and sucked up the pain. Blood spread between his fingers.

I moved in closer and sat on the table in front of him, keeping the gun out of his reach. "Who are you?" I asked.

"I told you, just a businessman."

"A businessman who fishes on the pier to oversee a hostage exchange?"

He stopped writhing. "You are good," he said through clenched teeth. "I could use you. You want a job? I'll pay you five hundred thousand a year to start, along with a generous profit-sharing package."

"Don't get off topic. Who are you? Tell me what's going on." I pointed the Sig at his other foot.

"Okay, okay. What do you want to know? I don't know what you're asking me."

"Those people working for you aren't street thugs, they're pros."

"You're right, you get what you pay for. I pay for the best. Hey, Son, can you get me a towel? I need to stop this bleeding or you're not going to get all of what you think you came for." I nodded to Bruno. He didn't move. He didn't care if Brodie lived or died.

He didn't have enough years in life to be so cynical or without empathy.

"I don't believe you," I said. "If you really don't have my brother, then you have to know where he is."

I watched his eyes for a deceptive answer. "I was only in it for the diamonds, that's all. I thought this would be an easy caper, a piece of cake with a nine-million-dollar payoff. Well, as you can see, it didn't turn out that way. I misjudged you."

"There aren't any diamonds," I said. "That's a myth, a rumor of pirates' lost treasure and nothing more."

"I'm not a fool," he said. "You think I'd be in this thing just based on rumor and supposition? Over there"—he took his bloody hand off his foot and pointed—"on the bar, in that cigar box. Jesus, you didn't have to shoot me. We're all civilized here."

"Yeah, kidnapping two innocent little kids, that's civilized. Watch what you say, you have no idea how pissed off I am."

I didn't have to tell him. Bruno moved over to the bar. I kept my eyes on the evil that sat in front of me. "What's he going to find?" I asked.

"A letter someone sent me anonymously, but I knew who it was from just like you will."

"What's it say?"

"Read it for yourself. Now get me a towel."

I still didn't take my eyes off Brodie. Behind, and to the side, my nephew opened the cigar box. The hinge creaked a little. After several seconds I said, "What's it say?"

He said nothing.

I got up from the table and backed up a little to see Bruno and, at the same time, keep my eye on Brodie. Bruno stood at the bar with the letter in his hand. "Well," I said, "what's it say?"

Bruno looked up, his expression one of shock.

I resisted the urge to go over to him and instead continued to hold the gun on Brodie. "Tell me."

"It's a letter from my father," Bruno said.

"And?"

Brodie spoke. "It says, 'you help me get out and I'll give you nine million in diamonds.'"

"My brother played you. He doesn't have any diamonds."

Bruno walked over, his open palm extended. The light caught the facets of a two-carat diamond. The sight shook me emotionally. "What the hell?"

"Ah," Brodie said. "You really didn't know, did you? Huh, that is interesting. I had it appraised. It is what it appears to be and is worth twelve thousand dollars. No one just mails you twelve grand like that. Not unless they have a lot more. Not unless they have another nine million. Don't you agree?"

I'd been played by my own brother.

For all those years I thought him a crook who deserved to be in prison. And then, after I got to know him again, through his valiant actions in the jail when I'd almost been shanked, and mostly through his son Bruno, I began to believe I'd been wrong about him all along. Now this.

Anger rose up hot enough to flush my face. The bastard had played me right from the gate. Worse, he'd played Dad, and that was unacceptable.

I reached down and took the edge of the coffee table, flipped it over onto Brodie, and jumped on it. He yelled, the first fear and emotion he'd shown. He couldn't move his arms, and the edge of the table pressed down just under his chin.

"Professional operators," I said. "Ex-special forces, silenced high-end weapons, you tell me the rest of it. And you tell me right now. Why would my brother send you a diamond and ask you to get him out? Why would he think you could get him out? I think I know, but you have five seconds to tell it."

He grunted and tried to get enough air. "I don't know—"

I stuck the gun barrel flush with the table and pulled the trigger. The gun kicked. The high-velocity nine millimeter went right through the table in the area of his leg.

"Aaahee. You son of a bitch."

"Next one goes in higher. Tell me."

"Okay, okay. There's a jeweler's loupe over there on the bar. Jesus, you black bastard, get off me. Get off."

Bruno got the loupe and put it to his eye. "What am I looking—"

"That's right," Brodie gasped. "The diamond has a serial number. That was state of the art back in the eighties."

I stuck the gun, with smoke still curling out the end, right on his nose. "So. Finish it, tell the rest."

"All right, I can't breathe, get off the table."

"Tell it."

He gulped. "All right, all right, no one will believe you anyway, and I'll only deny it if you tell anyone. In his book, that asshole brother of yours laid us all out. I was in the CIA at the time and made the deal with that corrupt asshole, Papa Dee. I brought the dope and Papa Dee never showed with the diamonds. He showed us half of the diamonds before the deal, gave us the serial numbers so we could check them when we made the exchange. Then, the night of the trade, he left us on that dock holding our dicks. He never showed." He gasped again. "Come on, man, get off."

"The rest of it." I shoved down harder on the table.

"Your brother wrote that book and sent me that letter to prove his bona fides. He wanted me to go to the government, to my old contacts, tell them he had evidence to hang the government out on that Iran-Contra bullshit."

"Did you do it?"

"Yeah, I did. I thought I'd have a chance at getting the diamonds once he got out. Nine million is still nine million."

"And what happened?"

"The State Department told me to go fuck myself. Said that the Iran-Contra shit was old news. They had that embassy thing in Benghazi they were trying to whitewash."

"So," I said, "you used some of your old cronies to kidnap my nephew's kids to force us to get my brother out. Is that it?"

"Yes."

"Then you rammed our Cadillac and took my brother Noble."

"No, I didn't. I thought he was with you."

"Bullshit."

"Think about it, why would I lie when I just told you all that other shit, huh? Why?"

CHAPTER SIXTY-TWO

"YOU RUN YOUR dope operation like some kind of spy shop with all the cells isolated and unable to communicate with each other so the cops can't get a foothold on you. You're smart. That means you have to have an intel branch feeding you information. Information is power. You have all the money you can possibly spend, so your thing is power."

"Aaah, come on, and your point is?"

"You have to have some idea who has my brother."

"I don't. I swear I don't."

I stuck the hot gun barrel in his eye socket and pressed down. "Then what good are you?"

"Wait. Wait. Okay, okay. Take that gun out of my eye, you damn nigger."

My finger almost went rogue and pulled the trigger all on its own. I eased up the pressure but didn't remove it.

"If I had to guess?" he said.

"I don't want a guess."

"That's all I got and, if it's not good enough for you, go ahead, pop me. Because that's what you're going to do anyway."

"What's your guess?"

"Get off me."

I got up. He pushed the table, his arms weak. The table slid off to the floor. The couch's soft ivory upholstery acted like a giant sponge and accepted all the blood Brodie's body offered. The cushion down by his leg swelled up and turned red. Brodie looked down at the same time I did and knew the truth the same as I did. "Ah, damn, now look what you went and did."

The color left his tan face all at once as the light in his eyes switched off. His lifeless body continued to stare at me.

From behind me, Bruno said, "Come on, Uncle, we have to jam. The cops will be here soon. Someone had to have reported those gunshots."

"I didn't mean to kill him." But in reality, I had. The man kidnapped my brother's grandchildren. He'd given the orders that ultimately caused my good friend Barbara to be shot. He also ruined tens of thousands of lives dealing his white powder. And the worst part was that the law worked in his favor, and he would have never been brought forward to answer for any of it. Dead on the couch, he'd received payment in full.

"I know," my nephew said. "Come on, let's go." He'd moved up close and had me by the arm.

"The round hit his femoral artery," I said, still half in a daze. I'd been hit in the head too many times recently, and my words didn't have the same impact as they should've had.

"Come on."

He moved us to the door, then stopped and scooped up the pink angora sweater. At least he kept his good sense about him. I'd just shot a man in cold blood. Right at that moment I realized I'd find Noble and do everything in my power to help him evade the law, even though he'd lied to me.

The night air helped clear the cloud of guilt obscuring logical thought. We moved along the path in between the other bungalows and made it halfway to the Dodge when the answer just bubbled up. My subconscious had known all along, had seen all the clues and put it together but had hidden the answer from me, the real reason Noble wanted out of prison.

And it wasn't just to get out of prison, or to recover the diamonds.

When we made it to the car, Bruno took the keys from me, got in, and fired up the Charger. "Where to?" he asked.

I reached over and shut off the car. "Tell me about your mother."

"Now? You need to know this now?"

"Yes, it's important."

"What do you want to know?"

"All I know about her is that she's buried in a cemetery in Hollywood."

"That's right."

"I know this is personal, but I need to know what happened and when?"

He looked away from me and out the windshield. "She had a heart attack while she was swimming. She drowned."

"Then that's where your father is. Take me to the pool where she drowned."

"That doesn't make—"

"Bruno, trust me, drive."

Bruno drove south and followed all the rules of the road. He left me alone to think, so I could recheck my facts to see if they fit. And they did. They all did.

After fifteen minutes, I pulled the Sig from under my shirt, popped the mag, and counted the rounds left. I'd fired two into Don the Don Brodie; that left thirteen in the magazine. Should be enough, but maybe not. Not with three experienced Los Angeles County Sheriff's detectives to deal with.

"You going to tell me what's going on?" Bruno asked as he exited the freeway. I hadn't been paying any attention to his route or where he'd ended up.

"What are we going to do?" he asked.

"Burn down the world."

CHAPTER SIXTY-THREE

BRUNO DROVE US right to Baldwin Hills, a district of Los Angeles that people called the Black Beverly Hills. The houses resembled estates, with big rolling front yards and Southern mansion designs. If you didn't know any better, a person might think he'd accidently driven into Beverly Hills.

"Don't go into the driveway," I said. "Park and we'll walk up like we did at Brodie's."

He slid up to a curb and shut her down. "Now tell me what we're doing here? Willy is a friend of the family. I've been here with the kids and Mom, swimming in his pool. If you think it was murder, it wasn't. Mom had a bad heart. She was taking nitro for it."

"I have to ask you an important question."

"All right."

"Do you trust me?"

He didn't hesitate. "Yes."

"This is real important now. Do you trust me more then you trust Willy Jessup?"

This time he hesitated.

"You better stay in the car." I pulled the door handle and bailed out of the car.

He followed me around the back to the trunk. I held out my hand for the car keys. He gave them to me.

"This is crazy," he said. "What are you trying to say?"

"I'm trying to say Willy is not who he says he is. Willy is a cold-blooded killer who has been batting your mother around for the last twenty-five years."

"What?"

"I'm only guessing, but it only makes sense. Papa Dee disappeared twenty-five years ago with the diamonds. Your father went to prison over killing two of Papa's thugs outside a Stop and Go store."

"Yeah, you did that. You arrested him. We talked about that already. And maybe with you talking smack like this, I don't forgive you anymore."

"Listen, I'm only guessing, but it stands to reason, with Papa Dee missing his diamonds *and* his dope, he went to the Department of Justice and they put him in the witness protection program. They did this because he threatened them that he'd expose the Iran-Contra deal. They gave him some plastic surgery, which they've been known to do, and the arrogant bastard left the program and came right back to the place he grew up. Tried to go legit. He knew the people, what they wanted, and ran for office and won."

Under the streetlight, my nephew's eyes went out of focus as his mind played back all this new information, checking for holes.

I reached into the trunk and pulled out an Ithaca Deer Slayer 12-gauge shotgun Barbara kept in a zippered gun bag.

"So you think Jessup drowned my mom and had his cronies with the county cover it up."

"That's what makes the most sense."

"My dad loved my mom more than anything. So he figured it

the same way and wrote the book to let everyone know about what happened to remind everyone about the coke and the diamonds."

"No, he wrote the book to get twelve thousand dollars, the price of one diamond. And the cost to have it engraved with a serial number."

The information all fell into place for my nephew. He grabbed the shotgun from me, gritting his teeth. "We talk to Jessup first. If he admits it, I get to shoot him."

Not such a good idea, not one I could condone. Bruno didn't need to have a body hit the floor by his gun, not at his age. Not if he could avoid it.

I reached in the trunk and unzipped the second zippered bag and took out an H&K MP5 nine-millimeter submachine gun. I stuck the magazine in and racked it. "You don't shoot anyone, and I mean absolutely no one, unless he is shooting at you first, you understand?"

"Yes."

"Promise me. And remember, you said you don't lie."

"I promise."

"Let's go." I eased the trunk deck down until it latched. Bruno racked the shotgun and led the way.

"Remember, there are three of them. They're deputies, and they are very good at what they do, so watch yourself."

Bruno kept walking, staying in the shadows along the edge of the sidewalk, and said nothing. He guided us into the driveway of the huge mansion, the kind a sports figure would own. Three cars sat under the portico by the front door. Bruno went on past the front entrance and around the north side. The walkway turned even darker as the shrubs closed in.

A yellow light bulb shrouded in opaque glass illuminated the side door and surrounding area. Bruno bent over and picked up a faux rock.

From inside the rock, he pulled out a key. I put my hand on his shoulder. "Let me go first."

He hesitated and then nodded.

I unlocked the door. The quiet little click sounded like a snare drum. I pushed the door open and went in with the MP5 in the lead.

Soft music massaged the air, Etta James's lyrical voice smoothing out the night.

We passed through the laundry room quickly and into the expansive kitchen, one large enough to service a restaurant. Soft talking came from the next room, the living room. I hung the MP5 around my neck from a team sling and eased down two of the copper-bottomed pots that hung over the center island.

I kicked off my shoes. Bruno didn't have to be told; he followed suit. The big shotgun in his hands was incongruent with his innocence. Marie's voice in my head kept saying, *This is a bad idea, Bruno*.

I shuffled over in my socks to the edge of the kitchen with my back to the wall. I did a quick peek and came back. In that brief glimpse I caught it all. My brother sat duct taped to a chair, his face beat to shit. Willy Jessup sat in a huge red velvet easy chair, holding court. Two of the thug detectives who'd bum-rushed our hotel room stood by my brother's chair. Both the men held items of torture: a phone book to beat him with and a half-empty bottle of coke to shoot up his nose.

I eased back and whispered to Bruno. The soft music covered our movement.

"Listen," I said, "we're missing one, the guy in the blue suit, the leader. He may not be here at all, but we can't chance it. You're going to bat cleanup. You're going to stay right here and don't come in no matter what, you understand? No matter what. You come in only when that guy in the blue suit shows himself, you understand? It's our asses if you don't do it exactly like I say."

He nodded.

I moved back to the edge, took two deep breaths. I tossed the pots long and hard. They landed on the tiled hall that led to the back of the house. They clattered and banged. I stepped out into the living room.

CHAPTER SIXTY-FOUR

THE TWO DETECTIVES, experienced over the years in violent confrontations, saw me first and started to move. I fired the MP5 above their heads into the large mirror over the mantel. Glass shards went everywhere. They bunched their shoulders, ducked their heads, and raised their hands.

"Nobody move," I said.

I hoped the five rounds I'd put in the mirror would smoke out Blue Suit. I moved into the living room in my stocking feet. "Put your hands on your head. Do it now."

They complied.

Willy Jessup, aka Papa Dee, chuckled, "Oh, look, it's a nigger Rambo."

I pointed the gun at him. "Shut up. You'd better shut up, or I will shoot you right where you sit."

He held up his hand. "Come in, come in, join the party. You coming here saves me the trouble of tracking you down."

Tracking me down? Was that where Blue Suit was—out looking for me? Looking for us? Was Marie still safe? I needed to call her. Mack was tied up at a different hospital, too busy to care about Marie's safety.

"You." I pointed my gun at one of the deputies. "You have a knife? Cut my brother loose, do it now."

Cotton-top, Papa Dee, chuckled again. "They're not going to do anything unless I tell them to. Come on in and sit—"

I shot one deputy in both legs. He went to the floor, screaming. I pointed the gun at the one still standing, his hands high in the air, his expression one of abject fear. He complied and sawed the duct tape holding Noble's hands and then he went down on his knees to cut his legs loose.

Noble pulled the tape off his mouth. "Behind you!"

"Game's over, asshole."

I whipped around.

Too late.

Blue Suit, now dressed in jeans and a button-down shirt, came into the room behind Bruno with a gun to the back of my nephew's head.

Papa Dee laughed. "I tried to tell you that—"

I turned the MP5 and shot him in the chest with a burst of five rounds. He slumped over dead.

Blue Suit froze, his expression stunned.

Noble, his face swollen from all the abuse he'd taken, yelled at me, "You son of a bitch. *You son of a bitch*. I had to do that. Me. Not you. Not you. Me. He killed my Sasha."

I ignored my brother, who picked up a gun from the downed deputy and held it on the other one. I turned my gun back on Blue Suit, who still hid behind my nephew, his gun held tight in Bruno's ear. "What are we going to do?"

Blue Suit said, "You're going to tell me you don't care what happens to your nephew?" He pulled the hammer back on his gun, a large semiautomatic. A pound-and-a-half trigger pull was all that remained from a bullet plowing into my nephew's head.

I raised the MP5. The memory of what happened not hours ago, returned vivid and clear. Barbara, in this exact situation, showed the balls and took the shot. Rebecca was not her child. Bruno was my nephew.

Out of my peripheral vision, Noble, too weak over his stabbing, the loss of blood, and the beating, wilted to the floor. I yelled at the deputy, "Don't you move, you hear me?"

I held the gun pointed low on my nephew. I didn't want to spook Blue Suit. "Bruno?" I said.

"Yes, Uncle."

"Do you trust me?"

"Yes, Uncle. Do what you have to do."

I looked at Blue Suit. "I'll trade you my nephew for nine million dollars in diamonds."

From the floor behind me, Noble said in a weak voice. "No, Bruno, don't. Don't do this."

Blue Suit must've thought Noble meant not to give up the diamonds.

Blue Suit said, "You have the diamonds? How do I know you have the diamonds?"

"Tell him, Nephew."

"My father told me where they were buried. I dug them up from under our porch. From under our porch on Nord Street. They were in a purple Crown Royal bag in a rusted-out Folgers can."

"I'm calling bullshit on this. You could've had this story all set up in advance. Drop your weapon, now."

"Show 'em, Nephew." I said.

Bruno said, "I'm going to reach into my pocket, okay?"

"Move slow. And you better not come out with any type of weapon."

My nephew came out with a fist. He held it away from his body and slowly opened his hand. The diamond's facets caught the light and sparkled.

Blue Suit took his eyes off me and looked at the diamond.

I raised the MP5 the last few inches and shot Blue Suit right in the eye.

CHAPTER SIXTY-FIVE

I HELD THE door to the rental, another Cadillac—an Escalade this time—and with the other hand, helped my pregnant wife from the wheelchair into the front seat. I thanked the attendant, ran around, and got in. I leaned over and gave Marie a kiss and a long hug. While in the hospital, I worried the law would figure the play and come and arrest us. Now, moving in the SUV, I could breathe a lot easier.

I started up and headed for Centinela Hospital to visit Barbara Wicks—soon to be Mrs. John Mack—before Marie and I left for the Mexican border. The cops wouldn't be looking for us there and we had our fake IDs. I wore an expensive wig, a Dodgers ball cap and sunglasses.

Two weeks had passed since the night Papa Dee went down. The media put their own spin on it:

Supervisor Willy Jessup was brutally and without motivation gunned down in his own living room. Three of Supervisor Jessup's personal protection unit, detectives from Los Angeles County Sheriff's Crime Impact Team, were shot trying to defend him. One died at the scene. The other two are rumored to be in line to receive the medal of valor.

* * *

John Mack said that he knew whose ear to whisper in. No way would an injustice like that happen. All the cops in three states were looking for my brother Noble. They wouldn't take him alive, not with Brodie shot and killed in a posh Beverly Hills hotel, along with a Los Angeles County Sheriff's deputy and a county board of supervisor dead. They'd blame it all on Noble, a real easy scapegoat.

"It's going to be nice to see Barbara and Mack again," Marie said. She held my hand and squeezed it. In her free hand she held a package, gift wrapped with transparent white tissue paper. A book dropped off for Marie by an unknown admirer. The book, *A Noble Sacrifice*, by Johnny Noble. By tacit agreement we knew the book came from Noble and possibly contained his signature and even a nice note.

"Yeah, maybe. But I don't think she's going to be too happy to see me."

"Ah, come on, Bruno, what did you do this time?"

The day after the shooting, I'd told Marie what had happened, just not who pulled what trigger and on whom. She didn't need to have that information. Emotionally and legally, it wasn't a good idea. At least, that's the argument I used to explain my position to Noble and Bruno when I dropped them off at a safe motel up the coast on the night of the shooting. Noble had been mad that I'd cheated him out of shooting the man who'd killed his Sasha. He didn't say a word to me the whole drive. I couldn't blame him. He'd been planning all along to shoot Jessup, aka Papa Dee, ever since he found out Sasha died in Papa Dee's pool, the victim of an *accident*.

Eighteen months ago Sasha had visited Noble in prison. She

told Noble everything. Wept. Told him that she had continued her relationship with Papa Dee after he got out of witness protection. While Noble was in prison. She hadn't wanted to; she absolutely hated the man. Papa Dee could be very persuasive. And to top it off, she was pregnant and alone. What Sasha didn't tell Noble was that the child wasn't his. She didn't have to. Noble saw the bruises on Sasha, watched his child as he grew, saw the resemblance to Papa Dee. A secret right in front of him, one he didn't want to see. So when Noble heard about the accident, he knew what had happened. It wasn't hard to guess, especially since it had happened eighteen months ago right after she visited him, told him about Papa Dee. Sasha married Noble during his life prison term. They had conjugal visits, safe and secure. Then she went back to the brutality of Papa Dee. What a horrible dual life.

I'd like to think Sasha didn't want to be with Papa Dee, that he forced her. Having a child with someone like Papa Dee would create an unholy alliance. Papa Dee and Sasha must have argued yet again and like before, when he'd beat and broke her arm, the argument turned violent. This time Papa Dee killed her. He made it look like an accidental drowning. For Noble, eighteen months was a long time to hold a grudge.

He wrote a book, an accomplishment in itself, and got it published in order to set his plan in motion. I truly admired my little brother for his discipline and determination.

"Yeah, I'm pretty sure Barbara's gonna be a little mad."

"Tell me."

"I used a gun from her trunk that could be traced back to her and would open up a lot of questions she couldn't answer, so I dropped it in the ocean."

"That's not that bad, is it?"

"It was a machine gun. All police departments have to register their automatic weapons with ATF, and she's going to have to report it stolen. She's the chief of police and she has to report that she lost a machine gun."

"Yikes."

"Exactly."

We rode for a while longer.

"Do you think Noble has all of those diamonds?"

"No, I told you he sold his book to get the twelve thousand dollars to buy the one diamond to make Brodie believe he had them so Brodie would pull some strings to get him out. The whole plan took a turn Noble hadn't figured on."

"But isn't there some way he could have the diamonds?"

I thought about it for a minute. "Well, based on what Noble wrote in the book, he could've followed Del in the shot-up Cadillac and relieved Papa Dee of the diamonds after Del crashed into the telephone pole. Not likely, though. Papa Dee would've had to be incapacitated or he would have fought Noble to the death over those diamonds. And if Papa Dee was incapacitated, he wasn't in the car when the cops arrived, so Noble would've had to help Papa Dee get away. Nah, no chance."

"So you're saying Papa Dee, who changed his appearance and his name to Willy Jessup, had the diamonds all along and bought that huge house in Baldwin Hills."

"Yep, it's the only thing that makes sense." I didn't want to tell her the rest, that I thought my nephew Bruno, really wasn't my nephew at all.

We rode in silence for a while.

"It's going to be good to get back to the kids, isn't it?" she said.

"Yes, it is."

Marie tore away the tissue paper to Noble's book and opened it. "Is there an inscription?"

I looked from the road to her when she didn't answer. She nodded and read it:

Bruno, my Big Brother,

Words cannot describe how much I appreciate all that you and your wife did for me and my family. I will never forget it. You are truly the best brother a man could ever have. Give Dad a hug for me and come see me sometime. I'll let you know where when I get settled. We've been apart far too long.

Always Yours
Your favorite Bro
Noble.
P.S. Check out page 100

Marie looked up at me. "He's going to be on the run for the rest of his life, isn't he?"

She said it as if this was a new and different concept when we'd been on the run from the law and hiding in a foreign country.

Marie turned to the page.

"Oh, my God, Bruno."

"What?"

She held up the open book. A rectangular chunk had been cut out of the pages. Glued to the inside were about fifty two-carat diamonds.

AUTHOR'S NOTE

Many years ago, almost four decades, I worked a patrol car with a valiant and heroic patrol officer. On that cold Christmas morning, *the day the house died,* I stood on the porch, helpless, and watched as my friend and partner kicked the door in to the burning house. Flames and black smoke billowed out. He wanted to enter despite the danger and would have if he could. I watched him as the intense flames rebuffed his every effort. Watched as he cried when they brought out the children we had arrived too late to save. Watched as the children's relatives tripped and stumbled over the bundled bodies laid to rest at the base of the tree. The officer was black and the children white. Race didn't matter that Christmas morning, as it never should.